PRAISE FOR

The Push

"[A] deft and immersive thriller…
The Push is an ingenious reincarnation of that most
forbidden of suspense narratives: the mommy-in-peril-
from-her-own-monstrous-offspring."
—**Maureen Corrigan**,
The Washington Post

"What makes [*The Push*] stand out is
Audrain's nuanced understanding of how women's voices
are discounted, how a thousand little slights can curdle a
solid marriage, and…how mothers really feel."
—**Los Angeles Times**

"Taut, chilling…
Audrain has a gift for capturing the seemingly small
moments that speak volumes about relationships."
—**The New York Times Book Review**

"A thrilling debut."
—**Harper's Bazaar**

"Ashley Audrain's *The Push* is
a taut tour de force that draws you in
from the very first pages and plunges you into the
most harrowing of journeys: parenthood."
—**Bill Clegg**,
New York Times bestselling author of
Did You Ever Have a Family

Dear Target Guest,

Thank you for reading *The Push*. I apologize in advance if you're up far too late tonight!

I started writing *The Push* when my first child was six months old. I thought a lot in those (very tired) days about society's expectations of mothers, and the expectations we have of ourselves.

So often, the reality of motherhood is different from the narrative we're taught, and yet that reality can be hard for women to speak about honestly. Motherhood has always been—and remains—a landmine of taboos. I've long been interested in the maternal experiences that women don't feel comfortable sharing openly.

I wanted to explore this darker side, one that so many women can relate to, through the journey of the character Blythe, who is forced to face her greatest fears about motherhood, in a marriage that is challenged by the weight of parenthood. As I wrote through those first few years of being a new mother myself, *The Push* was born.

The Push explores the often-ignored side of motherhood with page-turning, emotional suspense, and asks: What do parents owe their children? Can we really be different from the mothers we come from? What are the repercussions of silencing women's truths?

I'm so excited that Target has chosen *The Push* for its book club. I hope it sparks some meaningful conversations between friends—or even between mothers and daughters.

Warmly,

Ashley Audrain

Additional Praise for *The Push*

"*The Push* is uncomfortable and provocative, like a train wreck that demands your gaze."
—*The Washington Post*

"This taut and tense hurricane of a debut is best devoured in one sitting."
—*Newsweek*

"A chilling page-turner that asks provocative questions."
—*Real Simple*

"Well thought out, carefully crafted, vividly realized, and gripping . . . *The Push* turbocharges maternal anxieties with a fierce gothic energy."
—*The Guardian* (London)

"A psychological thriller that will make you question everything you know about motherhood."
—*Bitch*

"This book should come with a warning label! [A] buzzy debut novel that packs quite a few punches. With shades of *We Need to Talk About Kevin* . . . this GMA Book Club pick is a compulsively readable novel."
—*New York Post*

"This is a sterling addition to the burgeoning canon of bad seed suspense, from an arrestingly original new voice."
—*Publishers Weekly* (starred review)

"Both an absorbing thriller and an intense, profound look at the heartbreaking ways motherhood can go wrong, this is sure to provoke discussion."
—*Booklist*

"[A] dazzling exercise in both economy of language and vividness of expression . . . *The Push* announces Audrain as a sophisticated, compelling writer, perfect for fans of thrillers and intimate family dramas alike."
—*BookPage*

"With its riveting prose and deep convictions . . . Audrain's astute portrayal of motherhood is unsettling in its insights, yet highly entertaining on the page. Complex, nuanced, and unflinching, I inhaled this debut in one sitting."
—Karma Brown, bestselling author of *Recipe for a Perfect Wife*

"Intensely absorbing, gripping, until the final page."
—Kim Edwards, #1 *New York Times* bestselling author of *The Memory Keeper's Daughter*

"This is a thriller, yes, but one that probes deeply—with enormous intelligence—into what it means to be a mother. And, ultimately—like the best fiction of any genre—what it means to be a person in the world."
—Joanna Rakoff, internationally bestselling author of *My Salinger Year*

"A deeply provocative and fearless look at motherhood written in some of the prettiest prose you'll read all year."
—Aimee Molloy, *New York Times* bestselling author of *The Perfect Mother*

"Brilliant, insightful, compassionate, and horrifying. I wish I could read it for the first time over and over. One of the best books I've read all year." —Stephanie Wrobel, author of *Darling Rose Gold*

"Relentlessly compelling, distressing, and beautiful, Ashley Audrain's debut is the next *Gone Girl*, with shades of *We Need to Talk About Kevin*. I devoured it whole."
—Marissa Stapley, bestselling author of *Lucky*

"Visceral, provocative, compulsive, and with the most graphic and relatable description of childbirth I've read."
—Sarah Vaughan, bestselling author of *Little Disasters*

"Compelling, beautifully written, and wickedly entertaining . . . A tremendously thought-provoking read."
—Liz Nugent, author of *Our Little Cruelties*

"*The Push* is a force of nature, an unforgettable arrival that will linger in your heart—shimmer, darken, and then haunt you. Perhaps if Stephen King had experienced motherhood . . . he might have been able to dream up this book."   —Claudia Dey, author of *Heartbreaker*

"*The Push* is a freight train of a read—it barrels into you and propels you along, taking you places you're not sure you want to go. I found it disturbing, upsetting, and utterly compelling."
          —Beth Morrey, author of *The Love Story of Missy Carmichael*

"A tense and unsettling thriller that's immersive, chilling, and provocative. A book that's best read in one sitting."
          —Iain Reid, author of *I'm Thinking of Ending Things*

PENGUIN BOOKS

THE PUSH

Ashley Audrain's debut novel, *The Push*, was a *New York Times*, *Sunday Times* (London), and number-one international bestseller, and a Good Morning America Book Club pick. It has sold in forty territories, and a limited television series is currently in development. Audrain previously worked as the publicity director of Penguin Books Canada, and prior to that she worked in public relations. She lives in Toronto, where she and her partner are raising their two young children. She is working on her second novel.

Look for the Penguin Readers Guide in the back of this book. To access Penguin Readers Guides online, visit penguinrandomhouse.com.

The Push

A Novel

Ashley Audrain

PENGUIN BOOKS

PENGUIN BOOKS
An imprint of Penguin Random House LLC
penguinrandomhouse.com

First published in the United States of America by Pamela Dorman Books/Viking,
an imprint of Penguin Random House LLC, 2021
Published in Penguin Books 2022

A Pamela Dorman Book/Viking

ISBN 9780593511282 (Target paperback)

THE LIBRARY OF CONGRESS HAS CATALOGED THE
HARDCOVER EDITION AS FOLLOWS:
Names: Audrain, Ashley, 1982– author.
Title: The push: a novel / Ashley Audrain.
Description: [New York]: Pamela Dorman Books/Viking, [2021]
Identifiers: LCCN 2020010071 (print) | LCCN 2020010072 (ebook) |
ISBN 9781984881663 (hardcover) | ISBN 9781984881670 (ebook) |
ISBN 9780593296516 (international edition)
Subjects: GSAFD: Suspense fiction.
Classification: LCC PR9199.4.A9244 P87 2021 (print) |
LCC PR9199.4.A9244 (ebook) | DDC 813/.6—dc23
LC record available at https://lccn.loc.gov/2020010071
LC ebook record available at https://lccn.loc.gov/2020010072

Printed in the United States of America
1st Printing

Designed by Amanda Dewey

For Oscar and Waverly

It is often said that the first sound we hear in the womb is our mother's heartbeat. Actually, the first sound to vibrate our newly developed hearing apparatus is the pulse of our mother's blood through her veins and arteries. We vibrate to that primordial rhythm even before we have ears to hear. Before we were conceived, we existed in part as an egg in our mother's ovary. All the eggs a woman will ever carry form in her ovaries while she is a four-month-old fetus in the womb of her mother. This means our cellular life as an egg begins in the womb of our grandmother. Each of us spent five months in our grandmother's womb and she in turn formed within the womb of her grandmother. We vibrate to the rhythms of our mother's blood before she herself is born. . . .

Layne Redmond, *When the Drummers Were Women*

The Push

Your house glows at night like everything inside is on fire.

The drapes she chose for the windows look like linen. Expensive linen. The weave is loose enough that I can usually read your mood. I can watch the girl flip her ponytail while she finishes homework. I can watch the little boy toss tennis balls at the twelve-foot ceiling while your wife lunges around the living room in leggings, reversing the day's mess. Toys back in the basket. Pillows back on the couch.

Tonight, though, you've left the drapes open. Maybe to see the snow falling. Maybe so your daughter could look for reindeer. She's long stopped believing, but she will pretend for you. Anything for you.

You've all dressed up. The children are in matching plaid, sitting on the leather ottoman as your wife takes their picture with her phone. The girl is holding the boy's hand. You're fiddling with the record player at the back of the room and your wife is speaking to you, but you hold up a finger—you've almost got it. The girl jumps up and your wife, she sweeps up the boy, and they spin. You lift a drink, Scotch, and sip it once, twice, and slink from the record like it's a sleeping baby. That's how you always start to dance. You take him. He throws his head back. You tip him upside down. Your daughter reaches up for Daddy's kiss and your wife holds your drink for you. She sways over

to the tree and adjusts a string of lights that isn't sitting quite right.
And then you all stop and lean toward one another and shout something in unison, some word, perfectly timed, and then you all move
again—this is a song you know well. Your wife slips out of the room
and her son's face follows robotically. I remember that feeling. Of being
the needed one.

Matches. She comes back to light the candles on the decorated
mantel and I wonder if the snaking fir boughs are real, if they smell
like the tree farm. I let myself imagine, for a moment, watching those
boughs go up in flames while you all sleep tonight. I imagine the warm,
butter-yellow glow of your house turning to a hot, crackling red.

The boy has picked up an iron poker and the girl gently takes it
away before you or your wife notices. The good sister. The helper. The
protector.

I *don't normally watch* for this long, but you're all so beautiful tonight and I can't bring myself to leave. The snow, the kind that
sticks, the kind she'll roll into snowmen in the morning to please her
little brother. I turn on my wipers, adjust the heat, and notice the clock
change from 7:29 to 7:30. This is when you'd have read her *The Polar
Express*.

Your wife, she's in the chair now, and she's watching the three of
you bounce around the room. She laughs and collects her long, loose
curls to the side. She smells your drink and puts it down. She smiles.
Your back is to her so you can't see what I can, that she's holding her
stomach with one hand, that she rubs herself ever so slightly and then
looks down, that she's lost in the thought of what's growing inside her.
They are cells. But they are everything. You turn around and her attention is pulled back to the room. To the people she loves.

She will tell you tomorrow morning.

I still know her so well.

I look down to put on my gloves. When I look back up the girl is standing at your open front door. Her face is half lit by the lantern above your house number. The plate she's holding is stacked with carrots and cookies. You'll leave crumbs on the tile floor of the foyer. You'll play along and so will she.

Now she's looking at me sitting in my car. She shivers. The dress your wife bought her is too small and I can see that her hips are growing, that her chest is blooming. With one hand she carefully pulls her ponytail over her shoulder and it's more the gesture of a woman than a girl.

For the first time in her life I think our daughter looks like me.

I put down the car window and I lift my hand, a hello, a secret hello. She places the plate at her feet and stands again to look at me before she turns around to go inside. To her family. I watch for the drapes to be yanked closed, for you to come to the door to see why the hell I am parked outside your home on a night like tonight. And what, really, could I say? I was lonely? I missed her? I deserved to be the mother inside your glowing house?

Instead she prances back into the living room, where you've coaxed your wife from the chair. While you dance together, close, feeling up the back of her shirt, our daughter takes the boy's hand and leads him to the center of the living-room window. An actor hitting her mark on the stage. They were framed so precisely.

He looks just like Sam. He has his eyes. And that wave of dark hair that ends in a curl, the curl I wrapped around my finger over and over again.

I feel sick.

Our daughter is staring out the window looking at me, her hands on your son's shoulders. She bends down and kisses him on the cheek. And then again. And then again. The boy likes the affection. He is used to it. He is pointing to the falling snow but she won't look away from me. She rubs the tops of his arms as though she's warming him up. Like a mother would do.

You come to the window and kneel down to the boy's level. You look out and then you look up. My car doesn't catch your eye. You point to the snowflakes like your son, and you trace a path across the sky with your finger. You're talking about the sleigh. About the reindeer. He's searching the night, trying to see what you see. You flick him playfully under the chin. Her eyes are still fixed on me. I find myself sitting back in my seat. I swallow and finally look away from her. She always wins.

When I look back she's still there, watching my car.

I think she might reach for the curtain, but she doesn't. My eyes don't leave her this time. I pick up the thick stack of paper beside me on the passenger seat and feel the weight of my words.

I've come here to give this to you.

This is my side of the story.

You slid your chair over and tapped my textbook with the end of your pencil and I stared at the page, hesitant to look up. "Hello?" I had answered you like a phone call. This made you laugh. And so we sat there, giggling, two strangers in a school library, studying for the same elective subject. There must have been hundreds of students in the class—I had never seen you before. The curls in your hair fell over your eyes and you twirled them with your pencil. You had such a peculiar name. You walked me home later in the afternoon and we were quiet with each other. You didn't hide how smitten you were, smiling right at me every so often; I looked away each time. I had never experienced attention like that from anyone before. You kissed my hand outside my dorm and this made us laugh all over again.

Soon **we were** twenty-one and we were inseparable. We had less than a year left until we graduated. We spent it sleeping together in my raft of a dorm bed, and studying at opposite ends of the couch with our legs intertwined. We'd go out to the bar with your friends, but we always ended up home early, in bed, in the novelty of each other's warmth. I barely drank, and you'd had enough of the party scene—you wanted only me. Nobody in my world seemed to mind much. I had a small circle of friends who were more like acquaintances. I was so focused on maintaining my grades for my scholarship that I didn't have the time or the interest for a typical college social life. I suppose I hadn't grown very close to anyone in those years, not until I met you. You offered me something different. We slipped out of the social orbit and were happily all each other needed.

The comfort I found in you was consuming—I had nothing when I met you, and so you effortlessly became my everything. This didn't mean you weren't worthy of it—you were. You were gentle and thoughtful and supportive. You were the first person I'd told that I wanted to be a writer, and you replied, "I can't imagine you being anyone else." I reveled in the way girls looked at us, like they had something to be jealous about. I smelled your head of waxy dark hair while you slept at night and traced the line of your fuzzy jaw to wake you up in the morning. You were an addiction.

For my birthday, you wrote down one hundred things you loved about me. *14. I love that you snore a little bit right when you fall asleep. 27. I love the beautiful way you write. 39. I love tracing my name on your back. 59. I love sharing a muffin with you on the way to class. 72. I love the mood you wake up in on Sundays. 80. I love watching you finish a good book and then hold it to your chest at the end. 92. I love what a good mother you'll be one day.*

"Why do you think I'll be a good mother?" I put down the list and felt for a moment like maybe you didn't know me at all.

"Why wouldn't you be a good mother?" You poked me playfully in the belly. "You're caring. And sweet. I can't wait to have little babies with you."

There was nothing to do but force myself to smile.

I'd never met someone with a heart as eager as yours.

O*ne day you'll understand,* Blythe. The women in this family . . . we're different."

I can still see my mother's tangerine lipstick on the cigarette filter. The ash falling into the cup, swimming in the last sip of my orange juice. The smell of my burnt toast.

You asked about my mother, Cecilia, only on a few occasions. I told you only the facts: (1) she left when I was eleven years old, (2) I only ever saw her twice after that, and (3) I had no idea where she was.

You knew I was holding back more, but you never pressed—you were scared of what you might hear. I understood. We're all entitled to have certain expectations of each other and of ourselves. Motherhood is no different. We all expect to have, and to marry, and to be, good mothers.

1939–1958

Etta was born on the very same day World War II began. She had eyes like the Atlantic Ocean and was red-faced and pudgy from the beginning.

She fell in love with the first boy she ever met, the town doctor's son. His name was Louis, and he was polite and well spoken, not common among the boys she knew, and he wasn't the type to care that Etta hadn't been born with the luck of good looks. Louis walked Etta to school with one hand behind his back, from their very first day of school to their last. And Etta was charmed by things like that.

Her family owned hundreds of acres of cornfields. When Etta turned eighteen and told her father she wanted to marry Louis, he insisted his new son-in-law had to learn how to farm. He had no sons of his own, and he wanted Louis to take over the family business. But Etta thought her father just wanted to prove a point to the young man: farming was hard and respectable work. It wasn't for the weak. And it certainly wasn't for an intellectual. Etta had chosen someone who was nothing like her father.

Louis had planned to be a doctor like his own father was, and had a scholarship waiting for medical school. But he wanted Etta's hand in marriage more than he wanted a medical license. Despite Etta's pleas to take it easy on him, her father worked Louis to the bone. He was up *at four o'clock every morning and out into the dewy fields. Four in the morning until dusk, and as Etta liked to remind people, he never complained once. Louis sold the medical bag and textbooks that his own father had passed down to him, and he put the money in a jar on their kitchen counter. He told Etta it was the start of a college fund for their future children. Etta thought this said a lot about the selfless kind of man he was.*

One fall day, before the sun rose, Louis was severed by the beater on a silage wagon. He bled to death, alone in the cornfield. Etta's father found him and sent her to cover up the body with a tarp from the barn. She carried Louis's mangled leg back to the farmhouse and threw it at her father's head while he was filling a bucket of water meant to wash away the blood on the wagon.

She hadn't told her family yet about the child growing inside her. She was a big woman, seventy pounds overweight, and hid the pregnancy well. The baby girl, Cecilia, was born four months later on the kitchen floor in the middle of a snowstorm. Etta stared at the jar of money on the counter above her while she pushed the baby out.

Etta and Cecilia lived quietly at the farmhouse and rarely ventured into town. When they did, it wasn't hard to hear everyone's whispers about the woman who "suffered from the nerves." In those days, not much more was said—not much more was suspected. Louis's father gave Etta's mother a regular supply of sedatives to give to Etta as she saw fit. And so Etta spent most days in the small brass bed in the room she grew up in and her mother took care of Cecilia.

But Etta soon realized she would never meet another man lying doped up like that in bed. She learned to function well enough and eventually started to take care of Cecilia, pushing her around town in the stroller while the poor girl screamed for her grandmother. Etta told people she'd been plagued with a terrible chronic stomach pain, that she couldn't eat for months on end, and that's how she'd got so thin. Nobody believed this, but Etta didn't care about their lazy gossip. She had just met Henry.

Henry was new to town and they went to the same church. He managed a staff of sixty people at a candy manufacturing plant. He was sweet to Etta from the minute they met—he loved babies and Cecilia was particularly cute, so she turned out not to be the problem everyone said she'd be.

Before long, Henry bought them a Tudor-style house with mint-green trim in the middle of town. Etta left the brass bed for good and gained back all the weight she'd lost. She threw herself into making a home for her family. There was a well-built porch with a swing, lace curtains on every window, and chocolate chip cookies always in the oven. One day their new living-room furniture was delivered to the wrong house, and the neighbor let the delivery man set it all up in her basement even though she hadn't ordered it. When Etta caught wind of this, she ran down the street after the truck, yelling profanity in her housecoat and curlers. This gave everyone a good laugh, including, eventually, Etta.

She tried very hard to be the woman she was expected to be.

A good wife. A good mother.

Everything seemed like it would be just fine.

2

Things that come to mind when I think about the beginning of us:

Your mother and father. This might not have been as important to other people, but with you came a family. My only family. The generous gifts, the airplane tickets to be with you all somewhere sunny on vacation. Their house smelled like warm, laundered linens, always, and I never wanted to leave when we visited. The way your mother touched the ends of my hair made me want to crawl onto her lap. Sometimes it felt like she loved me as much as she loved you.

Their unquestioning acceptance about where my father was, and the lack of judgment when he declined their invitation to visit for the holidays, was a kindness I was grateful for. Cecilia, of course, was never discussed; you'd thoughtfully prefaced this with them before you brought me home. (*Blythe is wonderful. She really is. But just so you know . . .*) My mother wouldn't have been someone you gossiped about among yourselves; none of you had an appetite for anything but the pleasant.

You were all so perfect.

You called your little sister "darling" and she adored you. You phoned home every night and I would listen from the hallway, wishing I could hear what your mother said that made you laugh like you did. You went home every other weekend to help your dad around the house. You hugged. You babysat your small cousins. You knew your mother's banana bread recipe. You gave your parents a card every year on their anniversary. My parents had never even mentioned their wedding.

My father. He didn't return my message informing him I wouldn't be home for Thanksgiving that year, but I lied to you and said he was happy I'd met someone, and that he sends his best wishes to your family. The truth was we hadn't spoken much since you and I met. We'd communicated mostly through our answering machines, and even then it had become a series of stale, generic exchanges that I would have been embarrassed for you to hear. I'm still not sure how we got there, he and I. The lie was necessary, like the scattering of other lies I'd told so that you didn't suspect just how fucked up my family was. Family was too important to you—neither of us could risk how the whole truth about mine might change the way you saw me.

That first apartment. I loved you the most there when it was morning. The way you pulled the sheet over you like a hood and slept some more, the thick boyish smell you left on our pillowcases. I was waking up early then, before the sun most of the time, to write at the end of the galley kitchen that was always so damn cold. I wore your bathrobe and drank tea from a ceramic cup I'd painted for you at one of those pottery places. You'd call my name later on, when the floors had warmed and the light from behind the blinds was enough for you to see the details of my flesh. You'd pull me back in and we'd experiment—you were bold and assertive and understood what my body was capable of before I was. You fascinated me. Your confidence. Your patience. The primal need you had for me.

Nights with Grace. She was the one friend from college I stayed in touch with after we graduated. I didn't let on how much I liked her because you seemed a bit jealous of her time with me and thought we drank too much, although I gave her very little as far as female friendships go. But still, you gave us both flowers on Valentine's Day the year she was single. I invited her to dinner once a month or so, and you'd sit as our third on the garbage pail flipped upside down. You'd always stop for the good bottle of wine on your way home from work. When the gossip took over, when she brought out the cigarettes, you'd excuse yourself politely and open a book. One night we heard you speaking to your sister on the balcony while we smoked inside (imagine?). She was going through a breakup and she had called her brother, her confidant. Grace asked me what was wrong with you. Bad in bed? Temper? There had to be something because no man was this perfect. But there wasn't. Not then. Not that I understood. I used the word "luck." I was lucky. I didn't have much, but I had you.

Our work. We didn't speak about it often. I envied your rising success and you knew it—you were sensitive to the differences in our careers, our incomes. You were making money and I was dreaming. I had made next to nothing since graduating, except from a few small freelance projects, but you supported us generously and gave me a credit card, saying only: "Use it for whatever you need." By then you'd been hired at the architecture firm and promoted twice in the time it took me to write three short stories. Unpublished ones. You would leave for work looking like you belonged to someone else.

My rejection letters came in like they were supposed to—this was part of the process, you reminded me, kindly and often. *It'll happen.* Your unconditional belief in me felt magical. I desperately wanted to prove to myself that I was as good as you thought I was. "Read to me. Whatever you wrote today. Please!" I always made you beg and then you'd chuckle when I feigned exasperation and agreed. Our silly routine. You'd curl up on the couch after dinner, exhausted, your office clothes still on. You would close your eyes while I read you my work and you would smile at all of my best lines.

The night I showed you my first published story, your hand shook as you took the heavy-stock magazine. I've thought of that often. That pride you had in me. I would see that shaking hand again years later, holding her tiny wet head, marked with my blood.

But before then:

You asked me to marry you on my twenty-fifth birthday.

With a ring I sometimes still wear on my left hand.

3

I never asked you if you liked my wedding dress. I bought it used
because I saw it in the window of a vintage store and couldn't get
it out of my mind while I browsed the expensive boutiques with
your mother. You never whispered, as some awed grooms do, sweating
at the altar and rocking on their feet, *You look beautiful.* You never
mentioned my dress when we hid behind the redbrick wall at the back
of the property, waiting to float into the courtyard where our guests
drank champagne and talked about the heat and wondered when the
next canapé would pass. You could barely look away from my shining
pink face. You could barely let go of my eyes.

You were the most handsome you had ever been and I can close my
eyes now and see twenty-six-year-old you, the way your skin looked
bright and your hair still curled down around your forehead. I swear
you had remnants of baby fat in your cheeks.

We squeezed each other's hands all night.

We knew so little then about each other, about the people we
would be.

We could have counted our problems on the petals of the daisy in
my bouquet, but it wouldn't be long before we were lost in a field of them.

"There will be no table for the family of the bride," I had overheard the wedding planner say in a low voice to the man who set up the folding chairs and place cards. He gave her a subtle nod.

Your parents gave us the wedding bands before the ceremony. They handed us the rings in a silver clamshell that had been given to your great-grandmother by the man she loved, who had gone to war and never come home. Inside was engraved a proclamation from him to her: *Violet, You will always find me.* You had said, "What a beautiful name she had."

Your mother, cloaked in a fancy pewter-colored shawl, gave us a toast: "Marriages can float apart. Sometimes we don't notice how far we've gone until all of a sudden, the water meets the horizon and it feels like we'll never make it back." She paused and looked only at me. "Listen for each other's heartbeat in the current. You'll always find each other. And then you'll always find the shore." She took your father's hand and you stood to raise your glass.

We compliantly made love that night because we were supposed to. We were exhausted. But we felt so real. We had wedding bands and a catering bill and adrenaline headaches.

I forever take you, my best friend and my soul mate, to be my partner in life, through everything that's good, and everything that's hard, and the tens of thousands of days that fall somewhere in between. You, Fox Connor, are the person I love. I commit myself to you.

Years later, our daughter watched me stuff the dress into the trunk of our car. I was going to take it back to the same place I'd found it.

4

I remember exactly what life was like in the time that followed.

The years before our own Violet came.

We ate dinner, late, on the couch, while we watched current affairs shows. We had spicy takeout on a black marble coffee table with vicious corners. We drank glasses of fizzy wine at two o'clock on weekend afternoons and then we napped until someone was roused, hours later, by the sound of people walking outside to the bar. Sex happened. Haircuts happened. I read the travel section of the newspaper and felt it was research, realistic research, for the place we'd go next. I browsed expensive stores with a hot, foamy beverage in my hands. I wore Italian leather gloves in the winter. You golfed with friends. I cared about politics! We cuddled on the lounge chair and thought it was nice to be together, touching. Movies were a thing I could watch, something that could take my mind away from the place where I sat. Life was less visceral. Ideas were brighter. Words came easier! My period was light. You played music throughout the house, new stuff, artists someone had mentioned to you over a beer at an establishment filled with adults. The laundry soap wasn't organic and so our clothes smelled artificially mountain fresh. We went to the mountains. You asked about my writing. I never looked at another man and wondered what he'd be like to fuck instead. You drove a very impractical car every day until the fourth or fifth snowfall of the year. You wanted a dog. We noticed dogs, on the street; we stopped to scratch their necks. The park was not my only reprieve from housework. The books we read had no pictures. We did not think about the impact of television screens on brains. We did not understand that children liked things best if they were manufactured for the purpose of an adult's use. We thought we knew each other. And we thought we knew ourselves.

5

The summer I was twenty-seven. Two weathered folding chairs on the balcony overlooking the alley between us and the building next door. The string of white paper lanterns I hung had somehow made palpable the creeping smell of hot garbage from below. That was where you said to me over glasses of crisp white wine, "Let's start trying. Tonight."

We'd talked about it before, many times. You were practically gleeful when I held other people's babies or got down on my knees to play with them. *You're a natural.* But I was the one who was imagining. Motherhood. What it would be like. How it would feel. *Looks good on you.*

I would be different. I would be like other women for whom it all came so easily. I would be everything my own mother was not.

She barely entered my mind in those days. I made sure of it. And when she slipped in uninvited, I blew her away. As if she were those ashes falling into my orange juice.

By that summer, we'd rented a bigger apartment with a second bedroom in a building with a very slow elevator; the walk-up we lived in before wouldn't work for a stroller. We drew each other's attention to baby things with small nudges, never words. Tiny trendy outfits in store windows. Little siblings dutifully holding hands. There was anticipation. There was hope. Months earlier I had started paying more attention to my period. Tracked my ovulation. I'd made notes to mark the dates in my day planner. One day I found little happy faces drawn next to my *O*'s. Your excitement was endearing. You were going to be a wonderful father. And I would be your child's wonderful mother.

I look back and marvel at the confidence I found then. I no longer felt like my mother's daughter. I felt like your wife. I had been pretending I was perfect for you for years. I wanted to keep you happy. I wanted to be anyone other than the mother I came from. And so I wanted a baby, too.

6

The Ellingtons. They lived three doors down from the house I grew up in and their lawn was the only one in the neighborhood that stayed green through the dry, relentless summers. Mrs. Ellington knocked on our door exactly seventy-two hours after Cecilia had left me. My father was still snoring on the sofa where he had slept each night for the past year. I had realized only an hour earlier that my mother wasn't going to come home this time. I'd gone through her dresser and the drawers in the bathroom and the place where she stashed her cartons of cigarettes. Everything that mattered to her was gone. I knew enough by then not to ask my father where she went.

"Would you like to come for a nice Sunday roast at our house, Blythe?" Her tight curls were shiny and hard, fresh from the salon, and I couldn't help but reply directly to them with a nod and a thank-you. I went straight to the laundry room and put my best outfit—a navy blue jumper and a rainbow-striped turtleneck—in the washing machine. I had thought of asking her if my father could come, too, but Mrs. Ellington was the most socially appropriate woman I knew, and I figured if she didn't include him in her invitation, there was a reason.

Thomas Ellington Jr. was the best friend I had. I don't remember when I'd given him that distinction, but by the time I was ten, he was the only person I cared to play with. Other girls my age made me uneasy. My life looked different from theirs—their Easy-Bake Ovens, their homemade hair bows, their proper socks. Their mothers. I learned very early on that being different from them didn't feel good.

But the Ellingtons made me feel good.

The thing about Mrs. Ellington's invitation was that she must have somehow known my mother had left. Because my mother no longer allowed me to attend dinner at the Ellingtons'. At some point she had decided I needed to be home by a quarter to five every night, although there was nothing to come home to: the oven was always cold and the fridge was always empty. By then, most evenings my father and I ate instant oatmeal. He'd bring home small packets of brown sugar for the top, ones he stuffed in his pockets from the cafeteria at the hospital, where he managed the cleaning staff. He made decent enough money then, by local standards at least. We just didn't seem to live that way.

I had somehow learned that it was polite to bring a gift when invited to a nice dinner, so I had clipped a fistful of hydrangeas from our front bush, although late September had turned most of the white petals to a crispy dusty pink. I tied the stems with my rubber hair elastic.

"You're such a thoughtful young woman," Mrs. Ellington had said. She put them in a blue vase and placed them carefully on the table in the middle of the steaming dishes.

Thomas's younger brother, Daniel, adored me. We played trains in the living room after school while Thomas did his homework with his mother. I always saved mine for after eight o'clock, when Cecilia either went to bed or was gone for the night to the city. She did that often—went to the city and came back the next day. So doing my homework then gave me something to do while I waited for my eyes to get tired. Little Daniel fascinated me. He spoke like an adult and knew how to multiply when he was just five years old. I would quiz him on the times tables while we played on the Ellingtons' scratchy orange rug, amazed at how clever he was. Mrs. Ellington would pop in to listen and always touched each of our heads before she left. *Good job, you two.*

Thomas was smart, too, but in different ways. He made up the most incredible stories, which we'd write in the tiny spiral notebooks his mother bought us at the corner store. Then we'd draw pictures to go along with every page. Each book would take us weeks—we painstakingly discussed what to draw for each part of the story and then took our time sharpening the whole box of pencils before we began. Once Thomas let me bring one home, a story I loved about a family with a beautiful, kind mother who became very sick with a rare form of deadly chicken pox. They go for their last vacation together as a family to a faraway island, where they find a tiny, magical gnome in the sand named George, who speaks only in rhymes. He grants them the gift of one special superpower in exchange for bringing him home in their suitcase to the other side of the world. They agree, and he gives them what they wish for—*Your mom will live forever, until the end of time. Whenever you get sad, just sing this little rhyme!* The gnome lives inside the mother's pocket for eternity, happily ever after. I'd drawn the family carefully on the pages of this book—they looked just like the Ellingtons, but with a third child who didn't look anything like them: a daughter with Crayola-peach skin like mine.

One morning I found my mother sitting on the edge of my bed, flipping through the book, which I'd hidden deep in my drawer.

"Where did this come from?" She spoke without looking at me and stopped on the page where I'd drawn myself as part of the Black family.

"I made it. With Thomas. At his house." I reached for the book in her hands, my book. The reach was pleading. She yanked her arm away from me, and then tossed the book at my head, as though the spiraled pages and everything about them disgusted her. The corner clipped my chin and the book landed between us on the floor. I stared at it, embarrassed. Of the pictures she didn't like, of the fact that I'd been hiding it from her.

My mother stood up, her thin neck erect, her shoulders back. She shut the door quietly behind her.

I brought the book back to Thomas's house the next day.

"Why don't you want to keep it? You were so proud of what you two made together." Mrs. Ellington took it from my hands and saw that it was bent in a few places. She smoothed the cover softly. "It's okay," she said, shaking her head so that I didn't have to answer. "You can keep it here."

She put it on the bookshelf in their living room. When I was leaving that day, I noticed she'd opened the book to the last page and faced it out toward the room—the family of five, me included, our arms around one another, an explosion of tiny hearts coming from our smiling mother who stood in the middle.

At the Sunday dinner after my mother left, I offered to clean the kitchen with Mrs. Ellington. She clicked on a cassette tape and sang just a little as she cleared the table and wiped the counters. I watched her bashfully from the corner of my eye while I rinsed the dishes. At one point she stopped and picked up the oven mitt from the counter. She looked at me with a playful smile, slipped it over her hand, and held it up beside her head.

"Miss Blythe," she said in a funny high-pitched voice, her hand moving in the puppet. "We ask all of our celebrity guests here on the *Ellington After-Dinner Talk Show* a few questions about themselves. So. Tell us—what do you like to do for fun, hmm? Ever go to the movies?"

I laughed awkwardly, not sure how to play along. "Uh, yeah. Sometimes?" I hadn't ever been to the movies. I also hadn't ever talked to a puppet. I looked down and shuffled some dishes around in the sink. Thomas came running into the kitchen squealing, "Mommy's doing the talk show again!" and Daniel flew in behind him. "Ask me something, ask me!" Mrs. Ellington stood with one hand on her hip and the other hand chatting away, her voice squeaking from the corner of her mouth. Mr. Ellington popped his head in to watch.

"Now, Daniel, what is your very favorite thing to eat, and you can't say ice cream!" said the puppet. He jumped up and down while he thought of his answer and Thomas shouted options. "Pie! I know it's pie!" Mrs. Ellington's oven mitt gasped, "PIE! Not rhubarb, though, right? That gives me the toots!" and the boys screamed over each other in laughter. I listened to them carry on. I'd never felt anything like this before. The spontaneity. The silliness. The comfort. Mrs. Ellington saw me watching from the sink and called me over with her finger. She put the oven mitt on my hand and said, "A guest host tonight! What a treat!" And then she whispered to me, "Go ahead, ask the boys what they'd rather do. Eat worms or someone else's boogers?" I snickered. She rolled her eyes and smiled, as if to say, *Trust me, they'll love it, those silly boys.*

She walked me home that night, which she had never done before. All the lights in my house were off. She watched as I unlocked the door, to make sure my dad's shoes were in the hallway. And then from her pocket she pulled the book about the magical gnome and gave it to me.

"Thought you might want this back now."

I did. I flipped the pages with my thumb and thought, for the first time that night, about my mother.

I thanked her again for dinner. She turned around at the end of my driveway and called, "Same time next week! If I don't see you before then." I suspect she knew she would.

7

I knew as soon as you came inside of me. Your warmth filled me and I knew. I couldn't blame you for thinking I was crazy—we'd been trying for months—but nearly three weeks later we laughed together lying on our bathroom floor like drunken fools. Everything had changed. You skipped work for the day, remember? We watched movies in bed and ordered takeout for each meal. We just wanted to be together. You and me. And her. I knew she was a girl.

I couldn't write anymore. My head flew away every time I tried. To what she would look like and who she would be.

I began doing prenatal exercise classes. We started each class in a stretching circle where we introduced ourselves and said how many months along we were. I was fascinated to see what was coming, looking at the other women's bellies in the mirror as we followed an aerobic routine that barely seemed worth doing. My own body was still unchanged and I couldn't wait to see her make room for herself. In me. In the world.

Walking through the city to go about my day had changed. I had a secret. I half expected people to look at me differently. I wanted to touch my still-flat belly and say, *I'm going to be a mother. This is who I am now.* I was consumed.

. . .

There was a day at the library when I flipped through books for hours in the Pregnancy and Childbirth section. I had just started to show. A woman walked by me, searching the spines for a particular book. The one she slid out from the shelf was a well-used guide to sleep.

"How far along?"

"Six months." She scanned the table of contents with her finger and then looked at my middle before my face. "You?"

"Twenty-one weeks." We nodded to each other. She looked like she used to make homemade kombucha and go to 6:00 a.m. spin classes, but now settled for leftover puree and a walk to the store for diapers. "I haven't even thought about sleep yet."

"Your first?"

I nodded and smiled.

"This is my second." The woman lifted the book. "Honestly, just figure out the sleep and you'll be fine. Nothing else matters. I really fucked that up the first time."

I laughed, sort of, and thanked her for the tip. A child's wail broke from across the library and she sighed.

"That's mine." She gestured up and over her shoulder, and then pulled out a second copy of the same book she was there for. She held it out to me and I noticed she had pink marker on her hands. "Good luck."

She looked full and feminine from behind as she walked away, her wide hips, her shoulder-length hair creased from what sleep she had found. She felt, to me, so obviously a mother. Was it the way she looked, or moved? Was it the way she seemed to have more to care about than I did? When would this happen to me, this crossover? How was I about to change?

8

Fox, come see." It was the third huge box your mother had sent since we told them about the baby. She was relentless in her excitement and called every week to see how I was feeling. I pulled out fancy swaddle blankets and knitted newborn hats and teeny-tiny white sleepers. At the bottom there was a separate package on which she'd written "Fox's Baby Things." In it was a worn teddy bear with buttons for eyes, and a threadbare flannel blanket with silk trim that once had been ivory white. A small porcelain figurine of a baby boy sitting on a moon with your name in delicate gold script. I lifted the teddy to my nose and then to yours. You reminisced. I half listened but my mind was elsewhere, searching my past for the same kind of familiar tokens, blankies and stuffies and favorite books, but I couldn't find any.

"Do you think we can do this?" I asked you over dinner that night, pushing my food around the plate. I could barely stomach meat since I'd become pregnant.

"Do what?"

"Be parents. Raise a child."

You reached over and smiled as you stabbed my beef with your fork.

"You're going to be a good mother, Blythe."

You traced a heart on the top of my hand.

"You know, my own mother . . . she wasn't . . . she left. She wasn't anything like yours."

"I know." You were quiet. You could have asked me to say more. You could have held my hand and looked me in the eye and asked me to keep talking. You took my plate to the sink.

"You're different," you said eventually, and hugged me from behind. And then, with an indignation in your voice that I didn't expect: "You aren't anything like her."

I believed you. Life was easier when I believed you.

Afterward we lay together on the couch and you held my belly like the world was in your hands. We loved waiting for her to move, staring at my stretched skin, the blue-green hue of the veins underneath like the colors of the earth. Some fathers talk to their wife's belly—they say the baby can hear. But as we watched for her to show us she was in there, you were quiet and awestruck, like she was a dream you couldn't believe was real.

9

Today could be the day."

The baby felt heavy and low in the morning and I'd dreamed all night of my amniotic fluid soaking our bed. The panic came quickly and pulled me to a place I'd consciously avoided for the entire forty weeks of my pregnancy. I whispered to myself as I boiled the water for tea. *It's okay if she comes. It's okay if this is it. It's okay to have this baby.* I sat at the kitchen table and wrote these mantras on a piece of paper over and over until you walked into the room.

"The car seat's in. I'll keep my phone in my hand all day."

I slid the piece of paper under the place mat. You kissed me and left for work. I knew.

By seven thirty that night we were on the bedroom floor together, my knees splintered from the grooves in the old parquet flooring. You pressed on my hips while I tried to breathe deeply, evenly. We'd practiced this. We'd done the class. But I couldn't find that sense of calm I'd been promised, the intuition that was supposed to kick in. You were keeping track of things with chicken scratch, minutes and contractions. I ripped the scorecard from your hand and threw it back at you.

"We're going now." I couldn't be in our apartment anymore. She was volcanic and I was fighting to keep her in. None of what I'd prepared for felt possible. I wasn't open, I wasn't ready. I couldn't visualize her dropping into my open pelvis, I couldn't coax myself to expand like the mouth of a river. I was clenched and scared. I didn't know what to do.

What they say about the pain is true—I can no longer remember what it felt like. I remember the diarrhea. I remember how cold the room was. I remember seeing the forceps on a cart in the hallway decorated with Christmas tinsel garland as we walked between contractions. The nurse had hands like a lumberjack. When she shoved them in me to check my dilation I would whimper and she would look away.

"I don't want this to happen," I whispered to nobody. I was exhausted. You were standing two feet away, drinking the water the nurse had brought for me. I couldn't keep it down.

"You don't want what to happen?"

"The baby."

"You mean the birth?"

"No, I mean the baby."

"Do you want the epidural now? I think you need it." You craned your neck to look for a nurse and put a cold cloth on the back of my neck. I remember you holding my hair like a horse's mane.

I didn't want the drugs. I wanted to feel how bad it could get. *Punish me,* I said to her. *Rip me apart.* You kissed my head and I smacked you away. I hated you. For everything you wanted of me.

I begged for them to let me push on the toilet—I was most comfortable there and I was delirious by that point. I couldn't follow a thing anyone said to me. You coaxed me back to the bed and they ordered me into the stirrups. Nothing about it felt right. The burning. I reached down to feel the flames I was sure were there, but someone pushed away my hand.

"Fuck you."

"Come on now," the doctor said. "You can do this."

"I can't. I won't," I spat back.

"You have to push," you said calmly. I closed my eyes and I willed something horrible to go wrong. Death. I wanted a death. Mine or the baby's. I didn't think, even then, that we would survive each other.

When she came out, the doctor held her over my face, but I could barely see her in the assault of bright light. I shook vigorously from the pain and said that I might be sick. You appeared at my hip, next to the doctor, and he turned toward you instead, saying the baby was a girl. You put your hand under her slippery head and brought her carefully to your face. You said something to her. I don't know what—you had your own secret language from her first minute in this world. The doctor then cupped her belly, like she was a wet kitten, and handed her over to the nurse. He went back to work. My afterbirth splashed onto the floor. He tugged at my opening with suture thread while I stared at the light in awe of what I'd just done. I was one of them now, the mothers. I had never felt so alive, so electric. My teeth chattered so hard that I thought they might chip. And then I heard her. The howl. She sounded so familiar. "Are you ready, Mom?" someone said. They placed her on my bare chest. She felt like a warm, screaming loaf of bread. She had been cleaned of my blood and bundled in the hospital's flannel blanket. Her nose was speckled with yellow. Her eyes looked slimy and dark and they stared right into mine.

"I'm your mother."

The first night in the hospital I didn't sleep. I stared at her quietly behind the perforated curtain that surrounded the bed. Her toes were a row of tiny snow peas. I would open her blanket and trace my finger along her skin and watch her twitch. She was alive. She came from me. She smelled like me. She didn't latch for my colostrum, not even when they squished my breast like a hamburger and pried at her chin. They said to give it time. The nurse offered to take her while I slept but I needed to stare at her. I didn't notice my tears until they dropped onto her face. I wiped each one from her skin with my pinkie and then tasted it. I wanted to taste her. Her fingers. The tops of her ears. I wanted to feel them in my mouth. I was physically numb from the painkillers but inside I felt lit on fire by oxytocin. Some mothers might have called it love, but it felt more to me like astonishment. Like wonder. I didn't think about what to do next, about what we would do when we got home. I didn't think about raising her and caring for her and who she would become. I wanted to be alone with her. In that surreal space of time, I wanted to feel every pulse.

A part of me knew we would never exist like that again.

1962

Etta turned on the bath faucet to wash Cecilia's long, tangled hair. She was five years old and it wasn't often anyone made her brush it. Her elbows dug into the avocado green ceramic.

"Lean back," Etta said and tugged her hard. She pulled her head a few inches farther until Cecilia was square under the thunder of cold water. She gasped and choked and wrestled, until she pulled free of Etta's fingers clutched in her skin. When she caught her breath, she looked up to see Etta staring right at her. Etta didn't flinch. Cecilia knew she wasn't done.

Etta grabbed her ears and forced her back under again. Her nostrils stung as they filled with water. Her head started to feel like it was floating away.

And then Etta let go. She pulled out the moldy plug from the drain and left the bathroom.

Cecilia didn't move. She had shit herself during the fight and lay there, shaking and foul and cold, until she fell asleep.

When she woke up, Etta was in bed and Henry was home from work, sitting in the living room watching television, eating a plate of reheated roast beef, the tinfoil carefully folded on the table to be reused the next day.

Cecilia walked into the room with a towel draped over her shoulders *and startled him. He asked through a mouthful of food why on earth she wasn't asleep at nearly midnight. Cecilia told him she'd wet the bed.*

His face fell. He folded her up in his long arms and carried her to her mother's bed. She still stank like shit, but Henry didn't say a thing about it. He shook Etta awake.

"Dear. Can you fix Cecilia's sheets? She's wet herself."

Cecilia held her breath.

Etta opened her eyes and took Cecilia's hand in the same grip that had nearly killed her five hours ago. She walked her to her room and put a nightgown over her head and sat her firmly on the bed. Cecilia's heart pounded as they both listened to Henry's footsteps go back down the stairs. Cecilia was always listening for Henry's footsteps—he would change Etta's mood like the flip of a light switch.

Etta didn't say a word and she didn't touch her. She just left the room.

Cecilia understood that her instinct to lie was the right one. What had happened between her and her mother was to stay a secret.

There were other times over the next few years when Etta's problems with "nerves" were obvious to Cecilia. Some days she would lock her out of the house after school. The front door was bolted shut, the back door locked, the drapes all closed. But Cecilia could hear the radio playing or the kitchen tap running. She'd go to Main Street to kill time by wandering the aisles of stores, looking at things her mother never seemed interested in buying anymore, like fruit-scented soaps, or the mint chocolates she had once enjoyed.

After it had been dark for one hour, Cecilia would head home again. Henry would be there and dinner would be on the table. She would tell Henry she'd been at the library and he'd pat her on the head and say she'd become the smartest student in the class if she kept studying so hard. Etta would ignore her completely, as though she hadn't spoken at all.

Other days, Cecilia would come down for breakfast in the morning and Etta would be sitting at the table, looking down at her lap, her full cheeks white. Like she hadn't slept a wink. Cecilia didn't know what she did during those nights, but on those mornings, Etta seemed especially distant. Especially sad. She wouldn't look up until she heard Henry's feet hit the stairs.

You're anxious. She can sense it," you said. She'd cried for five and a half hours. I cried for four of those. I made you look up the definition of colic in one of the baby books.

"More than three hours, for three days a week, for three weeks straight."

"She's been crying longer than that."

"She's only been here for five days, Blythe."

"I mean hours. Longer than three hours."

"She's just gassy, I think."

"I need you to cancel your parents' trip here." I couldn't deal with your perfect mother being there for Christmas in a couple of weeks. She called constantly, and every conversation started with *I know things are different these days, but trust me. . . .* Gripe water. Tighter swaddles. Rice cereal in the bottle.

"They'll be a big help for you, honey. For all of us." You wanted your perfect mother there.

"I'm still bleeding through my pad. I smell like rotting flesh. I can't put my shirt on, my boobs are too sore. Look at me, Fox."

"I'll call them tonight."

"Can you take her?"

"Give her here. Go get some sleep."

"I think the baby hates me."

"Shhh."

I'd been warned about those hard, early days. I'd been warned about breasts like cement boulders. Cluster feeds. The squirt bottle. I'd read all the books. I'd done the research. Nobody talked about the feeling of being woken up after forty minutes of sleep, on bloodstained sheets, with the dread of knowing what had to happen next. I felt like the only mother in the world who wouldn't survive it. The only mother who couldn't recover from having her perineum stitched from her anus to her vagina. The only mother who couldn't fight through the pain of newborn gums cutting like razor blades on her nipples. The only mother who couldn't pretend to function with her brain in the vise of sleeplessness. The only mother who looked down at her daughter and thought, *Please. Go away.*

Violet cried only when she was with me; it felt like a betrayal.

We were supposed to want each other.

The night nurse had the softest hands I had ever felt. She barely fit in the nursery chair. She smelled like citrus fruit and hair spray and she was unflappable.

I was tired.

Every new mom goes through this, Blythe. I know it's hard. I remember.

But your mother must have been worried because she hired the woman without asking us and paid her fee. We were three weeks in and the baby wouldn't sleep longer than an hour and a half at a time. All she wanted to do was feed and cry. My nipples looked like raw ground beef.

You barely saw the night nurse—you were asleep most nights before she came. She brought me the baby every three hours, not a minute sooner or later. I would hear her heavy feet coming toward the door and startle from the glorious depths of sleep and fish my breast out of my nightshirt with my eyes barely open. I would hand her back when we were done. She would take her to the nursery and burp her, change her, rock her, and put her to sleep in the bassinet. We rarely exchanged a word but I loved her. I needed her. She came for four weeks until your mother said to me on the phone in her firm but delicate voice, *Honey. It's been a month. You need to do it on your own now.*

On the last shift she was with us, the night nurse brought the baby into our room for the early morning feed before she went home. But she didn't step out of the room like she normally did. You were snoring beside me.

"She's a sweet baby, isn't she," I had whispered to the woman. I shifted to relieve my stubborn hemorrhoids and then fiddled with my nipple in her mouth. I really didn't know if she was, but it felt like something a new mother would say of the warm, pink flesh she'd pushed into the world.

She stood over us and looked down at Violet and my huge brown nipple as she tried to latch again. We still hadn't got the hang of it yet and milk sprayed the baby's face. She didn't answer me.

"Do you think she's a good baby?" Maybe she hadn't heard me. I winced. The baby was on. The nurse stepped back and watched us as though she were trying to figure something out.

"Sometimes she opens her eyes so wide and looks right at me, like . . ." She let her words trail off and then she shook her head and sucked through her teeth.

"She's curious. She's alert," I clarified with words I'd heard other mothers use. I wasn't sure what she was implying.

She stood still and silent while I fed. She nodded sometime later. Too much time later. I wondered if there was something else she wanted to say. When the baby was done, she lifted Violet quietly and patted me on the shoulder. She left to put her down and I never saw her again.

You were irritated when it took weeks for the smell of the woman's hair spray to leave the nursery, but sometimes I went in there just for the scent of her.

12

The month with the night nurse helped. Violet and I emerged from the fog and found ourselves a routine. I focused a lot on that routine. Our day was bookended by you leaving for work and you arriving home again. All I had to do was keep her alive in between. One thing a day—that was always my goal. A few groceries. Her doctor's appointment. Exchanging a onesie I'd bought that she never wore and had already grown out of. Coffee and a muffin. I'd sit on the park bench in the cold and pick away at the dry bits of bran while I stared at her stuffed in a down-filled snowsuit, and waited for the next nap time.

I'd met a small group of women in the prenatal exercise class who had all been due around the same time as me. I didn't know them well, but was added to their email chain at some point. They often invited me to meet for a walk, or lunch somewhere that would accommodate our brigade of strollers. You loved when I had plans with them—you were excited for me to be like other moms. I mostly went for you. To show you I was normal.

Like all of our days, the conversations had a mundane routine. How the babies slept and when and where, when they ate and how much, the plan for solid foods, day care or nanny, what contraptions they'd bought that they couldn't live without that the rest of us needed to buy, too. Eventually it would be nap time for one of the babies, which was allowed only at home in the crib so as not to disturb the hard-earned schedule. And so we'd pack it up and go. Sometimes, as we paid the bill, I'd find the courage to say what really was on my mind. I threw it out like bait:

"This is pretty hard some days, isn't it? This whole motherhood thing."

"Sometimes. Yeah. But it's the most rewarding thing we'll ever do, you know? It's all *so* worth it when you see their little faces in the morning." I studied these women closely, trying to find their lies. They never cracked. They never slipped.

"Totally." I always gave some indication of agreement. But then I would stare at Violet's face in the stroller all the way home, wondering why she didn't feel like the best thing that had ever happened to me.

Once, weeks after I'd stopped joining those girls, I passed the window of a coffee shop where at the counter inside, overlooking the street, a mother sat staring at her baby. Maybe three or four months old, just a bit younger than Violet. The baby was slumped in the grasp of its mother's fingers, staring straight back at her. The woman's mouth did not move. There was no assurance from between her lips: *You're Mama's baby, you're my sweet baby. You're such a good baby, aren't you?* Instead, she turned the baby ever so slightly to one side, and then to the other, as though she were examining a clay artifact for marks of imperfection.

I lingered outside the window and I watched them, looking for love, looking for regret. I pictured the life she might have had before the baby had confined her to choose between the option of a stuffy, messy apartment that smelled like her own soured milk or the lonely window of a coffee shop.

I went inside and ordered a latte that I didn't want and sat on the stool next to her. Violet was asleep in the stroller and I pushed it back and forth gently so she wouldn't wake up. The diaper bag slipped from the handle and her bottle fell out and rolled across the floor. I collected it and decided I would not wipe off the nipple. I felt a rush of power when I made clandestine decisions like this, decisions other mothers would not make because they weren't supposed to, like leaving a wet diaper on too long or skipping her overdue bath again because I couldn't be bothered. The woman turned to me and we shared a look. Not a smile, but an acknowledgment that we had both morphed into a version of ourselves that didn't feel as good as had been advertised. Curds of milk came out of her baby's mouth and she wiped it with a rough paper napkin.

"Tough days, aren't they?" I had said, lifting my chin toward her baby who was still and expressionless, staring at her.

"There's that saying, the days are long but the years go fast." I nodded and looked at my own baby, who was starting to stir, her chin crinkling. "But I guess we'll see," she said flatly, like she, too, did not believe her experience of time would ever change again.

"Some women say being a mom is their greatest accomplishment. But I dunno, I don't feel like I've accomplished much yet." I laughed a little bit, because it was feeling too personal all of a sudden. But I needed this woman. She was everything the lunchtime friends were not.

"A girl?"

I told her the baby's name.

"Harry," she said of hers. "He's been here fifteen weeks."

We sat in silence for a few more minutes. And then she said, "It's like he just happened to me, all of a sudden. Slammed into my world and knocked over the furniture."

"Yeah," I said slowly, looking at her baby as though he were a weapon. "You want them and grow them and push them out, but *they* happen to *you*."

She took Harry off the counter and put him in the stroller. She tucked the blanket under him sloppily, like a poorly made bed. She still hadn't spoken to her son in a singsong voice, like all of those other mothers, and I wondered if she ever did.

"See you around," she said, and my heart sank. I was worried we'd never find each other again. I stammered, trying to find something else to say to keep her there.

"Do you live around here?"

"No, I don't actually. We live a bit north of the city. I'm just down here for an appointment."

"I'll give you my number," I said, my face flushed. I had never been comfortable making friends. But I suddenly flashed forward to late-night texting, when we would exchange brutally honest grievances and lament our existence.

"Oh. Sure. Here, I'll put it in my phone." She looked uncomfortable, and I wish I hadn't offered as I told her my cell number. She was never in touch and I never ran into her again.

I still think of that woman sometimes. I wonder if she eventually felt she'd achieved something, if she looks at Harry today and knows she did well as a mother, that she raised a good person. I wonder how that feels.

13

She smiled at you first. After bath time. You were wearing your reading glasses and said she must have seen her own reflection in the lens. But we both knew she wanted you the most from the beginning. I could never comfort her when she cried like you could—she melted into your skin and seemed to want to stay there, a part of you. My warmth and my smell seemed to mean nothing to her. They talk about the mother's heartbeat and the familiar sound of her womb, but it's as though I were a foreign country.

I listened to you placate her with soft whispers that soothed her to sleep. I studied you. I imitated you. You told me it was all in my head—that I was making a big deal out of nothing. That she was just a baby and babies didn't know how not to like a person. But it felt like two against one.

We were together around the clock and so yes, there were inevitably times she gave in, falling asleep on my chest or at my breast. You'd point this out like it was proof I was wrong—*See, honey? Just relax more around her and she'll be fine.* I believed you. I had to. I would run my nose over the fine hair on her head and breathe her in. Her smell was good for me. Her smell was a reminder that she had come from within me. That we were once attached by a living, throbbing cord of blood. I would close my eyes and replay the night she came out. Looking, feeling, for our connection. Those first hours. I knew it had been there. Before the chapped, bleeding nipples and the utter exhaustion and the crippling doubt and the unspeakable numbness.

You're doing great. I'm proud of you. You would sometimes whisper this to me in the dark while I fed her. You would touch both of our heads. Your girls. Your world. I would cry when you left the room. I didn't want to be the axis around which you both spun. I had nothing left to give either of you, but our lives had just begun together. What had I done? Why had I wanted her? Why did I think I would be any different than the mother I came from?

I thought about ways to get out. There, in the dark, my milk flowing, the chair rocking. I thought about putting her down in the crib and leaving in the middle of the night. I thought about where my passport was. About the hundreds of flights listed on the departures board at the airport. About how much cash I could take out from the ATM at once. About leaving my phone there on the bedside table. How long my milk would take to go dry, for my breasts to give up the proof she had been born.

My arms shook with the possibility.

These are thoughts I never let leave my lips. These are thoughts most mothers don't have.

14

I was eight years old and it was far past my bedtime. I'd been standing in the hallway in my nightgown listening to my mother and father fight in the living room.

There had been the sound of breaking glass. I knew it was the figurine of the woman in the full Southern dress holding the sun umbrella. I'm not sure where it had come from—a wedding gift perhaps. They'd been arguing about something he found in her coat pocket, and then my mother's trips to the city, and then someone named Lenny, and then me. My father felt I was becoming too quiet, too withdrawn. That I could benefit from some more attention from her once in a while.

"She doesn't need me, Seb."

"You're her mother, Cecilia."

"She'd be better off if I wasn't."

When my mother started sobbing, really crying, something I hadn't heard from her before despite the vitriol they flung at each other on a near nightly basis, I turned to go back to my room; my face was hot and the strained shrill of her voice made my stomach clench. But then I'd heard my father say my grandmother's name. He said, "You'll end up just like Etta."

My father's footsteps headed for the kitchen. I heard the heavy bottom of two glass tumblers hit the counter and then the splash of whiskey. The drink calmed her down. They were done. I knew this part of the routine—the point where she tired herself out and my father drank himself to sleep.

But that night she wanted to talk.

I slid my back down the wall and crouched on the floor. I sat there for the next hour and listened to her speak to him, those fragments of her past burning my mind for the first time.

That night, my father slept in the bedroom with her, which he rarely did. When I woke up in the morning their door was closed. I made myself breakfast and went to school, and that night they didn't fight. They were calm, civil. I did my homework. I saw my mother touch his back as she put the plate of overcooked chicken in front of him. He thanked her and called her "dear." She was trying. He was forgiving.

This would become something I did often over the next few years after that night. In my bed upstairs, when I heard Etta's name and I knew something had set my mother off again, my heart would race. I barely breathed as she spoke so that I could hear every word she told my father. Those rare nights were like gifts to me, although she would never know it. I was desperate to know who she was before she became my mother.

I started to understand, during those sleepless nights replaying the things I'd overheard, that we are all grown from something. That we carry on the seed, and I was a part of her garden.

1964

Cecilia couldn't sleep without her doll, Beth-Anne, even at the age of seven. She loved the doll more than anything—the smell, the feeling of the silk hair between her fingers as she fell asleep. She searched for it frantically one night, trying to remember where she'd seen it. Etta shouted angrily from the bottom of the basement stairs and Cecilia knew she was irritated by her stomping all over the house when she should have been in bed.

"She's down here, Cecilia!"

There was a small pickle cellar in the basement, about the size of a dog kennel. Etta had stopped canning pickles years before, and they'd almost eaten what was left. She crouched at the cellar door, her bum sticking out toward her daughter.

"Way at the back. You must have put it in there."

"I did not! I hate that cellar!"

"Well, I can't fit in. Go in and get her."

Cecilia whined that her nightshirt would get dirty. That she didn't like it in there. But she could see Beth-Anne lying in the corner.

"Don't be such a scaredy-cat, Cecilia. If you want her, go get her."

Cecilia got down on all fours and Etta pushed her forward. She fell onto her forearms and started to whimper, but she wanted Beth-Anne badly, so she slowly inched toward the back of the small, dark cave. The *pickle jars that lined the walls looked like swamp water and she started having trouble breathing.*

Something creaked behind her, but the walls of the cellar were too narrow for her to turn around. She realized then that the last sliver of light she'd seen on the glass jars around her was gone. She couldn't get enough air and called louder for Etta. The rubble under her knees dug into her skin every time she twitched. She inched back and tried kicking open the door with her heel, but it was jammed.

She heard the phone ring from the living room. Etta's heavy footsteps pounded the stairs. "Hello?" she heard her say, and then it was quiet for a moment, until the television set came on, and then the familiar voice of the evening news. Cecilia heard Etta's muffled voice again speaking into the phone. It was September 1964 and the findings of the Warren Commission were being released. Etta, like everyone else, was obsessed with JFK's assassination.

Etta never came back. Henry levered the door open when he got home from his night shift. He hauled Cecilia out by the ankles. Her fists were scraped. There was an argument about taking her to the hospital to be checked out. He thought her breathing was shallow and her eyes didn't look right. But Etta won; they stayed home.

Henry sat near Cecilia's bed while she slept. He put cold cloths on her head and didn't go to work in the morning. None of them spoke to one another for days. Henry took the door off the cellar and moved the few remaining pickle jars to the pantry in the kitchen.

"That door never worked properly," he said and shook his head.

A week later Etta whispered something to Cecilia when she cleared her dinner plate. Henry was at work. They were listening to the news on the kitchen radio. Cecilia couldn't quite hear her, but what she thought Etta said was, "I meant to go back for you, Cecilia." She put her lips on Cecilia's cheek and lingered there for a moment. Cecilia didn't ask Etta to repeat herself.

15

T ime goes by so quickly. Enjoy every moment.

      Mothers speak of time like it's the only currency we know.

Can you believe it? Can you believe she's already six months old? Other women would say this to me, nearly chipper, idling their strollers back and forth on the sidewalk as their babies slept under expensive, gauzy white blankets, their pacifiers bobbing. I would look down at Violet, staring up at me from where she lay, her fists waving, her legs stiff, wanting, wanting, wanting. And I would wonder how we'd made it so far. Six whole months. It felt like six years.

It's the best job in the world, isn't it? Motherhood? This was what the doctor said at one of Violet's appointments for her shots. She was a mother of three. I told her about my recurring hemorrhoids the size of grapes, about how long it had been since we'd had sex, since I'd even thought of your penis in passing. Her eyebrows lifted with her smile— *Yup. I get it. I really do.* As though I were a part of the club now, privy to its unspoken truths. What I couldn't tell her was that I felt I'd aged a century since I'd given birth to Violet. That she seemed to stretch every hour we spent together. That the months had crawled by so slowly

I'd often splash cold water on my face during the day to see if I was just dreaming—if that's why time never made any sense to me.

It's like you blink, and they're suddenly such big girls. They become these sweet little people right before your eyes. Violet seemed to grow so slowly. I never noticed a change in her until you shook it in front of my face. You would tell me her clothes were too small, that her belly was hanging below her shirts, that her leggings came up almost to her knees. You would pack away her baby toys and buy her things on your way home from work that blinked and beeped, things for tiny humans who are developing, learning, thinking. I was just trying to keep her alive. I was focused on her eating and her sleeping and the probiotic drops that I could never seem to remember. I was focused on getting through the days as they rolled like boulders into one another.

16

U s. No couple can imagine what their relationship will be like after having children. But there's an expectation that you'll be in it together. That you'll be a team where the teamwork is possible. Our operation functioned. Our child was fed and bathed and walked and rocked and clothed and changed and you did everything you could. I had her all day, but when you came through the door, she was yours. Patience. Love. Affection. I was grateful for everything you gave her that she didn't want from me. I watched you two and I was envious. I wanted what you had.

But this imbalance came at a cost. We had shifted away from our easy, treasured decade of comfort. Instead, my presence made you withdraw. Your judgment made me anxious. The more Violet got from you, the less you gave to me.

We still kissed hello and conversed over dinners at restaurants on the odd night we got out together. You always put your hand on the small of my back as we walked closer to our apartment, closer to the nest we'd built together. We had established certain motions and we still went through them. But there were subtle absences. We stopped doing crosswords together. You didn't leave the bathroom door open when you showered. There was space where there hadn't been before, and in that space was resentment.

I tried to do better. Becoming a father had made you so beautiful. Your face had changed. Warm. Soft. Your brows lifted more and your mouth was always agape when she was near you. Goofy. You had become a brighter version of the man I knew. I yearned for those things to happen to me, too. But I had become hardened. My face looked angry and tired where life had once lifted my cheekbones and glowed through my blue eyes. I looked like my mother had, right before she left me.

17

Somewhere in our seventh month together, Violet finally started napping for more than twenty minutes at a time. I went back to my writing. I didn't mention it to you—you always insisted that I sleep while she napped during the day, and asked me when you got home if I had. That was the only thing you cared about. You wanted me alert and patient. You wanted me rested so I could perform my duties. You used to care about me as a person—my happiness, the things that made me thrive. Now I was a service provider. You didn't see me as a woman. I was just the mother of your child.

And so I lied to you most days because it was easier that way: Yes, I napped. Yes, I got some rest. But actually, I had been working on a short story. The sentences poured from me. I couldn't remember words flowing this easily before. I'd been prepared for the opposite to happen; other women writers with babies warned of drained energy and brains that couldn't function on the page like they used to, at least for the first year. But I seemed to come alive when my screen went on.

Violet would wake like clockwork after two hours, and I was deep in the zone every time—I felt physically and emotionally elsewhere. I got into the habit of letting her cry, promising myself just one more page. Sometimes I slipped on my headphones. Sometimes one page turned into two. Or more. Sometimes I wrote for another hour. When her pitch became frantic enough, I'd flip down my laptop screen and rush to her as though I'd just heard her for the first time. *Oh, hello there! You're awake now! Come see Mommy.* I don't know who I was doing this performance for. I felt deeply embarrassed as she pushed me away when I tried to soothe her. How could I have blamed her for rejecting me?

The day you came home early.

I didn't hear you walk in over her screams and the music in my ears. My heart stopped when you whipped my chair around. You nearly tipped me over. You ran to the bedroom as though the baby was on fire. I held my breath as I listened to you calm her down. She was hysterical.

"I'm so sorry, I'm so sorry," you told her.

You were so sorry I was her mother. That's what you had meant.

You didn't bring her out of the nursery. I sat on the floor in the hallway knowing nothing would be the same between us again. I had broken your trust. I had confirmed every doubt you quietly held about me.

When I finally went in you were rocking her in the chair and your eyes were closed and your head was back. She hiccuped on the pacifier.

I walked toward the chair to take her from you, but your arm lifted to hold me back.

"What the fuck were you doing?"

I knew better than to make excuses for myself. I had never seen your hands shake with anger before.

I went into the shower and I cried until the water was cold.

When I came out you were scrambling eggs while she sat on your hip.

"She wakes up from her nap every day at three. It was four forty-five when I walked in."

I watched the spatula scrape the frying pan.

"You let her scream for over an hour and a half."

I couldn't look at either of you.

"Does this happen every day?"

"No," I said firmly. As though that would save my dignity.

We still hadn't looked each other in the eye. Violet began fussing.

"She's hungry. Feed her." You passed her to me and I did.

In bed that night you rolled away from me and spoke toward the open window.

"What's wrong with you?"

"I don't know," I answered. "I'm sorry."

"You need to talk to someone. A doctor."

"I will."

"I'm worried for her."

"Fox. Please. Don't be."

I would never have hurt her. I would never have put her in danger.

For years afterward, long after she began sleeping through the night, I would wake to the sound of her crying. I would clutch my chest and remember what I'd done. I would remember the cramp of guilt and the overruling satisfaction of ignoring her. I remembered the thrill of writing over the fusion of music and tears. How quickly the page filled. How fast my heart raced. How shameful it felt to be exposed.

18

My mother couldn't be in small spaces. The pantry closet in my childhood home was unused, the shelves dusty and scattered with turds from mice that had come for the stale peanuts and an old, open bag of sugar. The backyard shed was locked. The basement, with its low ceiling, was boarded up with three two-by-fours and rusty nails from the garage that Cecilia had hammered in herself.

When I was eight, on a deathly hot day in August, I sat outside our stifling home and watched my mother smoke at the plastic table on the rough, yellow grass that covered our yard from one rotting chain-link fence to the other. There was silence in the air, as though even the sounds from the neighborhood couldn't travel through the thickness I could barely force into my lungs. Earlier that day I'd been at the Ellingtons' house and Mrs. Ellington had sent us into the cold, dank basement for a reprieve. We'd pretended we were having a picnic down there. She brought us a blanket and boiled eggs and apple juice in paper cups with balloons on them, left over from Daniel's birthday party. I asked my mother if we could go down to our basement, too. Couldn't we take the boards off? Couldn't we use the back side of the hammer to pull the nails out, like Dad did to fix the front porch last weekend?

"No," she snapped. "Stop asking."

"But, Mom, please, I feel sick. It's too hot everywhere else but the basement."

"Stop asking, Blythe. I'm warning you."

"I'll die out here thanks to you!"

She slapped me across the face but her hand slipped on the sweat of my cheek, so she wound up and hit me again. Only this time it was with a closed fist and right on the mouth. Square and firm. My tooth hit the back of my throat and I coughed speckles of blood on my T-shirt.

"It's a baby tooth," she said as I stared at it in my palm. "They all come out eventually anyway." She put her cigarette out on a patch of dirt in the brittle grass. But I could see her disgust with herself in her twisted tangerine lips. She had never hit me before. And so I had never felt that particular collision of shame and self-pity and heartache. I went to my room and made an accordion fan with a grocery flyer from the mail and lay on the floor in my shirt and underwear. When she came in an hour later she took the fan from my hand and smoothed the creases and said she needed the coupon to buy chicken thighs.

She sat on my bed, something she rarely did. She couldn't stand to be in my room for long. Her husky throat cleared.

"When I was your age, my mother did something very cruel to me. In the basement. So I can't go down there."

I didn't move from the floor. I thought of the things I'd overheard late at night as she cried to my father. My face flushed with her secrets. I watched her bare feet rub against each other, her toes freshly polished in bright, cherry red.

"Why was she so cruel to you?" She could have seen my heart jumping under the bloodstains on my shirt.

"Something wasn't right with her." Her tone suggested the answer should have been obvious to me even then. She tore the chicken thigh coupon off the bottom of the flyer and folded the rest back into an accordion. I reached out to touch her toe, to feel the smooth polish, to feel her. I never touched her. She flinched, but she didn't pull her foot away. We both stared at my finger on her nail.

"I'm sorry about your tooth," she said and then stood up. I slowly took my hand away.

"It was starting to get loose anyway."

It was the first time she told me herself about Etta. I think she might have regretted it afterward, because she was especially cold in the weeks that followed. But I remember wanting to touch her more, wanting to be near her. I remember standing at the side of her bed in the mornings to run my finger softly along her cheekbone, and then tiptoeing out when she started to stir.

19

For the next few months I decided not to write. I decided to focus on Violet.

My doctor didn't think I was suffering from postpartum depression, and so neither did I. I'd done a quiz on the clipboard in her waiting room:

> Have you been stressed or worried for no good reason? *No*
> Have you been dreading things you used to look forward to? *No*
> Have you been so unhappy that you can't sleep? *No*
> Do you have thoughts of harming yourself? *No*
> Do you have thoughts of harming your baby? *No*

She recommended I make more time for myself and get back to the things I used to enjoy before I had the baby. Like writing. This, I knew, wouldn't go over well with you. Instead I told you she suggested some exercise and more time outside and a follow-up in six weeks. I began walking with Violet in the morning as soon as you left the house. We'd go for hours. I'd take her all the way downtown to your office, and you'd meet us for coffee. You loved the way Violet squealed when she saw you step off the elevator, and you loved to see me with a rosy-fresh face, looking like I was enjoying myself. She was almost a year by then and seemed lit up by the world around her, and so I signed us up for Mommy and Me music classes and a swim program. You warmed to me again—you liked this version of me and it felt good. And by then I had a lot to prove. We kept busy and I kept quiet.

Were there good moments? Of course there were. One night I put music on while I cleaned the kitchen. Food was everywhere—all over my clothes and her face and the floor. She laughed in her chair as I danced with the whisk in my hand. Her arms reached out for me. I swooped her up and twirled across the kitchen and she threw her head back and squealed. I realized we had never had these experiences together—we had never found the comfort, the silly, the fun. Mrs. Ellington and her puppet. Maybe we could have that, too. Instead I was always looking for what was wrong with us. I smothered her in kisses and she pulled away to stare at me—she was used to this kind of affection only from you. She leaned into my face with her wet open lips and made an *ahhhh* sound.

"Yeah. We're trying, aren't we?" I whispered.

You cleared your throat. You had been watching us there in the doorway. You smiled. I could see the relief as your shoulders relaxed. We were picture-perfect in that kitchen.

When you came back from changing, you poured two glasses of wine and kissed me on the head and then you said, "I was thinking. You should get back to writing again."

I'd passed whatever test you were putting me through. We desperately wanted life to feel good; we both had hope that it could. I put my nose in Violet's sticky neck and took the glass of wine from you.

20

S he said it. I swear to God. Say it again." You crouched down
and jiggled her hips. "Come on. *Mama*."

"Honey, she's eleven months old. It's too early, isn't it?" I had
met you back at the park, coffee for us in my hands. We were surrounded by other young families doting on their kids, looking various
stages of cold and tired. I smiled at a mom who was standing nearby
clutching a snotty tissue. "I mean, I spend every day with her, she's
never said it before."

"*Mama*," you prompted her again. "*Ma-maaa*."

Violet pouted and ambled toward the swings.

"I can't believe you missed it. Right when you left for the coffee.
She pointed in your direction and said *Mama. Mama.* Three times, I
think, actually."

"Oh. Okay, well—that's amazing. Wow." It didn't seem like something you'd lie about, but it was hard to believe. You lifted her into the
baby swing.

"I wish I'd caught it on video. I wish you heard it." You shook your
head and watched her in awe, your baby genius, rocking in her seat so
you'd push her higher. I gave you your coffee and slipped my hand in

the back pocket of your jeans like I used to do. We felt so normal among the other young families like ours, killing time on Sunday morning, savoring the caffeine.

"Mama!"

"Did you hear that?" You jumped back from the swing.

"Oh my God. I heard it!"

"Say it again!"

"Mama!"

I spilled my coffee lumbering toward her in the playground sand. I grabbed the front of the swing and pulled her close to kiss her square on her wet lips. "Yes! Mama!" I said to her. "That's me!"

"Mama!"

"I told you!"

You squeezed my shoulders from behind and we stared at her as I pretended to tickle her feet when the swing came toward us. She was laughing then, saying my name over and over to watch our reactions. I was mesmerized by her. We swayed ever so slightly together, and I reached up to feel the weekend's scruff on your chin. You turned my face toward you and kissed me, brief, happy, carefree. Violet watched us. We stood like that for what felt like hours.

She fell asleep in the stroller on the way home. It had been so long since I'd felt this connected to either of you, and I clung to the bliss of it—the lightness of my legs as we walked, the satisfying depth of my long, full breath. You carried her to her crib, careful not to wake her, and I slipped her tiny boots off while she slept. I turned in the hallway toward the kitchen, to clean the mess of breakfast we'd left for later. But you tugged at my arm. You pulled me into the bathroom and ran the shower. I leaned on the counter and watched you undress.

"Come in with me."

I thought of the half avocado still sitting on the counter, the rubber eggs left in the pan. It had been so long since we'd touched each other.

"Come on, *Mama*."

I'd just stepped in when we heard her little voice start to crack from down the hall. She was waking up. I reached for the faucet, thinking you'd want to run for her before she cried.

"Stay, we'll be quick," you whispered, already hard, and so I did. Her noises became more urgent, a reminder she was there, but you didn't stop. You'd wanted me more than her. I was repulsed with myself for the satisfaction this gave me as we fucked, for letting this turn me on as much as it did. I listened for her through the echo of the water. I wanted to hear her wail, to imagine you ignoring her like I sometimes did. We came fast together under the weak flow of the showerhead.

You shut off the water abruptly as soon as we finished. She was quiet. She hadn't started screaming like I'd been waiting for, like she did when it was just me. You tossed me a towel like my teammate in a locker room—you used to dry my body off slowly, it had once been part of what we did together. Violet's voice was soft in the distance, a meaningless scale of sounds, and I pictured her on her back, legs in the air, pulling at her sweaty toes. It was as though she knew you'd be there to get her soon. You wrapped another towel around your waist, kissed my bare shoulder, and you went to her.

Back in the kitchen you made us grilled cheese sandwiches while I tidied up the browning scraps from breakfast. You hummed and touched me whenever I was in reach. She said it over and over again as she watched for your reaction, kicking her legs in her high chair: *Mama. Mama.*

1968

Etta wasn't always unpredictable. There were stretches of time when she figured out how to look and act like the kind of person a mother was expected to be. Cecilia sensed this wasn't easy for her—she saw it sometimes in the way Etta's hands shook nervously when another mother knocked on their door to say hello, or when Cecilia asked for a braid in her hair. But nobody was scrutinizing Etta by then. The truth was they'd all given up. And yet something inside her made Etta want to try anyway. Sometimes it worked, and sometimes it didn't. But Cecilia rooted for her each and every time.

When Cecilia was in the sixth grade, there was a school dance after the holiday break, and she had nothing to wear—they didn't go to church and didn't celebrate much. This wasn't something Cecilia cared or complained about, but Etta said she would make her something special to wear. Cecilia was speechless—she'd never seen her mother make a thing. The next day, Etta came home from the fabric store and called up the stairs.

"Cecilia, come see!"

She'd laid out a tissue-paper pattern for a shift dress, and yards of dark yellow cotton. Cecilia stood still while Etta measured her long, skinny body, one so unlike her own. Cecilia felt like she was being touched by a stranger as her mother's hands ran along the inside of her leg, across *her thin waist, and up to her shoulders. Etta wrote down the measurements on a napkin and declared that the dress would be beautiful.*

There was an old sewing machine left in the hall closet from the owners before them, and Etta brought it to the kitchen table. She worked on the dress in the evenings for five straight nights and the old motor kept Cecilia awake until the early hours. In the morning there'd be straight pins and bits of thread spread across the kitchen table. Etta would come down, her eyes bleary, and stare at the fabric as she held it up to Cecilia. The project gave Etta a purpose that Cecilia hadn't seen her mother have before. And less room, she knew, for the anger and sadness.

The morning of the dance, Etta was up early and went to Cecilia's room with the dress. It was finished—pressed and draped over her arm. She held it up to Cecilia's shoulders and ran her hands over the drop waist and pleated bottom. She'd trimmed the neckline and sleeves with a beautiful knotted silk.

"What do you think?"

"I love it." It was what Etta wanted to hear, yes, but Cecilia did in fact love it. It was the most beautiful thing she had, and the only thing anyone had ever made for her. She imagined walking into class that day and watching the heads of the other girls turn to stare in jealous disbelief.

Cecilia turned her back and took off her nightgown. The zipper of the dress was stiff, but she managed to get it down and then slipped her legs in. She pulled the dress up and felt the seams rough against her skin. The waist was tight and flattened her small bum, but it wouldn't go any higher. She wiggled the dress around herself and tried to yank harder. But the dress wouldn't move.

"Put your arms in. Go on."

She tried to crouch into the dress and slither her arms into the sleeves, but it was too tight. They heard the sound of fabric tearing.

"Come here." Etta yanked her closer and pulled and tugged around

her like she was dressing a doll. She whipped the dress down Cecilia's legs and then tried pulling it over her head. Etta didn't say a word. Cecilia let her wrangle the dress and jostle her however she wanted to. Etta's forehead was slick with sweat and her face had turned a deeper red than usual. Cecilia closed her eyes as tight as she could.

Eventually Etta let her go and stood up.

"You're wearing the dress, Cecilia."

Her heart sank. She couldn't possibly wear it. She couldn't even get it on.

Fifteen minutes later, Cecilia came down to the kitchen wearing her usual beige slacks and blue turtleneck. She didn't look at Etta. She sat at the table and picked up her spoon.

"Go back and put the dress on."

"You saw. It doesn't fit." Cecilia's heart pounded.

"Make it fit. Go upstairs. Now."

She wondered if Henry might hear her. She put her spoon down and tried to decide what to do.

"NOW."

Cecilia could hear Etta's thick breathing behind her. She could feel Etta's rage tickling her spine. She listened for Henry's footsteps, hoping he'd hurry up and come down.

"NOW!"

For the first time then, Cecilia realized she had a kind of power over Etta. She could make her angry. She could make her lose control. She could have gone upstairs and pretended to try again, but she wanted to see how far Etta would go if she ignored her. They were trading gunfire.

"NOW, CECILIA."

Etta was shaking and she screamed again. Now! Now! Every time she screamed, the rage seemed to pump through her like a drug and Cecilia could see the shame in her face as the high wore off.

Cecilia would come to know that feeling herself many years later.

Henry came into the kitchen just as Etta's mouth opened again. Somehow, she found a way to calm down and she poured him a coffee. Cecilia ran out the door without the dress.

She waited until dark to go home that night, when she knew Henry would be there. Etta didn't look at her. She went upstairs and saw that Etta must have taken the dress from her room. A few minutes later Etta walked to Cecilia's door, the yellow fabric folded in her hands. She sat on Cecilia's bed and held up the dress. She'd taken it apart and sewn extra panels in the sides. It looked boxy and crooked, but she had tried.

"You can save it for the next dance."

Cecilia took it from her and ran her fingers over the knotted trim and then she hugged her. Etta stiffened in her arms.

A few months later she wore the dress to the school's end-of-year dance. She sat awkwardly on the edge of the gym stage, trying to hide just how badly it fit. Cecilia didn't change when she got home—she wore the dress to dinner. Her mother didn't mention it, and neither did Henry, and Cecilia didn't wear the dress again.

21

The party was more for us than it was for her. A whole year of parenthood. I ordered a huge bouquet of balloons in pastel colors with a giant foil "1" in the middle and bought fancy paper plates that were scalloped around the edges. The straws were polka-dotted. Your mother gave Violet a beautiful corduroy jumper the color of butter and ribbed tights with ruffles on the bum. She looked like a baby duckling, waddling around the living room, her pink, wet lips blowing spit bubbles as she babbled to her guests. Your father followed her, crouched on his bad knees, recording her every move.

I bought the cake from the bakery where I often took her for a treat on our walks. Vanilla-cream icing with rainbow sprinkles on top. She squealed and clapped when I placed it on her high-chair tray, her eyes locked on the single tiny flame.

"Happy!" she said. As clear as day.

"I got that on film," said your doting dad, holding up his digital camera. Your mother smothered her in kisses and your sister, whom we rarely saw but who had flown five hours to be there, scrunched up tissue paper to make her laugh. Grace, who brought a bottle of tequila with her, cut and served the cake. We watched them all together from the comfy living-room chair, me on your lap, your arms folded across my chest.

"We did it," you whispered, and breathed me in slowly, your nose tickling the nape of my neck. I nodded and took a sip of your beer. Violet looked angelic in her high chair, her rapt audience, the icing smeared across her face. I felt your nose on my neck again. I took another drink and pulled you up.

"Let's get a family picture."

We stood in the natural light from our apartment windows and I held Violet on my hip between us. She felt unusually docile, and I pulled her in for a kiss on her sugary cheek. We smiled as they clicked away. You made her giggle with your duck noises. I held her above our heads as we squealed at one another with wide-open mouths. The three of us, exactly as we were supposed to be.

22

Very soon after her first birthday, Violet stopped sleeping through the night again.

You never heard her right away, and sometimes not at all, but it felt like my eyes opened a few seconds before she made her first noise from the crib down the hall. This unnerved me every time, the reminder that she was still so much a physical part of me. Every two hours she cried for her bottle. After a few weeks, I lined up six of them, full of milk, against the railing of her crib, hoping she'd find one when she wanted it. She never did.

I can't do this, I'd think every time she woke me up. *I won't survive this again.*

I would open the door of her nursery, put a bottle in her hand, and leave.

"Isn't that bad for bacteria, having all that milk sitting out? Isn't that dangerous?" you asked when you realized what I was doing.

"I don't know." It probably was, but I didn't care. I just needed her to go back to sleep.

This went on for months and left me ravaged. I woke in the morning with a headache that sat behind my eyes and made my thoughts come slower. I avoided having to speak with other adults for fear I'd make no sense. My resentment of you both festered. I hated hearing you breathe deeply and evenly when I came back to bed, and I sometimes tugged at the sheets in the hopes it would rouse you from the place I so badly wanted to be.

I brought up the idea of sending Violet to day care a few days a week. You'd said early on, before Violet was even born, that you didn't like the idea of day care. Your mother had raised her children at home until they were five and went to school. You wanted the same for your own. I had agreed, blindly, heartily. I would do the things you thought perfect mothers did.

But that was before.

I found a place three blocks away that had a spot open up for the fall. I'd overheard people rave about it, and they had a camera in the room that let parents watch remotely. The truth was I often felt sad for those day-care babies when I saw them lined up like eggs in a carton in those long strollers, tired underpaid staff pushing them around the city for something to do. But there was research about babies in day-care environments—better socialized, more stimulated, accelerated development, et cetera, et cetera. I sent you the articles every so often. At dinner I'd follow up delicately to emphasize the internal conflict you wanted me to have: Maybe Violet needed more stimulation now? Maybe it's time? Although perhaps she's better off at home. For naps and such. *What do you think?* I'd ask to feign concern, but we both knew the answer I needed.

"Wait to decide once she's sleeping better," you'd reasoned. "You're just tired right now. I know it's hard, but this *will* pass." You had the nerve to say this as you dressed for work, your face bright, your hair freshly cut. I had listened to you sing in the shower that morning.

I was miserable. She and I both were, it seemed. She was gravely unhappy when she was around only me. She wouldn't let me hold her anymore. She didn't want me near her. Most days she was irritable and troublesome when we were alone and nothing could soothe her. She screamed so loudly when I picked her up that I could imagine the neighbors next door stopping dead in their tracks. When we were in public, at the grocery store or the park, other mothers would sometimes ask in a sympathetic voice if there was anything they could do to help. I was humiliated—they pitied me either for having given birth to a child like Violet or for being the kind of mother who looked too weak to survive her.

We began staying home mostly, although I lied about this when you returned from work asking for a daily report as she eagerly climbed onto your lap. Confined to our apartment she would scamper around like a scorpion, looking for things to shovel into her mouth—fistfuls of plant dirt, the keys from my purse, even stuffing she'd somehow pull from our pillows. She nearly choked herself blue sometimes. When I scooped her mouth clean, she would flail like a fish out of water and then go limp. Like she was dead. My heart would stop. Her eyes would go wide, and then would come a scream from deep within her, so repellent that it made my eyes sting with tears.

I was so disappointed she was mine.

I knew some of her behavior could be classified as typical. You wrote it off as being just a phase, toddler crankiness, the symptoms of a developmental leap. Fair enough, I tried to convince myself. But she was missing the inherent sweetness of other children her age. She so rarely showed affection. She didn't seem happy—not anymore. I saw a sharpness inside her that sometimes looked physically painful. I could see it in her face.

We joked about toddler life with other people who had kids, as parents do, looking for reassurance. We would commiserate with the tables beside us as we all raced through early-bird dinners at restaurants with sticky high chairs. I would downplay how bad she could be, knowing you wanted me to. I would agree, as I was supposed to, that the moments in between the chaos made up for all the rest. But she was cyclonic. And I was increasingly scared of her.

I desperately wanted more time to myself. I wanted a break from her. These seemed like reasonable requests to me, but you made me feel like I still had to prove myself to you. Your lingering doubt, although it was silent, was so heavy that sometimes it was hard to breathe around you.

I could write only when she was asleep, but she never napped long, and so we'd fallen back into our secret routine, as much as I promised myself I wouldn't do that to her again. I let it happen only a few days a week. And I always tried to make it up to her—a cookie on our afternoon walk, a nice long bath time.

I knew these days were numbered—she would soon be able to talk, to tell you what happened in her day, and then I would lose this power I so shamefully held. Perhaps this was part of my justification. My behavior was pathological. But I couldn't stop punishing her for being there. How easy it was to slip on my headphones and pretend she did not exist.

One day was particularly tough. She became angry every time I went near her, kicking and slapping. She slammed her head against the wall and then looked at me to see what I would do. And then she did it again. She hadn't eaten all day. I knew she was starving but she wouldn't let food cross her lips because it was me who was offering. I had spent the entirety of her nap crying, looking up early signs of behavioral disorders on the internet and then deleting the history from the browser. I didn't want you to see it, and I didn't want to be a mother with that kind of child.

She gave up the fight mere minutes before you came home, as though she could hear your feet step off the elevator. I placed her on my hip while I cleaned the living room. She was stiff. Quiet. She smelled a little stale. Her sleeper was rough against my arm, the cotton pilled from too many washes.

I handed her to you, still in your nice office sweater. I explained how she got the red welt on her head. I didn't care if you believed me or not.

"Honey." You tried to laugh to quell your judgment as you tickled her on the carpet. "Is she really that bad? I thought things were getting better."

I slumped on the couch. "I don't know. I'm just so tired."

I couldn't tell you the truth: that I believed there was something wrong with our daughter. You thought the problem was me.

"Here." You held her out to me. She was licking a piece of cheese you gave her. "She's calm. She's fine. Just cuddle with her. Show her some love."

"Fox, this isn't about love. Or affection. I try that all the time."

"Just hold her."

I put her on my lap and waited for her to shove me away, but she sat there, content, sucking on her soggy cheddar. We watched you unpack your briefcase. "Dada," she said. "Baba."

You passed her the bottle from the coffee table and she sank back into me.

"I don't think you understand," I said quietly, careful not to disrupt her. Her weight on my body was comforting, and I began to calm down. I felt like someone who'd been lost at sea having human contact again. I ran my finger along her forehead, brushing back her wispy fringe. She let me kiss her. She pulled the bottle away from her mouth and sighed—we were both so tired of fighting each other.

"Are you napping when she naps?" You spoke quietly, too, studying us.

"I can't nap," I snapped, the calm draining from my chest. She wiggled away from me. "There's too much to do. Laundry. I'm trying to
write. My mind won't stop spinning."

I tossed the bottle onto the coffee table and a squirt of milk sprayed
on the pages I'd printed. I was thinking of showing them to you that
night—it had been so long since you asked about what I was working
on. I watched the beads of milk drip from the rubber nipple onto my
sentences, blotting the ink.

You changed your clothes and came back and fell onto the couch
beside me. Your hand patted my thigh. There was a time I would have
asked about your day. The sadness of the distance that had grown
between us again over the past few months was something we didn't
discuss. I was willing to let it fester in the background, and it seemed
you were, too.

"What's that?" You gestured to the wet pages.

"Nothing."

"Confirm her day-care spot, if you want to. But only three days a
week, okay? We didn't budget for this." You rubbed your forehead.

I tried my best for the rest of that week. But we fell back into our
daily combat. She started day care the following Monday and I can
still feel the enormous sense of relief that washed over me when I
placed her down on the welcome mat. She stared at her yellow rain
boots until the teacher came to take her hand. She didn't look at me
when I said good-bye and I never turned around as I walked away
across the wet lawn and out of the gate.

23

Your mother gave Violet her first doll.

"Maternal instinct starts young," she said as she unwrapped fresh fish from the market and gestured to Violet on the floor. Violet had the plastic-headed baby tucked under her arm and hadn't put it down since she'd gotten it. *Baaaybee,* Violet sang over and over, and poked the wide fluttering eyes that had lashes thicker than mine. The doll had an artificial scent like baby powder and was dressed in a pink sleeper.

I drank my wine and watched your mother make dinner—she'd insisted on cooking cedar-planked salmon with maple sauce even though I'd offered to order in. Violet brought the baby doll to me and put her on my lap. "Mama. Baby."

"Yes, sweetie. She's cute." I rocked and kissed the doll as she watched. "Your turn."

She reached up to put her wide-open mouth on the baby's bald head. I hadn't seen her act this affectionately before, except with you, although I didn't want to give your mother the satisfaction of saying so.

"Good girl. Kisses."

The smell of fish filled the apartment. Your father had taken you to the hockey game. They were staying in the city for three nights. A hotel. A matter of space, I had said, although we had bought a pull-out sofa just for them when we first moved in. I was still so tired even though Violet was sleeping better—I was too on edge to have your mother in our home for all that time. My feelings for her were complicated. I felt desperate for her help, anyone's help, but I had come to resent her capability, how easy she had made everything seem for your entire life.

"How's day care going for our sweet girl?"

"Good, I think. She seems to really like the teachers. She's learned so much in just a few weeks."

She topped up my glass and bent to kiss Violet.

"And you?" she asked.

"Me?"

"You've been enjoying your free time?"

She had spent nearly two decades taking care of you and your sister at home. Baked pies. Ran the PTA. She had sewn every pillow, drape, napkin, place mat, and shower curtain herself. I watched her blond bob swing as she cooked, the same length and flip she wore in every gold-framed family photograph in the hallway of your childhood home.

"I've been writing more and catching up on things around here."

"You must count down the hours until pickup. I always did, once they were in school. You want a bit of peace and quiet and then you spend all day thinking about them." She smiled to herself, chopping dill. "Fox seems to be enjoying her. I always knew he'd make a wonderful dad. Even when he was little."

Violet clanged the stove with a whisk, the doll's foot in her other hand.

"He's incredible. He's . . . the perfect father." It was what she wanted to hear, and in some ways it was true.

She smiled to herself and picked up a lemon and then watched Violet play for a moment before she grated the rind. I bent down to lift Violet and take her to the bath. She flinched when she felt my touch and I knew I had set her off—the ever-present knot in my stomach tightened. She wailed, thrashing her body against the floor tiles.

"Come on, honey, bath time." I didn't want to battle in front of your mother. I picked her up as she kicked and screamed and took her to the bathroom. I shut the door and ran the water. Your mother knocked a few minutes later and spoke loudly over the crying.

"Can I help?"

"She's just cranky, Helen. She's tired." But she came in anyway. By then I was soaked and Violet was nearly purple with rage. I rinsed the soap from her hair with a tight grip under her arm. When I lifted her out she could barely breathe from the screaming. Your mother watched us and passed the towel.

"Can I take her?"

"She'll be okay," I said and held Violet tight to restrain her. But her teeth cut into the fat of my cheek before I could move my face away— she had bitten me. I yelled from between my clenched teeth and tried to pull her head away, but she was clamped on too tightly. Your mother gasped and pulled her granddaughter's jaw apart with her fingers. She grabbed Violet from me and said only, "My God."

I looked at the mark in the mirror and ran the cold water. I pressed a wet cloth onto my skin.

I was humiliated. I could see your mother's face behind me, aghast.

Violet had stopped screaming now. She caught her breath between her whimpers in your mother's arms and looked at her for reprieve, as though she'd been defending herself in the arms of a torturer.

"I'm sorry," I said. To no one.

"How about you take the fish out, and I'll get her pajamas on?"

"No, it's okay." I took her from your mother, embarrassed, determined, but Violet screamed again, whipping her head back. Your mother's face was on fire. I passed Violet back to her and turned to the sink. She walked down the hall to Violet's bedroom, hushing in her ear like you always did, while I cried behind the sound of the running faucet.

T*hank you for dinner,* Helen. It was delicious."
        "The least I can do."

"I'm sorry about earlier. That was quite a scene."

"Sweetheart, don't worry." She lifted her wine but didn't drink. "I'm sure she's just tired. Do you think she's napping enough?"

"Maybe not." She was. We were both pretending that things weren't as bad as they were. That Violet's behavior could be easily explained. It was what people in your family preferred to do. I pushed around the last bit of food. "She's in a Daddy phase right now, I guess."

"Well, we can't blame her." She winked and cleared our plates. "You're both very lucky to have him."

And what about him? Isn't he lucky to have me, too? In the kitchen she poured me another glass. I was quiet.

"Things will get easier," she whispered.

I nodded. The tears came back and I felt my face redden. She didn't speak for a moment, but when she did, she had softened, like she suddenly accepted that things were worse than she wanted to believe. She covered my hand with hers and we both watched her grip me tightly.

"Look. Nobody said motherhood was easy. Especially if it's not what you thought it would be, or it's not what—" Her thin, pink lips pressed together between thoughts. She wouldn't dared have mentioned my mother. "But you figure out a way to get through. For everyone. That's what you have to do."

. . .

When you walked in the door, the first thing you asked was how Violet had been. *How was my girl tonight?* You were beaming. You loved when your mother spent time with our daughter.

"She was very good, for the most part." Your mother kissed both of your cheeks and turned to get her purse. You gave me a long hug and felt tipsy in my arms. You smelled of beer and spicy processed meat and the cold. When I pulled away, you asked what was wrong with my face—you touched the red mark from Violet's teeth and I flinched.

"Nothing. Just a mark from Violet." I lifted my eyes toward your mother.

"Yes, she put up a challenge before bed," she said, speaking to you. "She does have a bit of a temper, that one."

You frowned and then moved on. Hung up your coat. Your mother smiled at you tightly with raised brows, as though she expected you to say more. I looked away from her, grateful for her solidarity, and ashamed that I needed it so desperately.

"Hang in there, honey." She said this to me quietly and then left to meet your father in the cab.

The vivid memories of my childhood start when I was eight years old. I wish I didn't have to rely on these memories alone, but I do. Some people frame their perspectives of the past with worn photographs or the same stories told a thousand times by someone who loves them. I didn't have these things. My mother didn't either, and maybe that was part of the problem. We had only one version of the truth.

There is one thing that comes to me: the white lining of my stroller, the dark blue florets and an eyelet ribbon trim, and the middle of the chrome handle wrapped with cane. My mother's canary-gloved knuckles loom over me. I can't see her face looking down, just her shadow floating over me every once in a while, when she turns a corner to put the sun behind her. I can't possibly remember anything this early, I know. But I can smell sour formula and talcum powder and cigarette smoke, and I can hear the sound of the slow city buses bringing people home for dinner.

I play this game in my head sometimes about Sam.

What might he remember? The sharpness of the grass on the hill at the park, or the orange quilt we laid him on, three faces bobbing above him like umbrellas? Maybe the smell of the pumpkin muffins Violet liked to bake. The big spoon with the red handle that she always gave to him, slopping with batter. The bath toy with the spinning light you wanted to throw out. Maybe the painting in the nursery—the cherub child always seemed to catch his eye in the morning.

But here's what I think it would be: the tiles on the wall in the change room at the community swimming pool. I don't know why, but I think these would have become a part of him. Every week I put him on the wooden bench in the corner stall and held him still with one hand while I reached over to lock the swinging door with the other. He always looked up at the wall with searching eyes and touched the small colored squares placed in a random pattern as if they were alive. Mustard, emerald green, and a beautiful dark blue. A sailor's blue. The tiles calmed him. He made soft noises and widened his eyes as I put on his swim diaper and wrapped a towel around my still-puffy waist. I looked forward to Sam seeing those tiles every time we went. They were the thing in his little world that sang to him.

I go back to that change room often. Looking for him in those tiles.

25

Her hair came in thick and beautiful and people often stopped to tell us what a gorgeous little girl she was. She would smile coyly and say thank you, and for a split second I could see this tiny, remarkable, civilized person who couldn't possibly have the capacity to drag me by the ears to the edge of insanity. Those dark moments had become fewer and other parts of her personality were emerging. She was obsessed with her baby doll and brought it everywhere she went. She knew her colors by the time she was sixteen months old. She insisted on wearing tights with Christmas trees under her pants for most months of the year. She ate scrambled eggs for nearly every meal and called them yellow clouds. Chipmunks scared her and squirrels thrilled her. She loved the woman from the flower shop on the corner where we went for a stem every Saturday morning. She kept the flower beside her potty to hold while she peed. She made no sense at all, and yet all the sense in the world.

She gave me just enough space to hang from, to convince myself I could wrestle back onto the ledge. For a while, anyway, until I was reminded once again of where I belonged in her small but orderly world.

When she was three, after we came home from a weekend away at your friend's wedding, I had snuck into her room without taking off my coat.

It was after midnight. I had wanted to smell her. I had felt an unfamiliar panic on the plane that something was wrong, that she would choke in her sleep and your mother wouldn't hear her like I would, that the carbon monoxide detectors weren't working, that the plane would hit the runway in the wrong kind of way and blow us both up. I needed her. I rarely felt this yearning for her, especially when I should have, but when I did, I couldn't remember what it was like not to want her. Who was that other mother? The one who brought me so much shame?

The face of a sleeping child. She fluttered her eyes and saw me hovering above. Her lids fell down, disappointed. Her sadness was genuine. She rolled over and pulled the periwinkle duvet to her chin and looked out the dark window. I leaned to kiss her and felt her muscles tighten beneath my hand.

I left the room and saw you in the hallway. I told you she was asleep. You walked in anyway and I heard smacking noises on your cheek. She told you your mother had let her watch a movie with a mermaid. She asked you to lie down with her. She had been waiting for you.

I felt like I would never have with her what you had.

"It's all in your head," you said to me whenever I brought it up. "You've created this story about the two of you, and you can't let it go."

"She should want me. I'm her mother. She should need me."

"There's nothing wrong with her."

Her. There was nothing wrong with her, you said.

In the morning, over breakfast, your mother recounted the lovely weekend they'd had. You beamed, being back with your daughter, bouncing her on your knee.

"So everything was fine?" I asked your mother quietly afterward, as we filled the dishwasher together.

"She was an angel. She really was." She rubbed the small of my back for a moment, as if to soothe an ache she knew I carried. "I think she missed you both."

26

In third grade, our class spent a week making flower bouquets for our mothers, buttons glued to the inside of pink and yellow muffin cups, stems made of chenille pipe cleaners. We stuck them on thick construction paper and used our best cursive writing to copy the poem from the blackboard: *Roses are red, Violets are blue, You're the best mom there is, and I love you!* I was the last one to finish. I couldn't remember making a craft for her before, not one as nice as this. The teacher took it from my hands and whispered to me, "It's beautiful, Blythe. She's going to love it."

The teacher sent us each home with an invitation to a tea party. I threw mine in the garbage when I left school that day—I didn't want to invite my mother. Or more specifically, I didn't want to invite her in case she didn't want to come. I was nine, but I had already learned how to manage my own disappointment. On the morning of the party, as I ate breakfast alone in the kitchen while my mother slept in as usual, I rehearsed what I'd say to everyone when I got to school: my mother was ill, she had food poisoning. She couldn't come to the tea.

That afternoon we decorated the classroom with tissue-paper flowers before the mothers arrived. I was standing on a chair with a tack in my hand reaching for the bulletin board when I heard:

"Am I early?"

I nearly fell off the chair. My mother. The teacher greeted her kindly and said not to worry, she was just the first to arrive. That she was glad to see her feeling better. My mother seemed not to pick up on my lie— she looked too nervous. She waved quickly from the doorway. She was wearing something I had never seen her in before, a pretty peach suit and pearl earrings that couldn't have been real. I wasn't used to seeing her look so soft, so feminine. My heart pounded in my chest. *She came.* Somehow she found out and she came.

She asked me to show her around the classroom while we waited for the tea to begin. I pointed out the weather station and the counter beads and the multiplication times tables. She laughed as I explained how to do it in the simplest way I could, as though she'd never seen numbers before. As the other mothers came through the door, their children running to them, my mother looked up at each woman and studied her—her outfit, her hair, the jewelry she wore. I sensed even then that my mother felt self-conscious and this shocked me—she never seemed to care what the other mothers thought. She never seemed to care what anyone thought.

Mrs. Ellington came in the door next and Thomas called to her. He was carefully setting up the teacups and saucers the teacher had brought from home. Mrs. Ellington waved to him, but first walked over to where I stood with my mother on the other side of the room. She held her hand out to my mother.

"Cecilia, it's so nice to see you again. That color is lovely on you." My mother took her hand and then Mrs. Ellington leaned in, a sort of touch on the cheek that I'd seen other women do with each other, but never my own mother. I wondered what she smelled like to Mrs. Ellington.

"You, too." My mother smiled. "And *thank you*. For this." She lifted her chin toward the room, full of miniature tables with doilies and plates of crumpets. Mrs. Ellington brushed her hand through the air as though it were nothing. As though they liked each other. I had never heard them speak that many words to each other before.

"Your mom is so pretty, Blythe," one of the girls whispered to me.

"She looks like an actress," said another. I looked at my mother again and imagined what they could see, without the burden of everything I knew about her. I could tell by the way she tapped her foot that she wanted a cigarette. I wondered where her outfit had come from—was it in her closet? Did she buy it just for today? I watched my friends watching her as they sat next to their ordinary-looking mothers. For the first time in my life I was proud of her. She looked special. She was trying. For me.

The teacher handed out the flowers we'd made and the women fawned over our hard work. I held mine out to my mother and she read the poem under her breath. I'd never said anything like those words to her before. We both knew she wasn't the best mother. We both knew she wasn't even close.

"Do you like it?"

"I do. Thank you." She looked away and placed it on the table. "I'll have some water. Blythe, can you pour me some?"

But I wanted her to feel like a better mother than she was. I needed her to be a better mother than she was. I picked up the poem again and read it to her aloud, my voice shaking against the noise in the room.

"Roses are red, violets are blue, you're the best mom there is"—I paused and swallowed—"and I love you."

She didn't lift her eyes from the poem. She took it back from my hands.

"Five more minutes, class!"

"I'll see you at home, all right?" She touched the top of my head, picked up her purse, and left. I saw Mrs. Ellington's eyes follow her out of the room.

M*y mother made* shepherd's pie for dinner and still had on the peach suit when I got home. My father pulled his chair out and declared he was starving.

"So? Tell me all about the Mother's Day tea."

Mashed potatoes thumped onto his plate and my mother didn't say a word. He turned to me and lifted his eyebrows. "How was it, Blythe?"

"Good." I sipped my milk. She slid the hot casserole dish onto the table, straight from the oven, and dropped a spoon beside it.

"Jesus, the wood." My father jumped up to grab a kitchen towel and burned his fingers lifting up the edge of the casserole dish to slip it underneath. He glared at my mother, but she didn't seem to notice.

"I made Mom some flowers out of paper."

"That's nice. Where is it, Cecilia?" He filled his mouth with potatoes and turned to her. "Let me see."

My mother looked up from the sink. "Where's what?"

"The thing she made you. For Mother's Day."

My mother shook her head, confused, as though I'd never given her anything. "I don't know, I don't know where I put it."

"It must be somewhere. Check your purse."

"No, I don't know where it is." She looked at me and shook her head again. "I don't know what happened to it." She lit a cigarette and turned on the tap to fill the sink for the dishes. She never ate with us. I never saw her eat at all.

My heart sank. It had been too much—I'd said too much.

"Never mind, Dad."

"No. No, if you made your mother something nice, we'll find it. We'll put it on the fridge."

"Seb."

"Go find it, Cecilia."

She threw the dishcloth at his face. The smack made me jump and I dropped my fork on the floor. My father sat there with the wet cloth hanging from him, his eyes closed. He put down his knife and fork and squeezed his fists so his knuckles were the color of the potatoes. I wanted him to yell with the same rage that brewed inside of her constantly. He was so still that I wondered if he was still breathing.

"I went, didn't I? To the fucking tea? I was there. I sat at the little table and played along. What more do you want from me?" She grabbed her cigarettes and left for the porch. My father took the cloth off his head and folded it on the table. He picked up his fork and looked at me.

"Eat."

27

The spring after Violet turned four, her preschool teacher asked us for a meeting after school on a Friday.

"Nothing of major concern," she'd said on the phone, emphasizing the major. "But we should talk."

You were skeptical from the start, although I knew a part of you was nervous about what she would say. *What, she won't share the glue stick?*

We sat on tiny chairs and your knees nearly hit your chin. She offered us water in pink plastic cups that tasted like dish soap.

Everyone knows you open with the good news.

"Violet is an exceptionally bright child. She's mature for her age in many ways. She's very . . . astute."

But there were incidents that had caused her classmates to be uncomfortable with her. She gave us the example of a boy who was scared to sit near her because she sometimes twisted his fingers until he cried. A girl who said Violet stabbed her thigh with a pencil. And that morning, during recess, someone said Violet pulled down their pants and threw handfuls of rocks in their underwear. My face grew hot and I covered my neck, sure it was blotching. I was embarrassed that we'd created a human being who would act this way. I glanced out the window to the playground covered with small, dusty pebbles. I thought of the aggression she'd shown when she was younger. Of what little empathy I saw in her now. I could easily see her doing it all.

"She's apologetic when told to be, yes," the teacher said hesitantly when you asked her. "She's smart. She knows her behavior is hurtful, but this hasn't seemed to deter her like we'd expect. At this point, I think we need to introduce consequences."

We agreed on the strategy and thanked her for the meeting.

"Look, it's not good, but every kid goes through this kind of thing. Testing the boundaries. She's probably bored in there. Did you see all that plastic shit lying around? It looked like a room for babies. Remind me how much we're paying them?"

I watched the bubbles dance up the side of your glass. We'd gone for a drink, my suggestion. I thought it might ease the tension between us.

"We'll talk to her," you rationalized to yourself. "Something's obviously provoking her to act this way."

I nodded. Your reaction made no sense to me. You were such a sensible person in every respect. And yet when it came to our daughter, you lost all your levelheadedness. You defended her blindly.

"You're not going to say anything?" You were angry.

"I'm—I'm upset. I'm disappointed. And yes, we'll talk to her . . ."

"But?"

"But I can't say I'm surprised."

You shook your head—*here she goes.*

"Other kids her age would act out by biting or hitting or saying, 'You're not coming to my birthday party anymore.' What she's doing sounds . . . kind of cruel. Kind of calculated." I put my head into my hands.

"She's four, Blythe. She can't even tie her shoes."

"Look, I love her, I'm just saying—"

"Do you?"

How good that must have felt. It was the first time you'd said it aloud, but I knew you'd been thinking it for years. You stared at the ring-stained bar top.

"I love her, Fox. I'm not the problem." I thought of how carefully the teacher had chosen her words.

I walked home alone and gave the babysitter money for her taxi. Violet was fast asleep. I slipped into her twin bed and pulled the duvet over my legs and held my breath when she stirred. She wouldn't have wanted me in there but it's where I so often found myself. I was trying to find something in her stillness. I don't know what. Maybe the raw, sweet smell of her when she slept reminded me of where she came from. She was not perfect, she was not easy, but she was my daughter and maybe I owed her more.

And yet. As I lay there in the dark, I felt a twinge of vindication thinking about the meeting. I'd been living with a terrifying, unrelenting suspicion about my daughter, and I sensed that someone else could finally see it, too.

28

Sometime in the weeks that followed, I went to a gallery downtown after I dropped Violet off at school. There was a controversial exhibit that had been reviewed in the newspaper the day before, and I watched you read it over your morning coffee. Ever so slightly you had shaken your head before you turned the page.

I took one step inside the gallery and stared at the walls. On the matte white paint hung portraits used in media coverage of children who had been accused of gun violence. Unthinkable, sometimes deadly violence. Children, some barely old enough for acne, barely large enough to ride a roller coaster. I thought of how tiny those boys' genitals would have been, how juvenile they were, hairless, sexless.

Two of the children were girls. Each smiled widely, intensely, lips nearly curled under. One had braces. She would have gone with her mother to the orthodontist every month for an adjustment, picked out which color bands she wanted for her wires. Asked for strawberry ice cream after, because anything else in her mouth hurt too much.

For hours the children watched me. Could they recognize me as the kind of person they came from? Someone like their own mother? An employee with short, side-swept hair barely looked up from reading art catalogs at the lumbering oak desk in the corner. I touched the glass covering one young girl's school portrait. A perfect braid hung over each shoulder. Where does it begin? When do we know? What makes them turn? Who is to blame?

On the walk home, I talked myself through how irrational it was to think I'd find something familiar in those portraits. Going there was an absolutely mad thing to do.

I picked her up early from school that day and we went for hot chocolate and cookies. She offered me half of her cookie when we sat down.

"I think you're a very kind girl," I said. She licked the chocolate chips of her half while she thought about this.

"Noah said I'm mean. But I don't like Noah anyway."

"Noah doesn't know you very well, then."

She nodded and stirred the marshmallow goo with her finger.

We skipped dinner—the cookies had ruined our appetites. In the bath she closed her eyes and floated over a layer of bubbles like an angel in the snow.

"I'm going to hurt Noah tomorrow."

Her words stopped my heart. I wrung the facecloth and hung it on the tap, careful to measure my reaction. She wanted a reaction.

"That wouldn't be nice, Violet," I said calmly. "We don't hurt people. Instead why don't you tell him one thing you really like about him? Does he share nicely? Is he fun to play with at recess?"

"No," she said and put her head under the water.

The next day I told you I had an appointment and asked you to pick her up at school. Instead I circled the grocery store and bought nothing. My heart raced as I got closer to home. I'd been looking at my phone all day, sure the teacher would have called.

"How was she?" I was nearly out of breath.

"They said she had a really good day." You ruffled Violet's hair while she twirled her spaghetti. She looked up at me and sucked a strand through the gap in her front teeth.

Later, before I went to bed, as I collected her clothes for the washing machine, I found a huge fistful of curly blond hair in the pocket of the dress she had worn to school that day. I stared at it in my hand. The feeling of holding another human's hair in my palm was unsettling. And then I realized whose hair this was. Small, shy, pale little Noah with his head of messy curls. I walked down the hall unsure of what to do with it.

"Fox?"

"I have something for you," you'd called from the living room. Your voice was higher than it usually was. I closed my fist around the hair. You were sitting on the couch and handed me a small square box. And then I remembered you'd had your annual review that day. You'd been promoted. You'd been given a huge raise.

"You do so much for us," you said, your nose to my forehead. I opened the box. Inside was a thin gold chain with a small pendant engraved with the letter *V*. I lifted it up and held it against my neck. "Things aren't so easy right now, but I love you. You know that, right?"

You slipped off my shirt. You told me you wanted me.

The hair sat in the pocket of my jeans on the floor, and when we were done, I flushed the nest of blond hair down the toilet.

In the morning on the way to school I asked Violet what had happened to Noah the day before.

"He cut off all his own hair."

"He cut it himself?"

"Yes. In the bathroom."

"What did the teacher say?"

"I dunno."

"You had nothing to do with it?"

"No."

"Are you lying to me?"

"No. I promise."

She was quiet while we walked another block and then she said:

"I helped him clean up, so that's why his hair was in my pocket."

When we walked into the playground that morning, Noah looked at Violet and ran back to his mother and buried his face in her legs. His head had been buzzed clean. Violet walked right past him and through the front doors. His mother bent down to ask him what was wrong. *Nothing*, I heard him whine. She held a tissue at his nose and told him to blow. I gave her a look of sympathy and smiled. She looked tired. She did her best to smile back and waved, the dirty tissue in her hand. I should have walked over to say, *I know the feeling. Some days are hard.* But my knees were weak, and I needed to get out of there.

On the way home, I thought of the photographs hanging in the gallery from the day before. The women behind those children. *But her mother was so normal. She was just like one of us.*

After school that same day, I came up from doing the laundry and found her standing on the edge of a chair at the kitchen counter, her little fingers dancing leisurely through the pickle juice.

"What are you doing?" I had asked.

"Fishing for whales," she had said. I looked over her shoulder and watched her try to catch the last few warted pickles as they gracefully breached and dove in a jar of soggy dill weed, and you know what, they did look just like whales. She had a brilliant, beautiful mind and sometimes I longed to be inside it. Even though I feared what I might find.

29

You might not remember that his name was Elijah. His funeral was on a Saturday in early November, and it had been raining for two full days, and there was a heaviness to us all that sometimes came when the apartment felt damp, when our bones felt cold. We left Violet at home with the babysitter. She drew a picture while we were gone of two children. One was smiling, and one was crying, with a red scribble on the chest that I assumed was blood. I held it out for you to see, but you said nothing. You put the picture on the counter and called a taxi for the sitter. Violet was almost five years old.

When we got into bed that night, I rolled toward you and asked you if we could talk. You rubbed the spot between your eyes—we'd had a long, upsetting day but I couldn't help myself. You knew what I wanted to talk about.

"For fuck's sake, did you learn nothing today sitting there in that church?" you spit through closed teeth. And then, "It was just a picture."

But it was so much more. I rolled onto my back and stared at our ceiling and fingered the chain on my neck.

"Just accept her for who she is. You're her mother. That's all you're supposed to do."

"I know. And I do." The convincing. The lying. "I do."

You wanted a perfect mother for your perfect daughter, and there wasn't room for anything else.

In the morning Violet's picture was gone from the counter. I couldn't find it in the garbage. I checked the trash can in the kitchen, the one in the bathroom, the one near my desk. I never asked you what you did with it.

*A*t Elijah's funeral, the priest spoke about how God has a plan for each of us, that Elijah's soul was not meant to grow old. I could not reconcile this with what I feared had really happened at the park after school the week before.

I think I saw something happen right before that poor boy fell off the top of the slide.

I was so tired—Violet was having trouble sleeping again, wanting more water, wanting the light on. It had been weeks since I'd slept through the night. I might not have been thinking straight.

Ten seconds, I would estimate. That's how long she watched Elijah run from one side of the big play structure to the other, where Violet stood at the top of the highest slide. She kept her hands behind her back, her eyes on the boy. He bounded toward her along the wobbly bridge, openmouthed, squealing, the fresh fall air blowing back his long hair.

The thud had a sharpness to it when he hit the ground. *Thuck.* More like that.

She had looked down at me without any remorse in her eyes when she saw, on the gravel below her, that his crumpled body did not move in his striped shirt and drawstring jeans. She was expressionless when we heard his nanny scream for someone to help, the woman's shrill panic enough to ring my ears. She was unflinching when the ambulance came to take him away on a tiny person's stretcher, as a crowd of mothers and nannies stood and watched in horror, their children's scared little faces buried safely in their necks.

I stood, staring at the top of the slide, replaying what had just happened.

In the moments before he ran toward her, Violet had looked over the steep slide platform, as though she were a professional diver, visualizing her splashless entry into the water. *Be careful, please!* I'd shouted. *It's too high up there! It's dangerous!* The panic of a mother. If I'm honest, my mind went there: Danger. Death. But hers. A mother's mind is always there. She stepped back and leaned against a wooden post of the play structure. I hadn't known why she stood there waiting.

I saw her leg lift. At just the right moment.

I think his head hit the ground first.

In the echo of sirens, Violet asked in a quiet voice if we could go for a treat. Her eyebrows lifted in anticipation of my reaction. Was this a test? What had I seen? What would I do to her? The fact that she might have tripped him was so absurd, so unthinkable, that it almost instantly disappeared. No, no, it didn't happen. I looked up at the gray sky and said aloud, "That did not happen." *Blythe, that was not what you saw.*

"Mom? Can we go for a treat?"

I shook my head and put my trembling hands into my coat pockets and told her to walk.

Follow me. Now. NOW.

We walked the seven blocks to our apartment in silence.

I left her in front of the television, and I sat on the toilet for the next hour, unable to move, visualizing what I might have seen. This wasn't a fistful of someone's hair or taunting in the schoolyard. That platform must have been twelve feet high. I took off the *V* necklace you gave me. My neck felt red. Hot.

Strange things flooded my mind, things like tiny pink handcuffs, and child social workers, and reporters in trench coats knocking at our door, and the paperwork involved in transferring schools, and the outrageous cost of divorce, and that poor child's electronic wheelchair. I stared at the mold in the grout of our shower tiles and I replayed her reaction over and over. And then I decided: No. She didn't trip that child. She wasn't close enough to him. No, I was not the mother of someone who could do something like that.

I was so very tired.

I made her a peanut butter sandwich. She touched my arm when I put the plate on the coffee table and her fingers on my skin made me flinch. I stared at her hands and they looked so small, so innocent, the knuckles still dimpled with baby fat.

No. No, she had not done anything wrong.

I told you that night about the horrible accident that had happened to Elijah.

The accident, I called it.

Violet did a puzzle at the other end of the kitchen. She looked up at me when my phone buzzed on the counter. I stared at her while I answered. It was one of the other mothers from the playground telling me Elijah had died at the hospital.

"Dead. My God. He's dead." I felt winded. You glared at me for such candor, such poor maternal judgment for having said that out loud, and you went to Violet's side to comfort her. But she was fine. She shrugged. She asked if you could find the corner piece she was looking for.

She just needs some time to process.

Of course.

Maybe you should have thought that through, Blythe. Did she need to hear he was dead? Bad enough she was there when he fell.

And then not until much later that night when we got into bed, *You doing okay? Come here. That must have been terrible to see. I'm so sorry, Blythe.* You pulled me close and fell asleep with your leg wrapped around mine. I stared at the ceiling in the dark, waiting for Violet to wake up again.

The next day I left a frozen quiche and expensive protein smoothies in a cooler outside the family's apartment door, with a note that said we were thinking of them. I sent flowers to the funeral home, big white lilies.

All our love, The Connors.

The police looked into the incident briefly, a matter of routine. They questioned me. I told them what I told you: we did not see anything. Violet had already come down the slide when I heard the sound of his body hitting the ground when he fell. That the wood planks are too worn and slippery. That I'd always thought it was a dangerous playground. That I was thinking of his poor mother.

30

The pediatric intensive care unit was on the eleventh floor. I left my coat and purse in the car, and still had my pajama bottoms on. This and the McDonald's Happy Meal I'd bought before getting on the elevator were enough for the nurse at the station to assume I belonged there. Parents who have children on the brink of death aren't often asked for their identification.

I sat on a metal bench at the end of the hallway under a window that overlooked the employee parking lot. The air vent above made the noise of a hungry stomach. I put the Happy Meal down beside me.

I was disgusted with myself for being there. The place where Elijah died.

For two weeks I thought of the accident every minute of every day. Every time I closed my eyes, I was there at that playground, yelling up at her on the platform to be careful in the moments before it happened. I saw their little legs, his running, hers standing still against that pole. And then her leg lifting just as he passed.

But I don't know—I couldn't be sure.

I listened. To the listless sounds of a toddler having vials of blood drawn, and to the gentle voice of his mother telling him he was brave.

Across the hall from that child, a tired-looking man carried a little girl out of the room. She held a teddy bear, and waved good-bye at whomever she'd left as her ratty winter boots dangled at the man's hip. A nurse followed and shut the door quietly. Inside the room I heard a woman cry, her sobs bellowing. I could hear in her cries how angry she was.

And two doors down from that woman, a family sang a song that Violet had learned in preschool. The music was muffled, punctured with beautiful, childish squeals and the ding of a bell from a board game. Like the white noise of a carnival. I wished for a moment I could join them.

Nurses came and went, banging the heels of their hands against sanitizer boxes outside each door. People left for coffee. Mothers paged for towels. A clown in a tutu with a cart of toys knocked gently door by door, asking if it was a good time. Whispers. Giggles. Clapping. *Good girl. What a big boy.* Long stretches of silence. A notification through the speaker system that the elevators in the west hall would be shut down for the next twenty minutes. I stared at a thick layer of grime along the baseboard of the peach and gray pebbled floor. Heavy double doors at the end of the hall clanked shut and then swung open, over and over and over.

"Do you need anything?" I hadn't noticed the woman in a pale green uniform approach me. I tried to swallow before I spoke and then winced; my throat felt stuffed with medical gauze. The air was stale. I shook my head and thanked her. I sat there for four hours.

On my way out, the box of cold fries in my hand, I stopped outside the closed door where I'd heard the woman weep earlier that afternoon. I looked through the gridded glass and saw her lying in bed, a tiny lump cradled beside her, a highway of tubes running into the blankets from bags of fluid that hung like storm clouds above them.

Raindrops came down, drip by drip. There was a whiteboard on the wall beside the bed that said "My name is ____ and my favorite thing to do is ____." Someone had filled in the blanks: *Oliver. Play soccer with my friends.*

Mothers aren't supposed to have children who suffer. We aren't supposed to have children who die.

And we are not supposed to make bad people.

There was a moment outside that door when I wanted Violet to be the one who was pushed off the top of the slide.

I sat in my car in the hospital parking lot and replayed it differently this time. I had to stop letting my mind go there; I had to believe my daughter had not tripped that boy.

That evening, you slipped your hand across my shoulders to rub my neck while I fried shrimp in a pan. When I pulled away you asked what was wrong. I wanted to tell you where I'd gone that day. I wanted to say, *I'm a monster for thinking the things I do.* Instead I mumbled something about a headache and stared at the spitting oil. You shook your head as you walked out of the room.

31

T oday's not a good day, I'm afraid." Mr. Ellington stood in the doorway with a wet cloth in his hand. I'd knocked on and off for five minutes until he answered. Thomas and Daniel had gone to their aunt's house, he'd said. Mrs. Ellington wasn't feeling well. He must have seen the disappointment in my face because as I turned to walk home, he reached for my shoulder.

"Just a minute, Blythe. Let me see if she's up for some company after all." I waited in the front hallway until he came back. "Go on up. She's in bed resting."

I'd never been in their bedroom before, but I knew it was the room at the end of the hall. I was nervous—it was such a private space—but I also felt special. The door was ajar, so I slipped through quietly and Mrs. Ellington sat up in bed.

"Come in, honey. What a nice surprise to see you today." She had no makeup on and her hair was wrapped in a silk scarf. Her eyes looked smaller and her eyebrows were thinner, but she looked just as beautiful as ever. She patted the bed beside her and I wondered if I shouldn't get so close, if that would bother her. But she patted again so I sat down and put my hands politely on my lap.

"I don't look so good today, do I?"

I didn't know how to answer. I looked around her bedroom instead. The gold curtains were pulled to the side with rope, and the textured, leaf-patterned wallpaper looked exactly like my mother's, only it was a deep yellow instead of the hospital green in our house that I had never liked. I ran my hand over her bedspread, which matched the curtains. Everything looked so luxurious and warm. I thought of my own mother's bed, never made, the sheets rarely washed.

"Are you going to be okay?"

"Oh, yes, I'll be okay. I'm not sick, not exactly."

"What's wrong, then?" I knew it was bold of me to ask, but I needed to know. I could smell something strange, pungent and sweet, like the yogurt other kids had in their lunches at school. There was a small container of pills on the table beside her, and I wondered if they were the same ones I had seen in my mother's room.

"I'm not sure it's my place to talk to you about the birds and the bees, but you're a mature ten-year-old." I must have turned red. My mother and I had never talked about sex or where babies came from, but I had an idea of how it all worked from kids at school. Mrs. Ellington lifted the comforter from her middle and pulled her white nightshirt down taut over her swollen stomach. I hadn't noticed her being fat there before, but she was always dressed so nicely in things that weren't tight and ill fitting, like my mother's.

"You're having a baby?"

"I was. I was pregnant. But the baby didn't make it."

I had no concept of what not making it meant, of what would have happened to the baby inside her. Where had it gone? What had happened? She must have sensed my confusion. She slowly pulled the comforter back over her middle, as though it hurt to cover it up, but she smiled through whatever pain was in her. I saw she had a hospital bracelet on her arm, the same kind I'd seen my mother come home with once years ago after she'd had a bad bout of the flu. I didn't know what to say. I pointed to the pills on her nightstand.

"Do you want more of those?"

She laughed. "Well, yes, but I can only have one every six hours."

"Will Thomas and Daniel be sad?"

"I hadn't told them they'd be big brothers yet. I was going to tell them soon."

"Are you sad?"

"Yes, I'm very sad. But you know what? God has a way of taking care of things." I nodded as though I understood, as though God were someone I trusted, too.

"She was a little girl. I would have had a daughter." She put her finger to my nose and her eyes welled with tears. "Just like you."

32

There was something special about the street of old row houses, the way the air smelled like winter-flowering honeysuckle when we stepped out of the car. I would learn that the backyard was full of them. Neighborhood basketball hoops lined the dead-end road, and the elementary school down the street was rated one of the best in the area. We could do most of the work ourselves. Offers were being accepted the following week, but we agreed on a number right then and there. Our real estate agent got the deal done by dinnertime. She called with the news while we anxiously ate pizza at a restaurant where we'd soon become regulars.

Three bedrooms. A quick closing. I was starting to believe that life would finally move along. I was desperate for it.

We had needed a change, although we didn't speak of the new house that way. We didn't speak of needing a change at all. It had been three months since the accident and I no longer dreamed of the playground. I no longer heard the sound of his body hitting the pavement when I poured cereal or closed the car door. Time had given me that. Time, and my will to forget. I no longer went to the park. I no longer walked anywhere near there. The boy's name was never mentioned. Violet had started sleeping through the night again, and the fog that muddled my brain seemed to have lifted.

You had come home one day and opened your laptop to the house listing on a real estate agent's website. I didn't even know you had been looking.

For the next two months the three of us spent every weekend there, breaking things up with tools we borrowed and meeting with tradesmen who did what we couldn't. We agreed we couldn't manage a full renovation right now, but there were things that couldn't wait: new flooring, new bathrooms. The list grew with your keen architect's eye. The week of the move, your parents came to town to help with Violet while we packed and unpacked. They brought her over to say good-bye to the apartment before we handed back the keys. Ceremony was your mother's thing, not mine. Somewhere along the way I'd lost the sentimental attachment to the place where our family began. Even you had— I could tell by the relief in your face when we left that building for the last time. The way you dropped the keys into the manila envelope and tossed it onto the doorman's desk.

Violet stayed with your parents at their hotel downtown while we worked until two in the morning. I moved her old baby stuff, packed in rubber bins, to the second small bedroom upstairs.

"Shouldn't those go in the basement?" you asked.

"We'll need them again sooner or later."

You drew a long breath. "Let's call it a night."

We slept on our mattress in the middle of the floor of our new bedroom. We hadn't remembered to turn on the heat and so we bundled up in hoodies and sweatpants underneath the blanket.

"We'll be happy here," I whispered and rubbed my socked feet over yours.

"I thought we always were."

33

She must have seen my naked silhouette in the moonlight. My thin nightshirt draped the intersection of our bodies, my catlike arch, my breasts like tiny sacks of sand swinging over your face.

I moaned low and long, my hands on the headboard, and I blocked out the room around us. The closet didn't have doors to hide the mess of laundry I hadn't yet done, and the row of dry cleaning I hadn't yet unbagged, and the box of clothing donations I hadn't yet dropped off. I was buried in "yets." The move was disorganized and the end of the renovations were slow.

Looking back, we were in the midst of the kind of mundane chaos I sometimes yearn for now.

I didn't hear the creak of the door or the smack of her flat feet along the new hardwood that had been laid the week before. I didn't know she was there, not until you shoved me off and swore and pulled the sheet over yourself. I lay at the end of the bed in a fetal position, where I had landed at the hand of your panic. *Go back to bed. Nothing is wrong,* I had told her calmly. She asked what we had been doing. *Nothing,* I answered. *Jesus Christ, Blythe,* you said, as though everything about the moment was my fault.

And it was, in a way. I was ovulating. You were tired. I had cried into my pillow. And so you rubbed my back and began kissing my neck, the kind of kisses that said you loved me but didn't want to fuck me. There would always be another time to try, you said.

You don't want another baby, I'd accused. *Why?* We lay together quietly, and later, you ran your fingers through my hair. *I do want another baby,* you whispered.

You were lying but I didn't care.

I rolled over and stroked you until I felt you give in. I slipped you inside me and pretended everything was different—you, the room, the motherhood I knew—and begged you not to stop.

Three weeks earlier I had brought up the idea again while we brushed our teeth. You spit in the sink and ripped us each a thread of floss. *Let's see. Later. We'll see.*

There was an uncharacteristic bluntness in your voice that would have triggered my suspicion on a different day. But not then. This wasn't about you. This was about me. The only way forward I could see for our family was to have a second child. Redemption, maybe, for everything that had gone wrong. I thought back to why we'd had Violet in the first place—you wanted a family and I wanted to make you happy. But I also wanted to prove all of my doubts wrong. I wanted to prove my mother wrong, too.

Blythe, the women in this family, we're different. You'll see.

I wanted another chance at motherhood.

I could not concede that I was the problem.

I often pointed to babies while I walked Violet to school. *Wouldn't that be nice? A little brother or sister?* She rarely replied to me. She was increasingly in her own world, but by then the distance that grew between us made life together easier, in a way. We saw the same mother at drop-off every morning with her newborn tucked into her chest while she carefully bent over to kiss her older child good-bye.

"Two looks like a lot of work," I once said to her, smiling.

"Exhausting, but worth it." Worth it. There it was again. She bounced and patted his head. "He's such a different baby. It's a whole different experience with the second."

Different.

Violet in our bedroom doorway, hands by her sides. She refused to leave until I answered her about what we had been doing. And so I explained. When two people love each other, they like to cuddle in a special way. We were silent, all of us, there in the dark. And then she walked back to her room. We should comfort her, I said to you. We should go make sure she's okay.

"Then go," you said. But I didn't. We rolled away from each other in a standoff that made no sense to me.

We didn't speak in the morning. I showered without putting on the coffee for you. On my way to the kitchen I stopped halfway down the stairs to listen to your breakfast conversation with Violet. She told you she hated me. That she wished I would die so that she lived only with you. That she did not love me. These words would have speared the heart of any other mother.

You had said to her, "Violet, she's your mom."

There were so many other things you could have said, but those were the words you chose.

That night I shamelessly begged you to try again. Just once more. And you agreed.

34

The mother was dressed in the same yoga clothes she always wore at drop-off, her shirt slightly wrinkled from the hamper. Her hair was leftover from the previous day's effort. Her son stood next to her and pulled his baseball cap off. The schoolyard was electric with morning energy, tummies filled with Cheerios, faces plump from sleep. She crouched. He found his spot in her neck. I could see from where I stood that there was pain in the boy's face; her hands closed around his head like the petals of a flower. Her mouth moved slowly in his ear. He coiled into her. He needed her. Behind him noise grew, shouts, the whip of basketball rubber on cement.

She slipped her hands down his slight shoulders and he pushed away, his small chest rising, but she pulled him back again. It was she who needed him this time. Now, her face in his neck, three seconds, maybe four. She spoke again. He squeezed his eyes. He nodded, put his hat on, pulled the brim low, and walked away. Not slowly, not with hesitation, but with anticipation, with haste, on legs that turned in slightly at the knees. She could not watch, not this morning. She turned away and left, looked down at her phone, and got lost in something that didn't make her ache in the way her son did.

My belly fluttered like a net of butterflies for the first time that morning. The baby was waking inside me. Violet had left her bag of orange slices with me at drop-off and I sucked the warm juice from them, tossing the rinds in a city garbage can as I followed the mother down the street and through two intersections. She stopped for salt from a corner market and I watched her from behind the pyramid of tomatoes. I wanted to see her face. To see if she carried him with her. I wondered how it looked—how it felt—to have that kind of connection to another person. I hadn't yet found the answer when I lost her one block later in a crowded section of sidewalk construction.

These kinds of things happened around us, Violet and me, in a language we did not speak. So I was desperate to learn. To be better with the one who came next.

On the way home, I walked by a woman setting up a small flea market stand on the side of the street. She leaned a stack of old paintings against the lamppost as she put colored dots on the backs to mark the prices. She pulled out one in an elegant gold frame and looked at it thoughtfully, deciding how to price it. I stood behind her and found myself clutching my chest as I took the painting in. It was of a mother sitting with her small child on her lap, the rosy baby dressed in white and cupping his mother's chin gently as she glanced down. One arm was around the child's middle, and the hand of the other held his small thigh. Their heads touched. There was a peacefulness to them, a warmth and comfort. The woman's long, draping dress was a beautiful peach with burgundy florets. I could barely speak to ask her the price. But it didn't matter—I had to have it.

"I'll take that one," I said as she put it back in the pile.

"The oil?" She took her glasses off and looked up at me.

"Yes, that one. The mother and the child."

"It's a replica of a Mary Cassatt. Not an original, of course." She laughed as though I should know how absurd it would be to have an original Mary Cassatt.

"Is that her in the painting? The artist?"

She shook her head. "She was never a mother herself. Maybe that's why she liked to paint them so much."

I carried the painting home under my arm and hung it in the baby's nursery. When you came home that night to find me straightening the frame on the wall, you stopped in the doorway and made a noise. A humph.

"What? You don't like it?"

"Not your typical nursery art. You hung pictures of baby animals in Violet's room."

"Well, I love it."

I wanted that baby. That cupped face. That chubby hand on mine. That palpable love.

35

Violet quietly watched my shape stretch and morph. He moved all day long, dragging his impossibly small heels across my belly and back again. I loved to lie on the couch with my shirt pulled up, reminding us all that he was here. That we would be a family of four.

"Is he doing it again?" you would call from the kitchen, finishing up the dishes.

"He's at it again," she'd yell back, and we'd laugh.

The baby had caused a shift in our relationship somewhere along the way, although I couldn't put my finger on exactly what that shift was. We were kinder to each other, although there was also a new distance between us, one you seemed to fill with more work. I took that space to turn inward. To him. We were happily each other's worlds, even as early as that. Mother and son.

When the technician rolled her wand over the mass of white static and said, *You've got yourself a boy in there*, I closed my eyes and I thanked God for the first time in my life. I kept the news to myself for two days—it took you that long to ask what had happened at my ultrasound appointment. This was uncharacteristic—you had cared enough during my first pregnancy to come to every one of them. We were, at that point, passing each other in the night. You had several big projects on the go, new clients with big money. I needed so little of you then. I had him.

Violet wanted to help me go through her old baby clothes. We sat together in the laundry room and folded the tiny sleepers as they came out of the dryer. She would lift each one to her nose as though she were remembering a time and place when she wore them. I let her dress her doll in a knitted sweater and she pretended to nurse him. I marveled at the unusual carefulness with which she touched everything, the softness of her voice.

"This is how you did it," she said, gently bouncing the doll twice to the right and then twice to the left, and then back to the right again.

At first I didn't know what she meant—I didn't remember doing that with her. But I took the doll from her and stood up and mimicked how she'd just rocked the baby. The familiarity of the motion came back to me instantly. She was right. I laughed as I kept bouncing the doll back and forth, and she giggled, nodding her head.

"I told you!"

"You're absolutely right."

It seemed impossible that she would remember this, that it would stay with her all these years. She put her hands on either side of my huge belly and mimicked that same motion for the baby inside me, rocking with my belly in her little hands. Soon we were dancing, the three of us, to the rhythm of the spinning washing machine.

36

I felt down with my hand as his head came through the hot ring of my cervix. The release was euphoric. You watched me guide him from my body's opening and then lift him quietly, carefully, onto the place he'd filled for 283 days. *You're here.* He looked for me and arched his back and then he began to slink up my stomach, like an inchworm covered in vernix and blood. His mouth was open and his glassy eyes were still black. His twitching, wrinkled hands looked covered in far too much skin. They found my breast and his little chin shook. He was my miracle. I pulled him to my nipple and tapped its nub on his bottom lip with arms that still shook from the oxytocin. *There you go, sweet boy.* He was the most beautiful creature I had ever seen.

"He looks just like Violet," you said, peering over my shoulder.

But he didn't look a thing like her to me. He was seven pounds of something so pure, so blissful, that it felt as though he might float away above me, a dream, something I would never deserve for as long as I lived. I held him for hours, my skin stuck to his, until they made me get up for the bathroom. The blood poured from me into the toilet and when I looked down at the mess, for some reason I thought of our daughter again. And then I stepped slowly back to my son in the glass bassinet outside the bathroom door.

I remember so little else about how he came into this world.

I remember everything about how he left it.

1969

Cecilia got her period when she was twelve years old. By then she had breasts larger than any other girl in her class. She walked with her shoulders rolled forward, trying to hide the new signs of her womanhood. Etta wasn't speaking to her much at that point, let alone broaching the subject of puberty with her. Cecilia had heard from other girls about the bleeding, but still her heart stopped when she saw her wet, red underwear. She went through her mother's cupboards looking for sanitary pads, but there were none. She doubled over in pain on the bathroom floor, saw the blood come through her pants, and decided she should tell her mother.

Etta didn't answer when Cecilia knocked on her mother's door, but there was nothing unusual about that—it was three o'clock and she slept most afternoons. She went to Etta's bedside and whispered her name until she startled awake. Etta sighed when Cecilia told her what had happened—in pity or disgust, Cecilia wasn't sure.

"What do you want from me?"

She didn't answer because she didn't know. Her throat tightened. Etta opened her bedside drawer and took out two pills from a small red makeup bag that she hid from Henry. She held them out to Cecilia and slipped her other hand under the pillow and closed her eyes.

Cecilia stared at the little white pills, placed them on the bedside table, *and left the bedroom. She found her mother's purse in the hallway and took whatever change she had to the pharmacy. Her face burned as she paid for the pads, looking away from the young man at the cash register. At home she ran a hot bath and Etta came in to use the toilet just as she sank into the tub. Etta peed with her eyes closed.*

Later that afternoon, Cecilia stood outside Etta's bedroom door. An unfamiliar rage crept up her chest. She charged inside and flipped on the light. Standing at the foot of her mother's bed with tight fists, she realized that she wanted Etta to hurt her. Being smacked by her at least meant that she existed in Etta's small, sad world. By then Cecilia had felt for months like she was dead to her mother. Etta stirred awake and looked at her.

"Hit me, Etta," she said, shaking. "Go on. Hit me!"

She'd never called her mother by her first name before.

Etta's expression was empty. She looked from Cecilia's trembling face to the light switch on the wall and she sighed again. She put her head back down and closed her eyes. Henry's footsteps traveled through the front foyer downstairs and into the kitchen. He'd been looking for dinner but there wasn't any. Not today. The two pills Etta had given her were still on the bedside table. Cecilia wasn't sure why she didn't want Henry to see them. She took them and flushed them down the toilet.

"Is she not feeling well again?" Henry was filling the kettle when Cecilia came into the kitchen.

"Headache," she said. They were all so good at lying for one another, at pretending things weren't as bad as they were. He nodded and looked again for leftovers in the fridge. Cecilia turned on the radio to fill the room so that they didn't have to say anything more.

37

I wonder if you ever noticed the things about him that I lived for?

The way he flung his arms above his head like a teenager while he slept. The smell of his feet at the end of the day, just before his bath. How he'd pop up on his arms when he heard the creak of the door in the morning, desperately seeking me through the bars of the crib. And so I never asked you to oil the hinges.

He's been heavy in me today. Sometimes this just happens. Distinct, dense, aching days that make everything around me taste sour. I want only him, but the real world threatens to quiet his noises, his smells.

I want to breathe him in deeply and never breathe out ever again.

Do you feel this sometimes, too?

Those first days. Sour milk and body odor. Nipple cream staining the sheets. A constant ring of tea on the bedside table. I cried without thinking, without knowing why, but the tears were a release of love. My milk came in and my breasts were boulders, and I barely moved from that spot. I jiggled him to sleep on my naked chest. He startled every so often, throwing his skinny little arms right up, and then curling back into me. And then we'd start again. There was no day or night. My nipples stung at the thought of feeding him next.

And yet. I didn't want that time with him to end. He was everything I had ever wanted. The connection we shared was the only thing I could feel. I craved the physical weight of him on top of me. *So this is it*, I would think. *This is what it's supposed to be like.* I drank him in like water.

He would lift his head from between my breasts and wobble it around like he was searching, trying to find his mama, looking for the person he loved. I would put my cheek down to touch his and then he would rest again, safe and happy and full. Of milk, of me.

Eventually I left my bed and turned my attention back to Life. I cleaned up Violet's breakfast, I made make-believe castles, I threw pile after pile of clothes in the dryer. But when he wasn't with me, my mind was with him, up in that nursery.

Violet didn't care much for Sam at first, although she watched carefully every time I latched him for a feeding. She would often feel her own flat chest as he drank from me, as though she was bewildered by the function of a woman's breasts. When he was done, she would leave the room, wanting to be alone most of the time.

Sam fell madly in love with her in the months that followed. Soon, he would light up when he heard her voice come out the school door at pickup.

"There's your sister!" I'd say, and he'd kick his legs, desperate to get near her, aching for her face to come up right in front of his. She would jiggle his foot and off we'd go, back to our home, to the part of the day I feared the most. The three of us, alone, the minefield of the late afternoon, waiting for you to walk in the door. You were the great neutralizer.

You and me. We were partners, companions, creators of these two humans. But we lived increasingly different lives, like most parents do. You were cerebral and creative, inventing spaces and sight lines and perspectives, your days concerned with lighting, elevation, finishes. You had three meals a day. You read sentences written for adults and you wore a very nice scarf. You had a reason to shower.

I was a soldier, executing a series of physical actions on a loop. Change the diaper. Make the formula. Warm the bottle. Pour the Cheerios. Wipe up the mess. Negotiate. Beg. Change his sleeper. Get her clothes out. Where's the lunch box? Bundle them up. Walk. Faster. We're late. Hug her good-bye. Push the swing. Find the lost mitten. Rub the pinched finger. Give him a snack. Get another bottle. Kiss, kiss, kiss. Put him in the crib. Clean. Tidy. Find. Make. Defrost the chicken. Get him up from the crib. Kiss, kiss, kiss. Change his diaper. Put him in the high chair. Clean up his face. Wash the dishes. Tickle. Change the diaper. Tickle. Put the snacks in a baggie. Start the washing machine. Bundle him up. Buy diapers. And dish soap. Race for pickup. Hello, hello! Hurry, hurry. Unbundle. Laundry in the dryer. Turn on her show. Time-out. Please. Listen to my words. No! Stain remover. Diaper. Dinner. Dishes. Answer the question again and again. Run the bath. Take off their clothes. Wipe up the floor. Are you listening? Brush teeth. Find Benny the Bunny. Put on pajamas. Nurse. A story. Another story. Keep going, keep going, keep going.

I remember one day realizing how important my body was to our family. Not my intellect, not my ambitions of a writing career. Not the person shaped by thirty-five years. Just my body. I stood naked in front of the mirror after taking off my sweater, which was covered in the pureed peas Sam had spit up. My breasts wilted like the plant in our kitchen that I could never remember to water. My stomach spilled over the indent from my underwear like the foam on the edge of my lukewarm latte. My thighs were marshmallows punctured with a roasting stick. I was mush. But the only thing that mattered was that I could physically keep us all going. My body was our motor. I forgave everything about the unrecognizable woman in the mirror. It never occurred to me then that my body would not be useful like that ever again: necessary, dependable, cherished.

Around that time, sex seemed to have changed even more for both of us. We were efficient. Rote. You were elsewhere while I straddled you. I, too, let my mind go. To the wet wipes I needed to buy. To the doctor's appointment I'd forgotten to make. Where had I seen that recipe for the curry carrots? Summer dresses. Library books. These sheets I'd need to wash.

W e can't do it this morning, Fox, he's got his swim class and then a playdate after, and I've already canceled on this mom twice. I told you this last week when I booked Violet for the dentist."

"I don't remember Violet having quite such a busy social life," you said.

I was packing the diaper bag. She looked up at me from the floor where she was carefully tying her shoes. I shot you a look that said *Not now*. But your remarks were constant. You were consumed with jealousy on behalf of our daughter, who could not have cared less about how close her mother was with her new baby brother. She had adjusted, to the surprise of us all, almost seamlessly. The baby had defused the tension between Violet and me somehow, as though we were both now free to breathe a little. In this new space, she offered me small, measured gestures of affection—she sat closer to me during bedtime stories, she lifted her hand for a brief good-bye at the school doors.

We were making progress.

It was you I struggled with. You were supposed to have been happy for the mother I had finally found within myself when Sam arrived in our lives.

Your mom had visited for a few days the week before. You two were in the kitchen having a cup of tea after dinner on her last night while I cleaned up the toys in the living room. You both must have thought I was upstairs. You had thanked her for coming. Anytime, she said. I stood still when I heard her mention my name—that I seemed to be in much "better spirits" than I was before Sam was born.

"She loves that boy. I just wish she felt that same way about Violet."

"Fox," she had chastised, although gently. And then a few moments later, "The second time around is easier for some women. An easier adjustment."

"I know, Mom. But I worry for Violet. She needs—"

I had marched into the kitchen with the bin full of plastic animals and dropped it on the floor at your feet. You jumped and stared at the toys.

"Good night, Helen." I couldn't look at you.

The next morning, before she left for the airport, she apologized for what I overheard you say, as though she still had some kind of responsibility for you.

"Everything okay with you two?"

I hadn't wanted her to worry.

"Just not getting enough sleep, that's all."

So you'll have to take her this morning, I'm sorry. Okay?" I bent down to tighten Violet's shoelaces.

"I've got a client coming in at ten. I can't make it from one end of the city to the other and back again by then."

"Well, you can make it to your office in time if you don't drop her off—just give her some paper and pencils to keep her busy during your meeting, and take her to school afterward. That would be fun, right, Violet?"

You rubbed your closed eyes and sighed. Sam had kept us both up most of the night. He was teething. You had always been able to sleep through Violet waking up at night, but you seemed to have a hard time sleeping since Sam came. "All right. Come on, kiddo, let's roll."

At dinner that night she told me all about her day. The treasure chest at the dentist's office, the hole punch she played with at your desk.

"And then I went for lunch with Daddy and his friend."

"Oh, how nice. And who was that?"

"Jenny."

"Gemma," you corrected her.

"Gemma," she repeated.

"Someone from the office?" I had never heard the name before.

"My new assistant. She took a liking to Violet while I was in the meeting, so I invited her along."

"That's nice. I didn't know you had a new assistant. And where did you guys go?

"A place with chicken fingers! She bought me an ice cream after! And a unicorn pencil and eraser."

"Lucky girl."

"She loved my hair."

"I do, too. You have beautiful hair."

"Her hair was long and curly, and she had pink paint on her nails."

Sam began to fuss in his high chair, fist in his mouth. Violet banged her hands on the table to distract him. "Sammy, look, it's a drum! Drum, drum, drum. Drum, drum, DRUM!"

"You'll clean up?" I asked. I took Sam for his bath without waiting for your answer.

I *read her a story in our bed,* Sam wiggling between us with his bunny, Benny.

"One more," she said when I finished the book. Always one more. I sighed and gave in. Sam tapped his fingers on his nearly empty bottle. *More, more.* You were changing into your jeans at the end of the bed.

"Mom, Sammy wants more milk."

"Going somewhere?"

"Back to the office," you said. "I have to finish a proposal tonight."

"Daddy, you have to tuck me in!"

You leaned down to kiss all three of us. One by one. With purpose. Sam held up his empty bottle.

"Mom will tuck you in, sweetheart. I have to run. Be a good girl for her, okay?"

"Sammy still needs more milk!" said Violet again.

"Love you," you said, to all of us.

I *sat on the edge* of her bed to say good night. She had been so good lately and yet I never told her this. I had started to take this new, peaceful normal between us for granted. I could barely remember a time before Sam. I could barely remember the mother I had been. Motherhood is like that—there is only the now. The despair of now, the relief of now.

Her face was maturing, a preview of what she would look like as a teenager. Her lips were round and plump, and I imagined her kissing someone. Loving someone. She had changed in those months since Sam was born. Or maybe it was me who had changed. Maybe I could finally see who she was.

"Violet? I want you to know what a very good girl you've been lately. You've been kind and gentle with Sam. You've been helpful. And you've been a good friend at school. I'm proud of you."

She was quiet, thinking. I turned out her night-light and leaned down to kiss her, and she let me.

"Good night. Sleep tight."

"Do you love baby Sam more than me?" Her words paralyzed me. I thought of you. Of what she might have overheard you say.

"Honey. Of course not. I love you both the same."

She closed her eyes, pretending to sleep, and I watched her lids flutter.

39

I didn't know she was in his room until she spoke.

The nights had been ours for months on end, more months than the baby books said was normal. I woke urgently at the slightest noise from Sam's crib, as though a rocket had launched in my ear. In the dark I stood, shifting my hips from side to side, the rhythm, like the scent of my skin and the taste of my milk, the way he knew it was me. *Go to sleep, sweet boy.* I would brush my lips on the fuzz of his head, careful not to rouse him. On the particular night I'm remembering, he barely nursed, wanting only the feeling of my nipple filling his mouth. The comfort. The sound machine hissed, a fusion of noises that were meant to be the ocean.

"Put him down," she told me. I gasped and startled the baby in my arms.

"Violet! Why are you in here?"

"Put him down."

She spoke calmly, directly. As though it were a threat. I sensed she was somewhere near the closet; I couldn't see her in the faint spread of light from under the closed door. I turned slowly, trying to catch a different perspective of the room, and waited, letting my eyes find the nursery's objects in the dark. Her voice came from the other end this time.

"Put him down."

"Go back to bed, honey. It's three in the morning. I'll come in and rub your back."

"I won't," she said slowly, her voice low, "until you put him down."

My chest began to tighten—that feeling again, the creep of anxiety. It was back in an instant, like she'd snapped her fingers to wake me up from her spell. That tone used to haunt me. *I can't go there again with you*, I thought, my mouth dry. Why had she been in here? What was she doing?

I'd huffed to show her how silly she was being, but I listened to her.

I laid Sam in his crib and felt around the mattress for Benny. He always held it near his face. I couldn't find it.

"Violet, do you know where Benny is?"

She tossed it at me and left the room. She'd taken the bunny from his crib. She'd been watching him while he slept.

She'd been so close to him.

I closed the door behind me and followed her to her room.

I sat softly on the edge of her bed. I slipped my hand up the back of her strawberry-patterned pajama top onto her perfect, silky skin. She loved to have her back rubbed. By you.

"Don't touch me. Get away from me."

I pulled my hand out of her shirt. "Have you been in there before to watch Sam sleep at night? Do you do that sometimes?"

She didn't answer.

My heart raced as I went back to our bed, slowing at Sam's closed door to make sure he was quiet. I was ashamed of myself for the thoughts that came to my mind. And then: *I could bring him to my bed. I could make sure he's safe. Just for tonight. Just this once.*

We were past this. We were supposed to be past this.

I took my phone out of the bedside table drawer and I looked at photos of her until you stirred gently beside me, bothered by the blue light. I was looking to find something in her face, but I didn't know what. I went to Sam's room and brought him back into bed with me.

40

S he's just been so good lately, you know? It came from nowhere."
We were in bed the next morning, early, Sam on the floor with
his board books. I lied and said Sam wouldn't settle after Violet
had been in his room and that's why I'd brought him into our bed. I
rolled into you, missing your warmth. You reached for your phone and
I studied you. Your chest, the new gray hairs, the way you twirled them
between your fingers while you read your emails.

"You're probably making something out of nothing. Again."

But here's what you didn't understand: There weren't many places
my mind wouldn't go. My imagination could tiptoe slowly into the
unthinkable before I realized where I was headed. While pushing a
swing or peeling sweet potatoes. The thoughts I had were awful, they
were harrowing, but there was something satisfying about letting myself go there. The extent of how far she might go. What could happen.
How my worst fears might feel if they came true. What I would do.
What would I do?

Enough. I'd snap back and cleanse my mind: The children. The
squeals. The life in their eyes. Everything is just fine.

I left the kids with the babysitter after school and joined Grace for a pedicure. The sitter was coming once a week then, a small break I cherished. I picked a color called Charcoal Dreams that felt suitable for the new chill in the air and tried not to breathe too deeply as the woman picked at my unloved cuticles. She put my foot on her thigh and seemed to be bracing herself for the work of a tradesman—the skin on my heels could have been shaved with a cheese grater. Petroleum jelly at night, she suggested, under a thick pair of socks. I didn't care enough about my heels to do something like that and almost told her, but this was her life after all—feet—so I simply thanked her for the tip.

Grace talked about the vacation she'd just returned from. Cabo with her mother for her seventieth birthday. The bartender had made them prickly pear margaritas at the swim-up bar. Something about a new self-tanner. I tuned her out. I thought of the kids at home, of how the babysitter said she would tidy the kids' bedrooms. Of how Violet would want to play in the basement instead, and Sam would whine until he was plopped down there, too. He wanted nothing more than to be near her lately, always reaching for her when she walked by, and calling out for her from the crib—"Bye-ette! Bye-ette!"—when he woke up in the morning. That made me smile, thinking of his broken baby talk. Grace moved on to some brothers she had met, something about a rancher from Iowa. Were there ranches in Iowa? I thought of that space down there in the basement where they'd be. It was unfinished, slightly damp, but clean enough for Sam to cruise around now that he was on the move. I thought of how we needed a new carpet. Something with a low pile, easy to clean. And some storage for toys. I thought of how you stored your sports stuff down there, too, how your golf bag barely fit down the narrow staircase. Of how you'd put your clubs down there the day before. Of how Violet liked to pull them out and pretend she was at the driving range. I thought of the sitter always wanting to clean, even though I told her she didn't have to. Of Sam obsessed with Violet's every move. Of the weight of the driver in her hand. Of the way I'd seen her swing it. Like a weapon. Of his small, feathery head. Of how easily she could do it. Of how it would take only a second. Of the crack. Of whether or not there would be blood. Brain damage, or just blood?

Now Grace talked about an open invitation to the ranch. She was thinking of March. The acetone started to hurt my lungs and I pulled my feet away from the woman's hands, the polish finished only on one foot. I leaned away to find air that didn't sting but the entire room felt toxic and my chest was closing in. I had to go. I grabbed my purse and I left the woman stunned, polish brush in hand. Grace called out about my shoes, about where I was going, and I started to run. The clubs. She could do it. She would do it. The sitter wouldn't watch them closely enough. I ran and didn't stop for the two red lights, holding my hand out for the cars to slow down as my numb feet carried me home.

"You'll kill yourself!" shouted a man on a bike.

No! I wanted to yell. *She will kill him. She hates me that much. You don't understand.*

"Violet!" I threw open the door. I ran to the basement stairs and screamed her name again. Nobody answered. "Sam! Where is Sam?"

The babysitter came rushing down the hall with a finger on her lips.

Sam was asleep. Violet was resting in her room with a book.

I fell back against the wall. Nothing had happened.

Nothing had happened.

nxiety attacks are very common. Especially for new moms. This is normal."

I wondered if I should have said more. The doctor blew on the end of her pen as though it were hot. She wrote me a prescription and explained when I should take them. I left the building thinking of my mother's translucent orange containers filled with tiny white tablets, dwindling over the course of each month.

knew something wasn't right. At first it was the emptiness she'd had in her eyes ever since I found her in Sam's room, the way she seemed to look through me when I was with him now. Her contempt had shifted from the wildly exhausting tantrums that had once left me in tears to a manipulative, premeditated coldness. Her calm, steadfast dismissal of me was far beyond her nearly seven years. The icy looks. The complete disdain. The passive resistance to doing what I asked her to: Can you finish your dinner, please? Can you put away your toys? She simply disengaged with zero reaction, nothing for me to work with. Punishments or threats were useless; consequences had no

meaning to her. Whatever attention I had gained from her since Sam
was born had all but disappeared. She wouldn't let me touch her. We
resumed our old stand-off. And you resumed your old place as the only
person she wanted in her world.

E ventually we learned to tolerate each other enough to coexist.
     She needed very little from me, to the point where she began to
feel like a boarder I had to feed with plastic dishes on a heart-shaped
place mat. I focused instead on Sam, on our routine, on the motions
required of me when she wasn't at school. And when you came home
in the evening, she came alive again.

     Sam was my light and I did everything I could to stop Violet from
dimming it. Some mornings we came home after dropping off Violet
and went back into our unmade bed with our suite of necessities—bottle,
tea, books, Benny. The mess in the kitchen and the laundry could wait
for us. Instead we passed the time staring at each other. We mused
about ducks and dinosaurs and belly buttons. Later on we napped in
the late-winter sun. He slept on my chest, even after he was weaned
from my milk and my smell had changed. It was as though he knew
how much I needed him.

     The anxiety stayed away for the next little while. I kept the unfilled
prescription in my purse—every time I saw the piece of paper when I
reached in for something, I would think of my mother. I couldn't bring
myself to go to the pharmacy. I didn't trust myself.

Cecilia's not here." My father's words were meant to be stern but I heard a ripple in his voice. "I don't know where she is." He placed the receiver on the phone cradle with a shaking hand. I'd been watching from the hallway. He had lied to the person on the other end. My mother was home and hadn't left her bed in a while. I didn't know why, or why my father needed to lie to whoever kept calling for her. The one time I had reached for the phone before him, he knocked it out of my hand, as though the voice on the other end would burn my ear.

He brought her soup and water and crackers. I asked if she had the stomach flu.

"Yeah. Something like that."

I was in the way. He passed me on the stairs, his back hunched over the tray he carefully carried to her. I hadn't seen my mother for days, not since she'd been dressed up for one of her nights out in the city. She was going out more often by then, gone overnight, sometimes two. Her disappearing act. I listened from my room but couldn't make out their words that night. She sounded weak and tearful and he was patient and calm. I tiptoed closer to their door.

"You need help."

And then a crash. A dish. She had thrown the bowl of soup. I jumped out of my father's path as he swung open the door in search of a cloth. I looked in the room and saw her in bed, upright, eyes closed. Her arms folded across her chest. I saw the same plastic bracelet I'd seen the year before on Mrs. Ellington when the baby in her stomach hadn't made it. My mother was thin, though, her waist the size of mine at eleven years old, and there wasn't any chance she wanted another child. I went to my room and got ready for bed, hoping to hear them continue the argument so I could piece together what was going on. I fell asleep to the sound of my mother crying.

In the morning I went to the bathroom to pee. The house was still quiet—my father hadn't stirred from the couch yet. I opened the toilet. The bowl was filled with blood and what looked like the guts of the mice the neighbor's cat sometimes left on our front porch. My mother's underwear was beside the toilet. I picked them up and saw that the heavy brown stains were dried blood.

"Dad? What's wrong with Mom?"

My father was standing over the pot of coffee, still wearing his clothes from the night before. He didn't answer me. He fetched the paper from outside the front door and tossed it onto the table.

"Dad?"

"She had a procedure."

I poured myself cereal and ate quietly. The phone rang as he flipped through newspaper sections, drinking his coffee. I stood to answer.

"Leave it, Blythe."

"*Seb!*"

He sighed and shoved his chair back. He poured a cup of coffee for her and left the kitchen. The phone rang again and, without thinking, I answered.

"I need to talk to her."

"Pardon?" I'd heard just fine but didn't know what else to say.

"Sorry. Wrong number." The man hung up. I heard my father's footsteps come down the stairs and I quickly turned back to my cereal.

"Did you answer that?"

"No."

He looked at me for a long time. He knew I was lying.

Before I left for school I went to my mother's door and knocked softly. I wanted to see for myself if she looked okay.

"Come in." She was drinking the coffee and staring out her window. "You're going to be late for school."

I stood in the door frame and thought of sitting beside Mrs. Ellington when she showed me her swollen stomach. My mother had the same strange smell. Two new containers of pills were on the nightstand. She looked tired and puffy. She'd taken off the hospital bracelet I'd seen the day before. The top of her hand looked badly bruised.

"Are you okay?"

She didn't take her eyes off the window.

"Yes, Blythe."

"There was blood in the bathroom."

She looked surprised, like she'd forgotten that I lived in the house, too.

"Never mind that."

"Was it from a baby?"

Her eyes lifted from the window and found a spot on the ceiling. I saw her swallow.

"Why would you say that?"

"Mrs. Ellington. She had a baby that didn't make it."

My mother finally looked at me. And then through me. She blew air through her teeth and looked back to her window, shaking her head. "You don't know what you're talking about."

I immediately regretted telling my mother about Mrs. Ellington. I wished I could shovel the words back into my mouth—I didn't want my mother anywhere near my relationship with her. It was the only thing I had in my life that was sacred. I left the room and went to school and when I got home everything seemed to be back to normal. My mother was standing in the kitchen, burning dinner on the stove. My father was pouring a drink. The phone on the wall rang, and he picked up the receiver to hit the hook and then let it dangle. We listened to the faint dial tone while we ate.

43

The day before Sam died we went to the zoo.

The weather was unseasonably warm and there was sun in the forecast.

We listened to Raffi in the car. *Zoo, zoo, zoo, how about you, you, you?* We packed our lunches and brought the nice camera, but we forgot to take pictures.

Violet tugged on your arm all day, wanting to run ahead. She always wanted to be ahead. The two of you against the world. I couldn't take my eyes off you from behind, the way you looked so much alike. The shape of you together. The way you leaned a little lower to the side where she stood, how she always reached up to feel the bend in your elbow.

I fed Sam outside the polar bear exhibit and you got Violet some apple juice from the vending machine because she said our juice boxes from home had a weird taste. A squirrel stole a leftover cookie from the bottom of our stroller. Violet cried. She wouldn't wear the hat I'd brought. Sam spit up his milk and I cleaned him with the brown paper towels from the bathroom because I'd forgotten our wipes. I made circles on his palm and then ran my fingers up his arm and tickled under his chin. His laughter was like a scream, spirited and expansive, and I lived for it. An older woman nearby with a little boy's mittened hand in hers said to me, "What a cute baby you have, such a happy little guy!" Thank you, he's mine, I made him. One whole year ago. He was so much a part of me that in the seconds just before he cried, my insides grew physically tight, like someone was blowing up a balloon in my rib cage.

"Wait until you see this!" you said to Violet, and we walked down the ramp to the dark, echoing underground, and you both stood at the glass wall. You were shadows against the electric green glow of the water in the tank, particles of dirt and fish scales floating around you like the dust from dandelions. I stood back, with Sam in my arms, and felt like I was watching someone else's family. That you were both mine seemed impossible in that moment. You were so beautiful together. The polar bear pressed his paw up to the glass right in front of Violet's face. She caught her breath and threw herself around your waist, in awe, in terror, in amazement, the kind of reaction you might catch only a few times in your child's life, a reminder that they are new to this world, that they can't possibly understand when they're safe or not.

We bought them a pair of tiny lions at the souvenir shop, and Violet threw hers out the window of the car on our way home. I was angry, looking back at the highway, wondering if the plastic toy had hit someone's windshield. You yelled and told her it was dangerous.

"Well, I didn't want the mom lion. I hate my mom."

I looked over at you and took a deep breath and turned the other way. *Let it go.* And then Sam started to cry, so Violet reached for Benny, which he'd dropped from his car seat, and tossed it back to him. She hushed him nicely and you said to her, "Good girl, Violet."

Her nose was sunburned—I hadn't thought of sunscreen in February. I squeezed aloe from an old tube and dabbed it on her nose with my finger. I counted the freckles on her face, wanting to hold her in that rare moment when I was allowed to touch her. She stared at me as though she had never heard anyone count before. I wondered if she might hug me and my muscles tightened, bracing for what she would feel like against me—it had been so long. But she looked away.

She watched as I bathed Sam before bed and then she sat with me on the floor and rubbed his tummy and said, "He's a good baby, isn't he?" She handed him Benny and he chewed on one of the ears while she watched him quietly. I let her put his pajamas on, an exercise in patience for us both, because she so rarely asked to do it. As she was pulling up the second leg, she said, "I don't want Sammy anymore." I clicked my tongue at her and wiggled his belly. He smiled at Violet and kicked his chunky legs. She gave him a kiss anyway, and then sat on the closed lid of the toilet and watched us as I rubbed a facecloth on his gums.

"He's teething again," I told her. "Before we know it, he'll have more teeth than you, if yours keep falling out."

She shrugged her shoulders and skipped away to find you.

You were kind that night. You were affectionate with me. We snuck into their rooms together before we went to bed and stared at their soft, gorgeous heads.

44

We left earlier than I'd planned for some reason. It was just one of those rare smooth days when nobody made a mess of their clothes at breakfast, and Violet let me brush her hair without a fuss. So I didn't have to yell things you aren't supposed to yell. *Hurry up! I'm out of patience!* The morning was distinctly peaceful.

The three of us were rarely alone together on a weekday, but Violet's school was closed for the day. I wanted to stop for tea on the way to the park. The owner of the coffee shop, Joe, talked to Violet like he always did while I stirred honey into my tea. He helped me get the stroller down the two big steps before he waved good-bye, and we walked to the corner, the fresh winter wind on our faces.

We stood at the intersection we crossed almost every day. I knew every crack in the sidewalk. I could close my eyes and see the graffiti tags on the redbrick building on the northwest side.

We waited for the light to change, Sam in his stroller watching for buses, Violet and I standing quietly. I reached for her hand, ready for our usual tug-of-war, but today there seemed no reason to argue.

"Careful near the road," I'd said instead, one hand resting on the stroller. Sam's arms reached toward Violet. He wanted out. I picked up my tea from the cup holder and brought it to my lips. Still too hot to sip, but the steam warmed my face. Violet looked up at me while we waited, and I thought she might ask me a question. When can we cross? Can I go back for a doughnut? I blew on my tea again as she watched me. I put it back in the holder, and then I touched Sam's head in the stroller, a little reminder that I was there, behind him, that I knew he wanted out. I looked down at Violet. And then I lifted the cup to my lips again.

Her pink mittens left her pockets and they reached for me. She yanked my elbow with both of her hands. So swiftly, so forcibly, that the hot liquid scalded my face. I dropped the cup and gasped as I looked down. And then I screamed: "Violet! Look what you did!"

As those words were coming out of my mouth, as I was clutching my burning skin with both hands, Sam's stroller rolled onto the road.

I will never forget her eyes in that moment—I couldn't look away from them. But I knew what happened as soon as I heard it.

The stroller was twisted by the impact.

Sam was still strapped into the seat when he died.

There was no time for him to think of me, or to wonder where I was.

I thought right away of the navy-striped overalls I'd dressed him in that morning. That Benny was in the stroller, too. That I would have to take Benny home without him. And then I wondered how I would get Benny out of the mess, out of that stroller, because Sam would need him that night to fall asleep.

I stared in disbelief at the curb in the middle of the chaos around me—the slight slope of cement and then a groove where the sidewalk met the asphalt—how had it not stopped him? The ice had melted in the warmth of the day before. The sidewalk was dry. Why hadn't the wheels slowed when they hit the groove? I usually had to shove it over the curb when we crossed, didn't I? Didn't I usually have to shove it?

I couldn't breathe. I stared at Violet. I had seen her pink mittens reach for the stroller when I let go. I had seen her mittens on the handle before the stroller hit the road. I closed my eyes. Pink wool, black rubber handle. I shook my head vigorously at the thought.

I *have no memory* of what happened next or how we got to the hospital. I don't remember seeing him or touching him. I hope I pulled him out of his straps and held him on the cold asphalt. I hope I kissed him over and over.

But I think maybe I just stood there. On that curb, staring at the groove.

A *mother was driving* the SUV with her two kids in the back, the same ages as ours. She went straight through the green light, as she had every right to, as she'd probably done three thousand times before. The two cars coming the other way slammed on their brakes when they saw the stroller, but she didn't have time. She didn't even brake. I've always wondered what thoughts had been occupying her mind when it happened. If she was singing songs with her kids or answering their trail of questions. Maybe looking in the rearview mirror, smiling at her baby. Maybe she was daydreaming, thinking about how much she'd rather be anywhere else but in that car, listening to her kids scream.

. . .

I *wish it hurt more.* I wish I could still feel it like it happened today. Sometimes I have moments when the pain is gone and I think, *My God, I'm dead inside. I've died with him.* I used to spend every minute of every day staring at his things, willing the pain to flood back. I sobbed because it didn't hurt enough. And then days later the pain would swell again and the world would become a little more alive in ways I loathed. I would smell banana bread from the house next door and it would paralyze me—that I could smell, that my glands would salivate, that someone on the other side of the wall was having the sort of morning that allowed her to bake banana bread for her children. I had been numb—the cruel lack of pain had been numbness. Later on, I would pray for the numbness to return. Even though I found satisfaction in the pain, I knew I wouldn't survive it.

When you met us at the hospital, you pulled Violet in close and held her head to your chest. And then you looked up at me, and you opened your mouth to speak, but nothing came out. We stared at each other and then we cried. Violet wiggled free of your arms and then you came to me. I folded down to the ground and leaned into your legs.

Violet watched us quietly. She came over and put her hand on my head.

"Sammy's stroller slipped out of Mom's hands and got hit by a car."

"I know, sweetheart. I know," you said.

I couldn't look at either of you.

The police came back and wanted to talk to you, to explain everything they'd already explained to me. That the driver wouldn't be charged, that we'd need to make some decisions about our baby's body. And his organs. They thought three of them would be viable for transplants in other babies, for mothers who had done a better job at keeping their children alive than I had. A nurse gave me a pill to calm me down.

I took Violet down the hall to the water cooler. As she overflowed the cone cup I threw up in a garbage pail full of discarded latex gloves and medical packaging. I listened to you sob down the hall, through the heavy glass door that separated us from the rest of the waiting area. Violet watched me and shifted her weight between her feet. She wouldn't dare speak to me. I knew she desperately needed to pee, but I wanted to let her wet herself. I watched the denim turn from light to dark as the wetness spread. I didn't say a thing and neither did she.

I had spoken to the police with the tone of ordering at a drive-through window: My daughter yanked my arm. I was burned by the hot tea. I let go of the stroller. And then she pushed it onto the road.

Anything else, ma'am?

No, that's all.

I didn't have the wherewithal to protect her with a lie. They'd asked me to repeat myself a few times, probably looking for signs of shock, inconsistencies. Maybe they found some. I don't know. I don't know what they told you when I was gone. But when I got back, the officer crouched down and put his hand on Violet's little shoulder, and said to her, "Accidents happen, okay, Violet? Accidents happen and it's nobody's fault. Mom did nothing wrong."

"Listen to him, Blythe. You did nothing wrong." You repeated this to me and held me.

"I think she pushed him," I said to you quietly as you dabbed ointment on my burned skin. I couldn't feel a thing. "I think she pushed him into the road. I told the police."

"Shhh." Like I was a baby. "Don't say that. Okay? Don't say that."

"I saw her pink mittens on the handle of the stroller."

"Blythe. Don't do this. It was an accident. A terrible accident."

"It must have been pushed. It wouldn't have rolled over that groove."

You looked at the police officer and shook your head, wiping the tears from your face. You cleared your throat. The officer's pale, chapped lips puckered. He nodded at you, an acknowledgment of some sort. The irrational mother. The incapable woman. *Look—I have to put her ointment on. I have to shush her.*

Violet pretended not to hear what I'd said. She drew flowers on a whiteboard next to a diagram of organs that someone had drawn when I wasn't there, maybe for my husband to understand what parts of my son they wanted. The diagram looked like a map of the Great Lakes. The police officer said he'd give us time in the room by ourselves.

You repeated it again to me slowly once he left, your voice cracking: "Blythe, it was an accident. Just a terrible accident."

I was in this alone.

O*n our way* to the park the weekend before, Violet had asked me a question at that very same corner, one she already knew the answer to.

"Do the cars only stop when the light is red?"

"You know that, you just turned seven! You know cars stop at all red lights. And a yellow light means be cautious because it's turning red soon. That's why it's dangerous to cross the road unless the cars are completely stopped at the red light." She had nodded.

I thought about how curious she was becoming about the world around her. I wondered if we should start teaching her about maps.

We could walk the neighborhood and look for street names and directions. How fun that might be for us to do together.

As I sat in the family room of the emergency department, I thought about that question over and over.

You took Violet home, but I couldn't leave. My son's body was still in that building.

Under a sheet? In the basement? On one of those trays that slide into the wall like an oven rack? Was my baby on an oven rack, and was he cold? I didn't know where they put him, but we weren't allowed to see him. Benny was in a plastic bag on my lap, his white tail stained.

I threw up everything I ate for eleven days. I cried in my dreams, and then I woke and I cried in the dark. My body shook for hours at a time.

The doctor came in his street clothes on a Saturday morning, someone whose house you had designed who had offered you the favor. He said I must have had a stomach bug, that it wasn't just grief, that sometimes the immune system can be compromised when dealing with something like this. You agreed and thanked him with a bottle of wine on his way out the door, and I didn't care enough to tell you both to fuck off.

Your mother came to stay with us. She brought me tea and tissues and sleeping pills and cold cloths to press on my face. I said what I needed to so that she'd leave the room. *I'll be fine, I promise. I just need some time to myself.* She tried her best, but her presence took up space in my brain, distracted me from the only thing I wanted to be thinking about. Him. Anger made it hard to breathe. Sadness made it hard to open my eyes, to let the light into me. I belonged in the dark, I was owed the dark.

Your mother took Violet to a hotel for a few days, thinking the change of scenery would help. I hadn't seen Violet since the hospital. The morning you went to pick her up, I sat under the window in our bedroom with a blade from the modeling kit you left on your desk. I lifted my shirt and I cut a faint line in my skin from my ribs down to my waist. I yelled for Sam until my voice was raw. The blood formed a perforated line, and tasted rancid, like I'd been rotting inside since the minute he died. I couldn't stop putting it on my tongue. I smeared the blood all over my stomach and my breasts and wanted more. I wanted to feel like I was murdered, like someone had taken my life and left me to die.

When I heard Violet's voice downstairs, I had to hold my hands tightly together to stop them from shaking. I locked the bedroom door and then I showered and put on a shirt that I had bought the week before Sam died, one I'd taken him out in the slushy frozen rain to buy, because I had felt like I had nothing to wear anymore. When that kind of thing had felt like a problem. I forgot his snacks. I had hushed his hunger impatiently in the long line and had made him late for his nap.

"Mommy's upstairs," I heard you tell her. You so rarely called me Mommy and neither did she.

You were wearing black sweatpants and a red flannel shirt. You didn't change your clothes for weeks after he died. That was the only thing about you that looked any different than before, although I know you were hurting immensely. I listened to you walk between the den and our bedroom and Violet's room and the kitchen. You never went into his room. A loop around our house, making the same creaks in the floors and the same noises: the toilet flushing, the hallway window opening, the fridge door shutting. Maybe you were waiting, respectfully, for someone to tell you that life could go on again, that you could set your alarm for the job you loved, and go to pickup basketball on

Tuesdays, and laugh with Violet as loudly as you had before. Or maybe you never expected to find these joys in life again.

Do you know you spoke to me just four times? Four times in almost two weeks. There was too much pain to bear in the sight of each other.

1. You said you didn't want a funeral. So we didn't have one.

2. You wanted to know where Violet's thermos was kept.

3. You told me you missed him, and then you lay down next to me on the bed, naked and wet from the shower, and you cried for nearly an hour. I lifted the blanket up, the only invitation I'd given you since he died, and you rolled in close. I held your head to my chest and realized that there would not be space for you in me, not that day, and maybe not ever. (This was the last time you would ever say those words to me—I miss him—of your own volition. "Of course I miss him," you would recite back at me for months after that, whenever I worked up the courage to ask.)

4. You asked if I would make dinner for Violet the night she came back, because you would be going out, you would be leaving the house at five o'clock. I told you no, I couldn't, and you left the room.

I hated you for trying to be normal. For leaving me there with her, alone, within the walls of Sam's home.

Violet never came up. I never went down.

When I woke up the next day and saw that you had taken the painting from his nursery and leaned it against the wall near the end of our bed, I became weightless for a moment. The pain stopped thumping in my bones. I had stared at that mother holding her child for nearly a year, while I rocked and fed and burped and whispered lullabies in his tiny ear. I realized when I saw the painting that I would live, and I don't know why. I knew I would crawl out of this place that crushed every ounce of me. And I hated you for it. I didn't ever want to feel normal again.

I walked to Violet's room in my underwear, my legs as heavy as they'd ever been. I opened her door and there she was, stirring under her sheets. Her eyes fluttered and then squinted at the light from the hallway.

"Get up."

I poured her cereal and looked around the kitchen. Someone had taken away his high chair, his bottles, his blue silicone spoon, the crackers he liked to suck on. Violet's feet scampered on the floor above into our bathroom, where you were shaving.

I *don't know why* you put the painting there. We never spoke of it. It's in our bedroom now, here with me, in this empty house. I barely notice its details anymore, like the finish on the faucets or the backward way the laundry door opens. But every once in a while, that woman, that mother, looks at me. The sun hits her in the morning and brightens the colors on her dress for hours.

46

Some days when I couldn't be at home any longer, I would ride the subway from one end of the line to the other. I liked the darkness outside the subway car windows, and I liked that nobody spoke to one another. The motion of the train was soothing.

I saw a poster stapled to a board on the platform and took a picture of it with my phone.

Two days later, the address took me to the basement of a church. The room was cold and I didn't take my jacket off, although everyone else's coats were stuffed on wire hangers on the rolling rack in the corner. I needed an extra layer between me and the damp chill that came through the white cement walls. An extra layer between me and them. The mothers. There were eleven of them. There were gingersnap cookies and a pot of coffee, and creamers placed in a basket that was lined with a Christmas napkin even though it was April. There were orange plastic chairs, the kind they used to set up for assemblies in my high school auditorium. Something profane was carved into the seat where I sat. Here we were, assembled, me and the mothers.

The group leader, an impossibly skinny woman with gold bangles up her arms, asked us to introduce ourselves. Gina was fifty and a single mother of three, and her oldest son had murdered someone in a nightclub two months ago. With a gun. He was awaiting trial, but he would plead guilty. She cried as she spoke and her skin was so dry that the tears made dark, defined rivers on her face. Lisa, who sat beside her, had patted the woman's hand even though they did not know each other. Lisa was a veteran of the group. Her daughter was serving a fifteen-year prison sentence for the attempted murder of her girlfriend and was barely two years into her time. Lisa had been a stay-at-home mother from the time her daughter was born. Her voice was soft, and she paused before the last word in each of her sentences. She had plum-colored hammocks under her eyes.

I was next. The fluorescent lights flickered just before I spoke and I wondered if I might be saved by a power outage. I told them my name was Maureen and that I had a daughter who was in jail for theft. Theft was the least-bad thing I could think of. Theft seemed like just one bad mistake, like everyone had done it but not everyone had been caught. Like I could still be the mother of a person who was good, and lovable.

I don't remember all the details now of what everyone else said, but I remember there was a rape, and a few possession charges, and some-one's son had killed his wife with a snow shovel. She said it was the Sterling Hock murder, like we all should have read about it in the newspaper, but I had never heard about it before. The group leader reminded us that we shouldn't use last names or details. We were to be anonymous.

I searched each of their faces for something familiar to me.

"I feel like I'm the one who committed the crime," one of the moth-ers said. "The guards treat me that way at the facility. The lawyers treat me that way. Everyone looks at me like I'm the one who did some-thing wrong. But I didn't." She paused. "We didn't do anything wrong."

"Didn't we?" One mother spoke up after thinking for a moment.

Some people shrugged and some people nodded and some sat perfectly still. The group leader looked as though she were silently counting to ten, a tactic she might have learned in her social work program, and then she reminded us there were cookies for the break.

"You gonna come back next week?" Lisa with the eye hammocks passed me a napkin for the coffee that dripped on my hand while I filled the small Styrofoam cup.

"I don't know yet." My forehead was beaded with sweat. I couldn't be in the room anymore with these women. I'd wanted to see other mothers like me, mothers whose children had done something as evil as mine had, but the basement walls were beginning to feel like they were closing in on me. I felt in my purse for the prescription I still hadn't filled. Instead I felt the softness of his diaper. I had always carried one in my purse.

"This is my second group. The other one happens Mondays, but I usually work Monday nights, so I can't go unless someone switches their shift with me."

I nodded and drank the lukewarm coffee.

"Your daughter, is she within driving distance?"

"Yeah." I looked around for the exit sign.

"Me, too. Makes it a lot easier, doesn't it? You go often?"

"Sorry—the restroom?"

She pointed me toward the stairs and I thanked her, desperate to leave the basement.

"We're not that bad," she said. I stopped in the doorway. "You'll find out for yourself, if you decide to come back from the bathroom."

"Did you always know?" The words felt like teeth yanked from my jaw. But I had to ask.

"Know what?"

"Did you always know something was wrong with her? When she was young?"

The woman raised her eyebrows at me and I think she knew then that I'd lied to them.

"My daughter made a mistake. You never made a mistake before, Maureen? Come on now, we're all human."

47

This city was suffocating. I wanted to go. To drive. Twenty-two weeks had passed, and I still had a hard time walking the streets. I still had a hard time thinking. I wanted the two of us to get in our car, and mile by slow mile, leave this place behind for a while. The sea. The desert. *Anywhere,* I had said, *let's just go.* You wouldn't leave town. You said it didn't feel right, not without Violet, and the familiarity of home was what she needed right now.

I hadn't looked her in the eyes since he died. I relapsed back to spending my days in bed. When I wasn't there, I'd be standing in the kitchen, staring at the dishes in the sink, unable to rinse them. Unable to do anything at all.

There were reminders of him everywhere. But most of all they lived in her. The tiny gap between her two front teeth. The smell of her bedsheets in the morning. The striped jumper she insisted on wearing all the time, the one that matched the overalls he died in. The walk to school. Bathwater.

Those hands.

I craved finding him in her, as painful as it was. And I hated her for it.

Nobody ever talked about him. Not our friends. Not the neighbors. Not your parents or your sister. They'd ask how we were doing, and their eyes ached with sympathy, but they never spoke his name. It's all I ever wanted them to do.

"Sam." Sometimes I would say it out loud when I was alone in the house. "Sam."

The mother of the boy who died in the playground two years before sent me an email a few months after Sam died. My heart raced when I saw her name.

I've been praying that you, like me, somehow find a way to move on. I don't know how, but I eventually found a sense of peace, even in the grief.

The peace she wrote about did not apply to me. I deleted her email.

"Maybe you should go away. Just you." You spoke from the bathroom doorway. I sank deeper into the tub water so that my ears were covered.

Later that night I asked you what you had meant. Go where? *Go.* You wanted me gone.

"There are places that can help you. With your grief. Counseling retreats."

"Like *rehab*?" I scowled.

"Like a wellness center. I found one out in the country. It's only a few hours away." You handed me a sheet printed on heavy-stock paper from your office. "They've got space right now. I called."

"Why do you want me to go?"

You sat on the end of our bed and put your head in your hands. The back of your ribs shook and the tears spilled onto your pants, slowly and evenly, like the drip from our kitchen tap. There was a confession brewing in you, something heavy that yanked at your gut, something that hadn't yet been said aloud. *Don't do it*, I begged you silently. *Please don't do it. I don't want to know.*

You rubbed your chin and stared at the painting from Sam's nursery that leaned against the wall.

"I'll go."

48

There were sound baths, energy healing circles, lessons about honeybees, and silk hammocks that hung from wood beams in the refurbished barn. My room had essential oils lined up on the bathroom counter and a pocket guide to natural healing in the bedside drawer. Therapy was at nine in the morning and three in the afternoon. Individual first, group second. They handed me the waiver when I checked in at the front desk. I ticked off the box that said: *I mindfully decline to participate in the therapy sessions that are included in my weekly rate.* I didn't want to have to say our daughter's name out loud while I was there. I had left to get away from her. I was not interested in talking about her, or you, or how fucked up my own mother was. I had a dead child. I just wanted to be left alone.

Our dinner was served at five sharp in the dining room. The solo tables were all taken so I sat on the bench of the long farm table and looked around at a sea of rich people. My sweat suit didn't seem up to snuff. I zipped my hoodie to my chin and reached for the black beans.

"Just arrive?" I nearly dropped the spoon and turned to my left—her voice sounded just like my mother's. The woman leaned over to look into my bowl and said she didn't feel I was eating the right foods for my energy field. By the end of the night, we were sharing a blanket by the fire pit and drinking ginger tea as I listened to her talk. Iris was the most intense woman I had ever met. But I liked her immediately.

She invited me to join her on a walk each morning, timed precisely so we'd cross over the field when the sun came up. She arrived at my cabin porch with a zircon crystal in her hand that she insisted she couldn't start her day without. We walked across the meadow that separated the guest cottages from the main building, and then down to a creek that lined the north of the property, and then up around the lavender fields through a marked trail. We'd go for an hour and a half each time and I was always a step behind her. Iris spoke over her shoulder in a constant stream of consciousness, with such particular emphasis on her words that it almost sounded as though she had rehearsed every sentence. She had a long, sharp nose. Her even sharper black bob barely moved while she walked briskly, and her hair never curled in the damp air like mine.

She mostly talked about her own life, her cancer, the miracles she'd witnessed as a doctor, and the losses she'd suffered. Iris had been married to another surgeon, who had a fatal heart attack while he was operating. She spoke about the incident as though the worst part of the whole thing was that he couldn't finish the procedure. When she was done telling me about whatever it was she intended to share that day— there always seemed to be an intention, like she was logging a lesson book—she would stop and stretch her calves and tell me to walk ahead of her for the rest of the way.

This is when her questions about Sam would begin. Questions that made me feel like I was under a lamp on her operating table, being ripped open at my rib cage. Crack by crack.

I had told her about Sam when we first met at dinner because she'd so pointedly asked me: "How many children do you have, and are they all still living?"

I had answered her calmly. I had one child. And he was dead. Iris offered little sympathy. She spoke flatly. She told me I needed to find a new way of living in the world now. I hated her and I loved her.

I got out of bed at five o'clock every morning. I brushed my teeth and stepped out into the fresh, dewy grass to talk with this woman I did not know. When I spoke to Iris about Sam, my legs ached and my chest felt heavy enough to pull me to the ground. I'd arrive back at my cabin at the end of the walk, feet wet and leggings damp, and I'd step under the steaming-hot outdoor shower and forget every last thing I had said that morning, every last question Iris had asked me. *What do you think he'd be like now if he'd lived? What was your favorite thing about him? What did he feel like to hold? How was he born into the world? What was the weather like on the day he died?* I scrubbed it all away, like an affair with another man, like illicit sex that nobody could ever know about.

The day before I was to leave, two weeks after you dropped me off, the groundskeepers found me in the ice-cold stream on the property. I was naked and frantic, flailing like an animal being eaten alive.

Let me touch him. I'm his mother. I need him. I need to take him home.

My voice was gone for hours.

I couldn't stand up when they pulled me out. The resident medic came and went. People whispered and held their hands gently to their clavicles as they watched me gain my footing and pull on a pair of sweatpants from the gift shop with the logo of the center embroidered on the hip. I dropped the blanket from my shoulders and let my shriveled breasts stare back at the small crowd around me. I was far beyond the place where shame could exist.

Iris brought tea to my cabin, but I didn't open the door when she knocked or when she apologized loudly through the cedar planks to say she had misjudged how fragile I was. Fragile. I wrote the word with my fingertip on the other side of the door.

A therapist who specialized in grief, the one I so mindfully declined, requested to do a formal assessment with me, and said that I should think about staying longer. She suggested I might not be safe on my own. She suggested she call you.

"No, thank you," I said and that was all. There wasn't much more to say.

The next morning, I sat on the porch of my cabin with my suitcase and waited for you. I stared at the trees across the lot, each swept orderly to the west.

"So?" You kept your eyes on the highway. I put my hand on top of yours, on top of the gear shift. You moved from fifth gear to sixth. I knew what I had to say next.

"How is she? How's Violet?"

49

We'll be fine. Go. Have fun." I flipped the puzzle pieces right side up on the floor and forced myself to look at Violet. She didn't lift her eyes. You had a work thing. They were more frequent than they used to be, it seemed, and you looked different when you left the house now. Layered your clothing, belted your jeans. You looked handsome and I told you so earlier, in our bedroom.

"Same old guy you married," you'd said.

I couldn't have said the same of myself, and we both knew this, our eyes meeting in the full-length mirror behind the door.

The solar system puzzle had one thousand pieces and hadn't been in our house before I left. Your parents had stayed with you and Violet while I was gone. Your mother and I hadn't spoken about much since Sam died, although she had called every two days for months to say a quick hello, to offer to come stay, to say she was thinking of me. She was trying, but she didn't know how to be around me, and I didn't know how to be around anyone. They'd been gone before I arrived home from the retreat, although the cookies she made were still warm on the counter. The babysitter was there when I came through the door—I hadn't seen her since Sam died. Her eyes were swollen and red. We hugged and I thought of the sugary smell she had left on him whenever I took him from her arms.

Three days. That's how long it took for Violet to speak to me after I walked back into our home. Sam had been dead for nearly seven months by then. She started at Neptune and I worked on Jupiter. Eventually we met somewhere near the sun.

"Why did you leave?"

"I needed to feel better."

I passed her the piece she was looking for.

"I missed you while I was gone," I said.

She punched in the piece and looked up at me. People always told me she looked older than her age, and I didn't see it until then. The color in her eyes looked darker to me. Everywhere I looked in the house, everything was different. Everything had changed. I looked away from her first. Bile filled the space under my tongue. She watched me swallow. And swallow again. I excused myself to the bathroom.

The puzzle was put away when I came back. I found her in her bedroom reading a book. She had no doubt heard me retching into the toilet.

"Do you want me to read that to you?"

She shook her head.

"My stomach's a bit upset. From dinner. You feel okay?"

She nodded. I sat at the end of the bed.

"Do you want to talk about anything?"

"I want you to leave again."

"Your room?"

"Leave us. Me and Dad."

"Violet."

She turned the page.

My eyes welled. I hated her. I wanted him back so badly.

50

After my mother left us, my father continued as if nothing had happened. Logistically this wasn't difficult—she'd become less and less a part of our routine as the years had passed, a casual observer of us, like she was watching a movie she might turn off before the ending.

The only thing that changed was that he moved my toothbrush and my hairbrush to the top drawer in the bathroom, which was stained with years of makeup and tacky hair products that had leaked from her aerosol cans. That I no longer kept my things under the sink made me feel like I had new responsibilities now, although I didn't know what they were.

My father began to have friends over to play poker on Friday nights. I would go to Mrs. Ellington's and stay there with Thomas, watching movies and eating popcorn, until she turned off the television and offered to walk me home, where I'd go straight to bed. But one night I lingered in the dark hallway outside the kitchen and listened. The house smelled of musky cologne and beer.

I didn't mind those nights, the house full of men and their smells—it was one of the only times my father seemed like a real person. My dad didn't drink much then beyond his one glass of whiskey after a shift, but the others did. They were swearing at one another over slurred words and then someone banged on the table. I heard a waterfall of poker chips hit the floor.

"You're a cheater," my dad had said in a way I'd never heard him speak before, like it was hard for him to breathe between those three words. And then someone said, "Your *wife* was the cheater, you weak piece of shit. No wonder she left you."

When I lifted my eyes from the hallway floor, I saw my dad staring at me, shaking with rage in the doorway to the kitchen. My legs had been too numb to move when I heard his footsteps coming. He yelled at me to go to my room. Someone slammed a bottle on the table. Someone said, "Sorry, Seb, things got out of hand. He's had too much to drink."

In the morning my dad said he was sorry I had to hear that, and I had shrugged and said, "Hear what?"

"Blythe, people might think bad things about you that aren't true. The only thing that matters is what you believe about yourself."

I drank my orange juice and he drank his coffee and I thought, My father is better than those men. But something had been said that night that rang in my ears—weak. *You weak piece of shit.* I thought of all the times he never stood up for himself, never asked her to stay home from the city. I thought of the wet dishcloth hanging from the side of his head. I thought of the man who'd called, of the clumps of fleshy blood in the toilet. Of the pills he never took away, of the smashed dishes he always cleaned up. Of his quiet retreats to the couch. I hated that my mother had left him, but I wondered if he ever really tried to stop her.

51

I started writing again by throwing out every word I'd written before Sam died. My brain had changed, as though it were on a different frequency than before. Before. After. After felt curt, my sentences abrupt and sharp, like every paragraph could hurt someone. There was so much anger on the page, but I didn't know what else to do with it. I wrote about things I knew nothing about. War. Pioneering. A mechanic shop. I sent the first short story I finished to a literary magazine that had published me before I had children. Their reply was as brusque as my submission letter, and it felt gratifying, the same way smearing blood across my stomach had felt after Sam died. *Fuck you. I didn't write this for you anyway.* None of it made any sense but it filled the hours I had to get through.

I started going to a coffee shop a short walk away where they didn't play music and the mugs were like bowls. There was a man I often saw there, a young man, maybe seven or eight years younger than I was. He would work on his laptop, never got refills. We both liked to sit near the back, away from the draft of the door. I liked the way he hung his jacket on his chair, so that the thick lining of the hood created a comfortable place for his back to rest on, and I started hanging my coat the same way.

One day he brought two older people with him, one of them with his very large nose and the other one his very dark eyes. He invited them to sit down and brought them coffee from the counter and a croissant to share. He placed two napkins gently on the table, one in front of each of them, like he was serving long-standing customers at a fine-dining establishment.

He had bought his first house! This news thrilled me. I listened as he explained each of the listing photos on his phone. The kitchen entrance is there, and this leads to the powder room, and oh, this will be the baby's room. He would be having a baby! Like my Sam. I wanted him to look at me so I could smile, so I could acknowledge that I cared about his future, that I had worried about whether this nice young man had someone in his life who loved him.

They talked about property taxes and a roof replacement and how long his new commute would be. And then the mother asked about her son's plans for when the baby was born in just a month's time.

"I can come back to the city for the week to help, whatever you need. Dishes, laundry. It's no problem for me, I've got the time. I can bring the cot from the spare room at our house." Her voice was so hopeful, and I knew before the son replied that it would be one of the hardest things she ever had to hear. He explained that Sara's mother would come instead. That it would just be better for Sara that way. That she could visit afterward, once they were settled, once they'd had some time together, just the three of them. And Sara's mom. He would let her know when she could come. Maybe a few weeks or so later. They'd have to see how things went.

The mother's head moved slowly forward and then back and she mustered the words, "Of course, honey," and she put her hand on his for the most fleeting moment before she tucked it back beneath her thighs under the table.

A mother's heart breaks a million ways in her lifetime.

I left then—I didn't want to eavesdrop anymore. I walked the long way home.

There was a moment in the car on our way home, I can't remember where from. We turned to look at each other in the front seat, muffling laughs and locking eyes, the same reflex we used to share when Violet said something funny. That was all that mattered—that we shared this intimate knowing of each other. That we'd created her together and now here she was, saying these impossibly grown-up things she'd learned from us in her twiggy, eight-year-old voice. How had I been able to find that moment of perfectly typical joy with you? With her? Not a day went by that I didn't replay what had happened at that intersection.

But life was moving on, I realized as I looked away from you, whether I wanted it to or not. We were together, the three of us, in the car without him, looking at one another like we had before. He had been gone for more than a year.

I missed him desperately. I wanted to say his name in the car so that you both had to hear it. He should have been there with us.

I reached down to the bag at my feet and pulled out a small package of tissues. I looked back at Violet in the seat behind you. I pulled one out and tossed it over my head into the backseat. She watched the tissue float up and then land on her lap. I pulled another one, and then another, and another. You looked away from the road and glanced at me once, and then again, and then to your rearview mirror to watch her. Violet's eyes met yours, and then she stared quietly out her window as the tissues sailed around the backseat.

We used to do this with Sam sometimes when he cried in the car. We used to toss the tissues all around him until his long, sad sobs became a crescendo of laughter. He loved them. We'd go through a whole big box sometimes, mad with giggles, the soft white parachutes filing the car, the children's squeals heightening, our tired, relieved faces grinning aimlessly ahead.

Neither of you said a thing while I did this for him that afternoon. I turned away from you when the package was empty, and I placed it on the dashboard, so that you'd have to see it as you drove. There were fields, I think, outside the window. I remember looking out and wanting to run through them until you caught me by the hood of my sweatshirt. If you ran after me at all.

That night I asked you if Violet should see someone. A child psychologist to help with the grief. She seemed so reluctant to talk about him.

"I think she seems to be coping pretty well. I'm not sure she needs it."

"Then what about us? Together. Couples therapy." We couldn't seem to talk about him either. You hadn't even mentioned what I'd done in the car.

"I think we're coping pretty well, too." You'd kissed me on the forehead. "But you should go. By yourself. You should try again."

I walked aimlessly through our quiet house.

You'd been building a model in your den and your things were spread across the desk under the swing arm of the lamp. Superglue and a cutting mat and a set of knives with interchangeable blades. The tiny foam-board walls were lined up at the side. Violet loved to watch you build models of your work.

I picked up the blades one by one and dropped them into the tin. They shouldn't have been lying out. I'd asked you to be careful about them before. I picked up the last one and ran it over my finger and flinched at the sharpness. How easily they could cut. How easily I could cut. I touched the scar beneath my shirt, the raised line of skin that had formed on my stomach. How good the blood had felt. I closed my eyes.

"What are you doing?" Your voice made me jump.

"Cleaning up your stuff. You shouldn't leave these things lying around for her to find."

"I'll do it. Go to bed."

"You coming?"

"In a bit." You took a seat on the stool and clicked on the lamp. I touched your shoulder and then rubbed the back of your neck. I kissed you behind your ear. You slipped a blade into the knife and then reached for the metal ruler. You always held your breath while you worked. I put my ear against your back and listened for your long inhale. "Sorry, honey. Not tonight. I need to finish this."

Hours later the sound pulled me from my sleep—one by one, slowly, the blades dropped into the tin. *Clink. Clink. Clink.* A pause. And then *clink, clink.* A pause. I opened my eyes and anchored myself in the room with the faint glare reflecting from our glass ceiling light. *Clink, clink.* My head fell to the side and the sound of those metal blades against the tin became the frozen pellets of rain against the drainpipe outside our window. The wind picked up. *Clink, clink. Clink.* I closed my eyes and dreamed of my baby boy in my arms, the smell of his warm neck and the feel of his fingers in my mouth, of blood dripping on him slowly like beads of water from a leaky faucet as he twitched with every drop. I watched the blood hit his fresh skin and trickle into jagged rivers that collected in the crevices of his tiny body. I licked him up like he was a melted ice cream cone. He tasted like the sweetness of the warm applesauce I fed him the summer before he died.

You never came to bed that night. In the morning I found you sleeping on her bedroom floor under the throw blanket from the living-room couch.

"The ice pellets scared her," you'd said at breakfast. "She was having a nightmare."

You rubbed her head and poured her more orange juice while I went back upstairs to bed.

It's freezing out there, Blythe, does she not bring mittens to school?"
Your mother winced as she bent down, pulling off her wet boots. She had come to stay for a few nights to spend some time with Violet and had gone to pick her up from school. Violet sat in a puddle of melting snow, brushing off her pants.

"They're in her backpack, but she won't wear them."

Violet wiggled past me to the kitchen.

Your mother fluffed her thinning hair in the hallway mirror and I could tell by the way she fiddled that there was something on her mind. I stood against the wall and waited for her to speak.

"You know, the teacher said Violet had a tough day. That she seemed angry. She wasn't willing to join in any of the class activities."

I felt my chest tighten. "Fox thinks she's bored there."

"She was sitting alone in the corner of the schoolyard when I arrived. Not playing with anyone at all." She raised her eyebrows and looked toward the kitchen to make sure Violet was still out of earshot. "It hasn't even been two years. You have to remember she loved him, too, like we all did. Despite everything."

Despite everything—her words surprised me. She never brought up the death of our son. I didn't know if she knew what I knew. I had always wanted to ask her. She was the closest thing I had to an ally.

"Helen," I whispered. "Has Fox talked to you about the day Sam died? About what I told him happened?"

She looked away and then turned to straighten the coat she'd hung in the entryway. "No. And I don't know if I can talk about that, to be honest with you. I'm so sorry. I know you were there, you lived it, but— I can't."

"You said 'despite everything,' I thought—"

"I meant how seemingly unaffected she's been." She spoke sharply. "How well she's adjusted at home even though you haven't been available for her." I shot a look toward the kitchen and she lowered her voice again. "I don't mean that as a criticism, Blythe, I promise you. You've been through hell."

I nodded to defuse any tension I'd caused. She looked so feeble to me then, so much older than her sixty-seven years, and I realized then that losing her grandson had taken a toll on her, too. Of course you hadn't told your mother what I believed. Violet called out for her to make chocolate chip cookies and I could hear her digging through the cupboard for mixing bowls. Your mother had walked to the store in the snow that morning to buy all the ingredients. I reached out for her hand and squeezed it.

"You're a strong person," she said quietly. Those words meant nothing to me—they weren't true. She loved me, but she didn't know me at all.

When you came home that night, I saw her pull you aside into the dark living room. You spoke together in low voices. I heard your hands pat her back. Afterward you smelled like her strong rose perfume and I thought of that embrace all night.

54

There's a story of me and Violet that goes through my head sometimes.

That story goes like this:

She sucks milk from me until she turns one. I am fueled by the feeling of her hot skin on mine. I am happy. I am grateful. I do not want to cry when I have to be near her.

We teach each other things. Patience. Love. Simple, joyful moments with her make me feel alive. We build towers after nap time and we read the same book every night until she knows each page, and she can only sleep if I rock her first. I do not hate you when you're late to come home, late to take her from me. It is me she calls for when she wakes up in the night. She squeals good morning when I come into her room, and we spend a quiet hour together before you get up. She doesn't need you like she needs me.

We walk to preschool together and she waves at me from behind the gate. I miss her all day in the back of my mind. She makes me a card for Mother's Day with words she came up with, something the teacher prints for her, and it makes me weepy when I open it. I do not feel dread when I pick her up at the end of the day.

She smiles at me. She hugs my legs. I ask her for kisses.

She cares for him like a baby doll. She touches his head while she holds him. She watches me feed him and she cuddles up beside us and wants to share in the warmth of our bodies. I do not wish he and I were alone without her. She talks about him when he's not there. She tells strangers about him. Every once in a while, she asks if we can go to the park alone because she misses time with just me. We do, and we swing side by side, and get vanilla ice cream cones. We go home and he is waiting for us, safe with you. I do not quietly pretend that he is my only child.

She sits on my bed while I get changed and we talk about things mothers and daughters talk about. I am gentle, and I am warm. She is curious. She likes to be near me. Her eyes are soft. I trust her. I trust myself to be around her. I watch her grow into a young woman who is respectful and kind. Who feels like she is mine. We have a son and she has a brother. We love them both equally. We are a family of four who eats the same kind of dinner every Sunday, who argues over which television show to watch on Fridays, who goes road-tripping on spring break.

I do not spend my days wondering who we could have been.

Or what life would be like if she had died instead of him.

I am not a monster, and neither is she.

55

You'd gone to buy more sunscreen from the shop in the hotel lobby. We never did well with beach vacations; we burned too easily. But we were trying to be a normal family. Your mother suggested we go, that a change of scene would be good for us, and so you booked it. Violet loved to play in the sand, even at the age of nine. I read a novel under our striped umbrella and lifted the floppy brim of my hat every so often to check on her. She was digging a maze of canals to fill with water. A skin-and-bones boy, no older than three, lingered between her and the lap of the ocean, picking at the corner of his thumb.

She tiptoed over and crouched at his feet, the wind carrying their voices away from me. He looked like he was giggling. She toppled over with a silly look on her face and he laughed toward the sun. He followed her, and she handed him a bucket to help her fill the canals.

His mother had an elegance I'd admired when I saw her earlier that day near the pool.

"What a doll your daughter is, to be entertaining him like that. Does she babysit yet?"

I explained she looked older than she was. I invited her to have a seat on your empty lounge chair while the two of them played. We watched our children and exchanged the kind of pleasantries you do with other mothers. The boy looked up and called for her, waving, showing her the bucket he'd been given.

"I see, I see! How nice, Jakey!" They were there for the week. She had two other children who were on a boat for the day with their father, but she and Jake were prone to seasickness. Violet began burying him in the sand. His legs first. Then his torso. She patted the sand, smoothed it out over the mound, as the boy held as still as he could.

"Do you mind?" she asked, holding up her phone.

She had to make a call for work but the beach was too windy. She ran up to the boardwalk behind us and I watched the way her white caftan blew around her long legs.

The boy was buried up to his chin now, his hot, round head like a cherry dropped in the sand. Violet ran to the water and filled the largest bucket and walked slowly back to him, her arms shaking. How could she have carried such a heavy bucket? I sat up in my chair. She held the bucket over his head and her chest rose. She paused and looked up to see if I was watching. I stared back, my heart beating. The boy's eyes were closed. I scrambled to stand. Some water splashed out as she shifted to put one hand under the bucket. She was going to turn it over. There must have been a gallon of water, it would fill his airway in an instant. She stared at him, still, her hand ready to tip it. My legs went weak underneath me and I tried to yell but nothing came out. I hit my chest, trying to find my voice. And then finally I screamed. His name came out, barely audible, the pitch like fire in my throat.

"Sam!"

"What's wrong?" Your hand on my arm startled me and I swatted you away. Violet stood staring at us, the bucket down by her side. The boy craned his neck and the sand cast cracked like ice around him.

"You ruined it!"

"I'm sorry," he said and started to whimper.

She dropped to her knees and helped him up, brushing the sand from his back and his fine blond hair. "Don't cry. We can do it again. Are you okay?" Her hand draped around his little shoulders and he nodded. She looked over at me briefly, wanting to see if I was watching her still.

"Nothing," I said to you finally, and adjusted the bottom of my bathing suit. My heartbeat shook my chest. I watched her trying to cheer the boy up. Maybe I'd overreacted. I thought again of her pink mittens pushing the stroller and then quickly batted the image away. You handed me the plastic bag and seemed untroubled—you hadn't heard me say his name. Or at least you pretended not to.

We stayed for two more hours. I finished reading my book. You flew a kite with the kids. We ate dinner that night with the boy's family, the elegant mother and her three seersuckered sons.

I watched Violet put marshmallows on the ends of the kids' sticks and show them how to make s'mores. I felt you looking at me. I turned to meet your eyes and you smiled. You finished your wine. I got up to break another chocolate bar into small squares and gave them to the children. I joined you on the Adirondack chair, on the lap in which I used to spend long stretches of child-free time, and slipped my hands up your shirt to warm them. You kissed me on my lips. I watched the woman watching us from across the flames. Things could be so easy, if only I could let them.

56

A long, exasperated pause before an answer that should be easy to give. Closing the bathroom door when you had always kept it open. Bringing home one coffee instead of two. Not asking what the other is going to order in a restaurant. Rolling over to face the window when you hear the other person begin to wake up. Walking just that much farther ahead.

These slips in behavior are deliberate and noticeable. They eat away at what once was. This turn plays out slowly, and it almost doesn't seem to mean anything at all; when the music is just right or the sun slips into the bedroom just so, it can almost mean nothing at all.

On the morning of your thirty-ninth birthday, I went down to the kitchen and made myself breakfast. You had suggested the night before (you said it twice, in fact) that you'd like to go to the brasserie down the street for eggs.

But I wanted you to wake up in our bed and smell that I was toasting a bagel. You hated bagels. You would realize that I wouldn't be going to the brasserie for breakfast. I wanted to hurt you. I wanted you to think, *Maybe she doesn't love me anymore.* I wanted you to be so disappointed that you rolled over and went back to sleep and felt like you were not the kind of husband whose wife wanted to make him happy on a morning that should have mattered.

You came down the stairs twenty minutes later, dressed in the sweater I hated. The wool was pilled and ratty. I was rinsing the cream cheese off the knife. It was nine o'clock by then and you said you were going out for the newspaper. We subscribed to the *Times*, and I tossed it on the counter in your direction. You said you wanted the *Journal*. I didn't think you liked the *Journal* anymore. You came home after an hour and a half and said nothing. You didn't eat anything until we heated up bowls of leftover spaghetti well past lunchtime. And so you must have gone for the eggs without me. We never spoke of it and I never regretted doing that to you.

Three days before that you asked me the name of the flowers I had bought for the kitchen table the weekend before, *the white fluffy ones*. They were dahlias. I asked you why you wanted to know, and you said you were just curious, that you liked them, that I should buy them more often. This was strange. You never seemed to care about flowers before. You had never asked me about the name of a flower.

The week after that you sat in your reading chair and you had my phone in your hand. I had left it on the table. You were looking at a photograph of yourself that I had taken the month before. I was not in the photo with you, and neither was Violet. This was just a picture of you, handsome, grinning, two days of facial-hair growth, one elbow leaning on the table at a restaurant. Later that night in bed, I thought, Maybe he was wondering how he looked to other women; maybe he was imagining the kind of first impression he might give to a woman who might find him attractive. Maybe he was trying to find a different version of himself in that photograph.

But looking at a photograph of oneself is not proof of an affair. And asking a question about a type of flower is not proof of an affair. These are, though, the kinds of things that fester in a person's mind until she no longer feels loved; they are the happenings that took us from a place we could have survived, even in the grave face of a death that nearly killed me, too, to the place we simply could not come back from. These things became too heavy and too hurtful, habitual abuses in what once felt like the safest place in the world.

That's why I didn't go for breakfast with you on your thirty-ninth birthday.

57

You poured yourself a cup of coffee and slid the resignation letter toward me. I'd just come back from dropping off Violet and hadn't expected you to be home.

"But why?"

You sat back and crossed your legs. I noticed then that you hadn't shaved your face in a few days. Maybe three or four. There was so much about you I didn't see anymore.

"I want something more forward thinking. Maybe something focused on sustainability. There's no room for creativity there anymore. Wesley's got his hands in everything."

I watched your fingers rap slowly on the wood table. My eyes shifted to the letter and your signature. The note was brief. A few sentences. Dated the day before.

"We should have talked about this, don't you think?" I didn't really know how we were doing financially, or how much we had saved. My mind raced back, trying to remember the last bank statement I'd seen. You paid our bills. I didn't keep track of what we earned and spent. I felt the foolishness rise inside me. "I mean are we okay financially? This is a big decision."

"We're fine." You liked to keep me out of it. You tapped the table again. "I didn't want to bother you with this."

"So what now?"

"I've got some opportunities lined up."

You stretched back in your chair and bounced your heels. You seemed restless. And maybe relieved. I couldn't quite place it then.

"I'm going for a run."

"It's cold out today."

"Carry on. Do whatever you do during the day when I'm not here." You tousled my hair like you always did to Violet and left the kitchen to find your running shoes. You never went for runs anymore.

Something didn't feel right. My head was light. I had an urge to call your mother. She was walking the dog when she answered.

I told her I wanted to talk about the holidays early, to go over the plans for their visit. They were to book a flight for December twenty-second and we'd take Violet skating the next day with your sister. I asked about gift ideas for your father. We talked through who should cook what for the dinner.

"I know this will be hard again," she said. "Without Sam."

"I miss him."

"Me, too."

"Helen," I said, wondering if I should have just said good-bye. "Fox told me this morning that he resigned from his job. Did you know he was thinking of leaving?"

"No, he didn't mention it." She paused. "If money is a problem, you know we can always help. I don't want you to worry about that."

"It's not that. It's— I feel like I don't know him anymore. He's grown so . . . distant." I held my breath and rolled my eyes to myself. I didn't like talking to her about you, but I was desperate for some kind of reassurance. "I feel like something else might be going on."

"Oh, I don't think so, honey. No." Her tone suggested she understood what I was inferring. "You're still grieving parents, Blythe. This is a hard time for both of you. Maybe Fox is struggling more than you realize." She gave me space to agree, but I didn't speak. "Be patient with him."

"Please don't mention to him that I called, okay?" I rubbed my temples, trying to ease the tension.

"Of course." She changed the topic back to which day they should fly home and I watched for you from the window of the living room.

Your laptop was on and I knew your password. Your desk looked the same, tools scattered, a project in progress left wherever we'd interrupted you the night before. Nothing looked as though it were winding down, nothing looked different. I opened your in-box and scrolled through the messages. The email from your boss wasn't hard to find: *I'm glad we both agree this is the best outcome given the nature of the incident. I'm sorry it had to end this way. Perhaps we both could have used better discretion in how things were handled. Cynthia will be in touch with the details of the severance we agreed on.*

There was an incident of some kind. Severance—you had been fired.

I opened an email sent that morning from your assistant. You hadn't read it yet. She'd written only, *I just met with HR. Call me.*

I went to Violet's room and picked up the unicorn pencil and eraser she gave her. I smelled the rubber, as though it were possible to find some kind of confirmation. I put it back on her shelf and lay down on her unmade bed.

I clutched my pounding chest with both hands. The late nights at the office. The rejection when I touched you. The way your fingers had tapped the table as you lied to me. I closed my eyes and smelled Violet's pungent sleepiness on the pillow.

"I hate you," I whispered. To you both. I hated both of you. I wanted only Sam. If he was there, everything would have been okay. I cried until I heard you open the front door. Your shoes dropped on the tiles. Your feet hit the stairs. I lay still and you walked past Violet's bedroom door and into the bathroom for a shower. I'd left the email open on your laptop. You'd find it twenty minutes later and not say a word to me.

58

The next morning, I waited outside for a while before I came back in the house after drop-off. I wanted you to be gone, but the house still smelled too strongly like you. You were somewhere. I didn't call for you. I shut the bathroom door and got into the shower and I scrubbed myself hard. Every piece of me. I stood under the showerhead until the water ran cold.

I could hear you on the other side of the door, the sounds I had heard nearly every morning of our life together. Your drawers opening and closing. Your fresh underwear. Your undershirt. And then the closet. Your dress shirt—you must have been trying to impress someone that day. The metal clips on the hangers clanged. Your suit slipped off the heavy wooden shoulders and onto your arms.

And then the bathroom door opened. I was naked. You stared at my body differently that morning; the hanging skin that had held your children; the breasts those children had sucked dry; the patch of scraggly pubic hair that hadn't been cared for in years—all there, for the eyes of a man who had something better, younger, firmer to look at. I imagined her skin was smooth and free of purple veins and enduring hairs. I watched you watch me. And I wondered what this body meant to you now. Was it just a vessel? The ship that got you here, father of one beautiful daughter and a son you'd barely known?

You saw me watching you and then you looked away. You knew you'd lingered too long on my naked body. You knew that I knew. You reached out for the towel on the hook and you handed it to me.

We didn't say a word to each other that morning. You were gone until ten at night. And then you came home and fucked me so hard that I bled. I had begged you to. I imagined you'd fucked her that night, too. But I wanted to feel used, in a mechanical type of way that made my body feel separate from who I was. I wanted to feel like a barge in the sea. Rusted, trusted, dented.

There are days, like that one, that mark the moments in our life that change who we are. Was I the woman being cheated on? Were you the man who betrayed me? We were already the parents of a dead boy. Of a daughter I couldn't love. We would become the couple that split. The husband who left. The wife who never got over any of it.

1972

There came a time when it was clear to everyone that Etta was slipping away. She'd stopped cooking and stopped eating. She'd stopped doing much of anything by then. The house had a rank smell to it, like damp towels that had been left too long in the washer. She wandered the second floor some days, but others she didn't leave her bedroom.

It was a tough time for Cecilia as well. She was wasting away, swimming in the clothes that had fit her earlier that year. She'd lost her appetite and stopped caring for herself in the way other fifteen-year-old girls knew how to do. She didn't want to ask Henry for money to buy sanitary pads, so she started stuffing her underwear with socks during her period. There was never laundry soap in the house, so she let them pile up under her bed. When Henry found them, Cecilia was humiliated. He asked his sister to move in for the time being. She lived overseas and as far as Cecilia could remember, Henry hadn't spoken about her before, so she figured things were desperate. They kept their distance from one another as best they could—Henry's sister understood that the situation was delicate. She cleaned the house and bought groceries for the fridge.

One day, Cecilia overheard Henry's sister suggest that Cecilia should move away to a boarding school. She didn't think it was safe for her to be living with her mother anymore. Henry's fist rattled the silverware.

"She's her daughter, for God's sake. Etta needs to be with Cecilia."

"Henry. She doesn't want to be. She doesn't love that girl."

Cecilia peered around the corner and watched him. He covered his face with his hand for a minute. And then he shook his head. "You're wrong. Love doesn't have anything to do with it."

A few days later, Etta hanged herself from an oak tree in the front yard using one of Henry's belts. It was a Monday morning and the sun was just coming up. They lived on the same street as Cecilia's school. Etta was thirty-two years old.

59

I wondered if the pain of spending my days imagining you fucking another woman would mean I'd start to miss Sam less. Surely there is a limit to how much sadness one person can hold. And so I thought if I just focused more attention on what you did to me, maybe the pain of Sam would start to feel less suffocating, less consuming.

But that never happened. I couldn't find enough heartbreak in your betrayal. What happened with Sam had blunted me, knocked me so hard that I still couldn't feel anything more deeply than his loss. You wanted another woman? Fine. You didn't love me anymore? I understood.

The doctor at the hospital who spoke with us after Sam died said this before you left: "Be strong together. Many relationships don't survive the death of a child. You have to be aware of this and work hard on your marriage."

"What kind of thing is that to say to us?" you'd said to me later about her comment. "We have enough to worry about."

I didn't confront you for eight days about what I suspected. We went about life quietly so that Violet wouldn't sense any tension. You were extra kind. Extra thoughtful. I didn't want any of it. I never asked

where you were going during the days because I didn't much care.
To see her, to find a new job? I didn't know. I told you to cancel your
parents' visit for Christmas, although it seemed like a punishment for
us both.

"Why don't *you* call my mother?" you said. "You seem to enjoy
keeping her up to date about me."

She'd told you I'd called.

I don't know what excuse you gave her when you canceled. I didn't
answer her calls after that, although it hurt each time I ignored her.

On the eighth night, I found you in the den cleaning up your desk.
All of your projects were put away, handed off to the people taking
over your clients. The long arm of your lamp was tucked against itself
now, as though it would be put in bubble wrap and packed for a move.
Maybe it would be. I looked for the tin of blades and didn't see it anywhere.

"Where did you put all your things? Your modeling tools?" I held
my breath and felt the shame of needing to know where the blades were.
The anxiousness tickled in my chest, threatening me. You pointed
to the closet while you sorted through a box of loose papers. I slid open
the door and scanned the messy shelves. Old board games and stacked
empty picture frames and dictionaries I'd saved from college. The tin
was there, on the second shelf, between your architecture books and
a bin of rulers and pens. I closed the door and turned to you. Your
shoulders were starting to build the same hunch your father had. I
wondered if she liked to run her hand against the bristles of hair on
the nape of your neck, if she would one day shave them for you like I
did every so often.

"What is she like?"

You lifted your head. The room felt so different without the shadows from your lamp that had always danced over the wall as you

worked. You were so still. I held my breath again and wondered what you would say next. But you didn't speak. I asked you again: "What is she like, Fox?"

And then I left. I went to bed. I wondered if you'd be gone in the morning, but a few hours later, or maybe it was just one, I felt your side of the mattress move.

"I'm not seeing her anymore."

You'd been crying. I could hear the thickness in your nasal. There was nothing inside me. No relief. No anger. I was just tired.

In the morning I brought coffee to you in bed before Violet woke up. I sat next to you while you drank it.

"We lost enough when Sam died," I said. You rubbed your forehead. "You never dealt with your grief properly. You've never faced it."

I waited for you to speak.

"Sam isn't why our marriage is falling apart. He doesn't have anything to do with it."

The door to our bedroom opened and Violet walked in and stared at us. You looked at me slowly, your sleepy eyes now as wide open as hers. And then you looked back at our daughter.

"Morning, honey," you said.

"Breakfast?" she asked. You left the room behind her.

60

It had been a stupid place for me to leave it. Under the bed. I'd tossed it there when I heard you come home midafternoon. You never took notice of the books I had lying around anyway. And I hadn't thought of her, if I'm being honest; I barely existed in her world, and she barely existed in mine beyond the logistics of the routine we kept.

I don't know why I bought it. I knew it wouldn't help, but it felt like something I could do to try to make it real. To make me feel something other than desperately curious. Two months had passed since I confronted you about the affair. And all I could think about was: Who is this woman? What's she like? You refused to say a word about her—all I knew was that she'd been your assistant. The woman you'd taken our daughter out to lunch with.

Every time I asked you to tell me more, you shook your head and said only, quietly, "Don't."

I found the book in her backpack. *Surviving an Affair: How to Overcome Betrayal in Your Marriage.* Violet was eating yogurt at the kitchen counter, her after-school snack, and looked up as I stared at it in my hands. I didn't know what to say to her—she was ten. Could she have known what an affair was? I thought of the older kids at school whom she wouldn't have hesitated to ask.

"Why did you have this?" I asked nervously. She raised her eyebrows knowingly and went back to stirring her bowl.

"Answer me."

"Why did *you* have it?"

I walked away.

An hour later, I knocked on Violet's door and asked if we could talk. She spun her desk chair around slowly and looked at me blankly. I held the book out and said that I wanted to clear something up—that this book was research for something new I was writing. That we should talk about what this grown-up word "affair" meant—what she *thought* it meant. That I didn't have this book because there was something wrong between her mom and dad. That we loved each other very much.

"Okay," she said. And then she put her head back down to her workbook.

I knew she knew who the woman was. Maybe that day you took Violet to your office wasn't the only time they'd met—I didn't know what secrets you two kept. It was so strange to me that she'd never used the unicorn pencil or eraser the woman had given her. She'd kept them on her bedroom shelf, on display like trophies, prized possessions that must have meant more to her than I had realized.

I threw the book in the trash can outside, and I wondered about other lies I could tell her that would corroborate the one I'd just told. I wanted to walk back in there and convince her, with the authority that a mother should have, that she was wrong. I didn't want her to think I was the kind of woman a husband cheated on. And despite my ten years of resentment for the relationship you and Violet shared, I didn't want her to believe you were the kind of man who would do that.

I was hanging on to my family by a thread, I knew. But I had to. I had nothing else left.

When you came home that night, I touched you with affection when I thought she might be looking, and I called you "honey" instead of your name. I slipped in beside you on the couch while you watched the hockey game. I put my hand on your lap and my chin on your shoulder, and I called her into the room to ask if she had handed in the money for the school pizza lunch. She glared at me and looked down at my hand on her father's thigh and shook her head just slightly, just one sharp back-and-forth, just enough to tell me she knew what I was trying to do. She had a remarkable ability to make me hate myself.

One month later—three months after I discovered the affair—I woke up on a Sunday and I knew. We were over. We needed to stop pretending we would simply float past this, like it was something unpleasant on a riverbank. The sitter took Violet out for the afternoon and we went to the bar down the street.

"You're still seeing her, aren't you?"

You looked out the window and then impatiently waved for the server. I asked you again if you could just, please, tell me about the woman. Tell me why you loved her. You didn't avoid my eyes. You looked like you were talking yourself through the decision of how much to tell me, what secrets you were willing to part with. An urgency welled inside me and I could no longer be there across from you—we needed to get this done. I wanted you gone.

I walked home briskly, with my coat clutched at my chest. I brought up the suitcases from the basement. I packed all of your clothes neatly inside and zipped them shut. I called a moving company and booked

four large packing bins and a small moving van to arrive the next day.
I found a pad of sticky notes in your desk drawer and I walked through
the house and stuck one on each item we shared that I wanted you to
take: the small rolling island in the kitchen, the record player, the set
of dishes from your parents, the runner in the front hallway that had
marks from the shoes you never took off when I asked you to, the sofa
in the living room that had been imprinted with the shape of your ass
for years, the green glass vase, the chopping board stained with the
blood of red meat, the chairs you commissioned for the dining-room
table that hurt everyone's backs, all the furniture in your den, and most
of the art in the house. And then I went to the closet in your den and
found the tin of blades. I took the longest one and wrapped it in a silk
scarf, and I put it in my bottom drawer.

"I don't care where you stay tonight. Just come back tomorrow to
pack everything else." I even kissed you good-bye, a habit, a reflex of
a married woman. As I walked up the stairs I thought of Sam's things.
Everything we kept that had belonged to him was in boxes in the basement. Maybe you would want something—a blanket, a toy. Maybe I
should ask you. Maybe you were owed the faint smell of him still lingering in the fabric after nearly three years. I turned on the tap of the
bath and took my clothes off. The sound of the water had muffled your
footsteps and so the sight of you in the doorway startled me. I clutched
my breasts and turned away. You felt like an intrusion now. All those
years, and now you felt like a stranger.

"What about Violet?" You didn't take your eyes off me as I stepped
into the tub. The water was too hot, but I forced myself lower.

"What about her? This is your doing. You can figure out what to
tell her."

You looked up and away, as you did whenever I said something that made you wish I wasn't so stubborn or vague or difficult or indecisive. Or flippant. Or sarcastic. Those were some of the things you didn't like me to be. You rubbed your forehead. I seemed to make you tired. I seemed to make you wish I hadn't ever existed at all.

"I've tried my best to keep this from her because I don't want her to think badly of you. I don't want things between you two to change," I said. "But I think she knows."

I waited for your reaction. I wanted you to be grateful to me, to concede that you were the one doing this to us. But all you said was:

"I want to share custody. And split the time evenly."

"Fine."

You watched me slip into the tub until my whole body was magnified under the water. You stared at me, the woman you'd been inside for twenty years. I wondered if you might try to come in with me. If despite all my faults, all the ways I disappointed you, you still wanted to feel my skin one last time. I looked up and felt nothing for you—not love, not hate, not anything in between. Is this what the end was supposed to feel like? There are people who work through it, who fight for one another, who do it for the children. The life they thought they needed. But I had nothing to fuel the fire. Nothing to give.

And then what you said hit me—shared custody. I'd be alone with her. That's what you had meant when you'd asked, "What about Violet?" You'd meant, "What about you and Violet, what about the life you'll have to endure together without me? What about the days you don't speak to each other, what about the nights she needs someone, and you just won't do? What about the times she knows you're pretending to care as much as you should? Who will believe her? Who will defend her? Who will comfort her? Who will light her up in the morning when she wakes? Who will love her on those days when she's alone with you and needs to know everything will be okay? Who will believe her?"

You stood in your jeans and your gray sweater with your hands in your pockets and you watched me. Bare. Inadequate. I met your puncturing eyes.

"We'll be fine," I said. "I'm her mother."

61

Our brains are always watching. Looking for danger—a threat could come at any time. Information comes in and it does two things: it hits our consciousness, where we can observe and remember it. And it hits our subconscious, where a little almond-shaped section of the brain called the amygdala filters it for signs of danger. We can sense fear in less time than it takes for us to be aware of what we are seeing or hearing or smelling—just twelve-thousandths of a second. We respond so fast that it can happen before we're consciously aware that something is wrong. Like if we see a car coming. Like if we see someone about to get hit.

Reflexes. They tell you about the most natural reflex in the world when you give birth to your baby—the oxytocin reflex. The mothering hormone. It makes the milk flow, fill ducts, stream into the baby's mouth. It starts to work when the mother expects she needs to feed. When she smells or touches or sees her baby. But it also affects a mother's behavior. It makes her calm, it reduces her stress. And it makes her like her baby. It makes her look at her baby and want to keep him alive.

There was a viral video circulating online of a famous woman, a young British aristocrat the tabloids loved, and her rambunctious young son. Three different times she's catching him in perilous moments—swooping in to grab his hand as he falls down the wet steps of an airplane, yanking the neck of his shirt on the slippery bow of a yacht, pulling him back from a polo pony's path in the nick of time. Like a viper snapping a mouse in the clutches of her jaw. The instincts of a mother. Even that mother—flanked with nannies, brooched and heeled, with a fascinator pinned to her curls.

Violet picked up my phone one Sunday morning not long after you moved out and found the video on YouTube. She took the seat right next to me on the couch, in the beam of warm weekend sun. I'd been reading. She held the phone up.

"Have you seen this?"

I watched it. She stared at me intently for the entire sixty seconds.

"The mom saves her kid every time," she said.

"So she does." I put my book down and reached for my tea. My hand trembled holding the cup. I wanted to smack her. I wanted to knock her head back into the couch and make her mouth bleed.

You stupid fucking little girl. You killer.

Instead I left the room and cried quietly over the kitchen sink as the water ran. I was so sad. I missed him desperately. It was almost his fourth birthday.

62

I stared at the empty space you left in our bedroom. You'd taken Sam's painting when you moved out. I sat on the floor and visualized it there, the mother, the cupped hand on her chin, her grasp on the baby's thigh. The warmth of their skin.

"I'm hungry." Violet was watching me from the doorway, still dressed in what she had worn to school. "What are you looking at?"

"We'll order in."

"I don't want takeout."

"I'll make spaghetti."

That worked—she left me alone. I didn't want her there. I couldn't lift my eyes from the nail hole in the wall.

I cooked while she finished her homework at the table. She had the same habit you did, putting her nose so close to the paper it nearly touched it as she wrote. I saw the hunch in her back and smiled without thinking. And then remembered you were gone. That you weren't a person I should smile about anymore.

"You want to have ice cream after dinner and watch a show?"

"We don't have a television anymore."

"Right. We could play a game?"

She didn't need to answer that one.

"What time is it? We could probably still make a movie, a later show."

"It's a school night." She vigorously erased something and brushed the flakes of rubber on the floor.

"Well, I was going to make an exception."

I slipped an apron on while I stirred the sauce. I'd gone shopping for new clothes while you moved out of our house. I wore one of the sweaters, a cream-colored cashmere wrap, straight home from the dressing room at the department store. I never did this sort of thing, buy piles of expensive new clothes at once, but I had wanted to feel reckless that day and it was the best thing I could think of. You were still paying the Visa bill.

"She has that sweater you're wearing."

She. I stopped stirring, as though if I were still enough, I wouldn't spook the animal. In the periphery I saw Violet retreat back to her work, nose inches from the page. I wanted her to say more.

"That's nice," I said.

She looked up at me—was it?

"I guess she has great taste, then." I winked and put her spaghetti on the table. She let it cool while she finished up and I leaned on the stove, wondering what else she might tell me.

"So, you're going to Dad's tomorrow. Are you excited to see his new place?"

"It's their place."

I didn't know if she was lying to me or not—she seemed to know more than I did. I assumed you were living on your own, but I never made a point of asking. I wondered if you'd talked to Violet about our separation much earlier than you and I had discussed it. I took the apron off and looked at the sweater, wondering if it was too late to return it. But there was a splatter of sauce on the sleeve now.

"Okay, well, their place. Are you excited?"

"There's something you should know about her." She spoke sharply. I held my own dish of spaghetti, about to sit down with her. I found myself nearly out of breath all of a sudden—maybe it was the fear of what she'd say next.

"What?"

She shook her head and looked down again and I could tell she'd never intended to tell me. Or maybe there was nothing to tell.

"We don't need to talk about her. That's your dad's business, not mine." I smiled. I twirled the noodles and stuffed them in my mouth.

63

My mother reinvented herself when she left me, although perhaps reinvention is being generous. I learned this when I was twelve and saw her at a diner just outside the city. She was standing between two stools at the milkshake bar asking for a clean fork in a voice I had not heard her use before. But I would have recognized the back of her anywhere—the round of her shoulders, the curve of her hips. When she was given the fork, she said thank you in a voice that sounded different than it had when she was my mother. Her words, with their superiority, had come out of her mouth as she spun on her black heels. She handed the new fork to the man she was with and he said, "Thanks, Annie, honey." Anne was her middle name.

Later, I'd come to find out the bulky man was Richard. I'd known another man existed, the one on the phone before she left, the one who I suspected had something to do with the blood in the toilet. But I hadn't pictured him looking this way—he was handsome but slippery, with wet hair and shiny skin, and he wore a huge gold watch. His face looked tanned from the sun although it was only March. He was nothing like my father, nothing like the life I imagined she had left me for.

I sank into the booth beside Mrs. Ellington, who had brought

Thomas and me to celebrate our first-place win in the regional school science fair. She had watched us from across the gymnasium as we presented our findings to the judges, standing in front of the cardboard poster we'd made, our experiment written in Thomas's careful cursive, with detailed pictures I'd drawn for each section. Something about ultraviolet light—I can't remember now. But I remember Mrs. Ellington nodding along with the presentation we gave, like she could hear every word we said through the hum of one hundred students. I watched her in the distance and straightened my shoulders as I spoke, like she did. I wanted to make her proud.

I watched my mother and Richard for what felt like hours as they ate their meal and then folded their napkins like proper people did. She wore a black sheer blouse with big rose embroidery on the collar; I'd never seen her in something sexy like that. He put cash on the table before they'd even seen the bill. Mrs. Ellington glanced over at her, too, but she didn't say anything to me then, nor I to her, and so we just had our milkshakes and Thomas talked about what we could do with our fifty dollars in prize money. I was numb with anxiety, wondering if my mother might turn her head around and catch a glimpse of me. A small part of me hoped she would. She never did, and I was mostly relieved when they left—I wasn't sure if she would have come to say hello had she seen me. We left the restaurant and drove home in Mrs. Ellington's car.

"You okay, Blythe?" Mrs. Ellington let Thomas run into the house while she walked me to the end of their driveway. I nodded and smiled and thanked her for the drive. I didn't want Mrs. Ellington to know how much it hurt to see my mother. Happy. Beautiful. Better without me.

That night I got on my hands and knees before I went to bed and prayed that my mother would die. I would rather have seen her dead than as the new woman she had become, the changed woman who was no longer my mother.

64

I'd never been avoided before, at least not that I could remember or knew about. But it would have been easier to meet face-to-face with the queen than to have seen you in person the year after you left. You only ever wanted to hand Violet off at school drop-off and pickup, and your text messages were curt. I wanted to meet the woman you left me for, the woman who was living in the same apartment where my daughter would spend half of her time. I wanted to know how we compared. I wanted to be able to picture you two together. We were avoiding courts and legal counsel at your request, and so I had something of an upper hand in our stilted negotiations. But this one you were adamant about—you would introduce us when you were ready and there was no room for discussion otherwise.

"I'd love to meet Dad's new girlfriend," I said to Violet after she told me the woman had dropped her off at school that morning. It was Friday and I had her for the weekend.

"Maybe she doesn't want to meet you."

"Maybe."

Violet buckled her seat belt and looked at the key in the ignition, desperate for me to start the car and get her one step closer to not being in the seat behind me. I glanced in the rearview mirror and her face changed—a look of pity. I didn't know if it was genuine or not.

"There's a reason Dad doesn't want you to meet her." Her voice lowered, like she was telling me a secret, giving me a clue to a mystery I hadn't yet known I was solving. She looked out the window at the familiar row of brownstone walk-ups that we passed on the way home. She barely spoke to me for the rest of the evening.

And so I'm not sure you left me much choice but to do what I did.

V*iolet told me* you were going to the ballet together, just you and her, the following week; the woman couldn't go, she had standing Wednesday night plans at the same time. I'd looked up the show online and saw it began at 7:00 p.m. I knew you'd take Violet for pizza first.

Your low-rise apartment building was in a quaint part of the city that I knew well. I took a taxi over and got out a few blocks away. It was six thirty and traffic was still heavy. The driver stared at me in the rearview mirror like he could sense my nerves, see my fingers pulling over and over at the stray thread in the hem of my coat. I tipped him too much, not wanting to wait for the change, and pulled up the hood of my coat so the fur shielded most of my face. Walking was good for my nerves. I calmed down and watched my feet, one in front of the other, until I approached your building. I leaned casually against the redbrick wall and took my gloves off and pulled my phone from my pocket. I didn't really have a plan, but it made sense to look busy, distracted by texts, like any other person on the street.

I watched the door to the lobby from the corner of my eye—it became easier to see inside as the sky darkened. A few women came and went but I knew they weren't her—too old, too big, too many dogs. And then a woman in a puffy down jacket walked out of the building,

phone in hand, and smiled at the doorman. She had long curly hair
pulled to the side and a diamond earring that twinkled under the lights
of the lobby overhang. She reached her arms up to put a cross-body
purse over her head and then pulled on leopard-print gloves—it had
quickly become a cold, blustery night. I was pretty sure it was her. So
I took my chances and I followed her.

It was easy to keep up. Her suede ankle boots had a low, thick heel
and she walked at a slow pace, like she hadn't grown up in the city.
She hit every crosswalk button even though most people knew they
were useless. I thought I'd be nervous about being caught doing something like this, but following her felt so easy. She made a quick phone
call as I stood several feet back from her at a set of streetlights, and then
she hustled to catch the green she'd nearly missed, distracted. Half a
block later she turned into a place I'd gone to many times when I was
in the neighborhood—a small bookstore with ornately carved wall-to-
wall shelving and huge milky-glass spheres that swayed ever so slightly
from the soaring twenty-foot ceiling every time the door opened.

I double-checked the sign on the window—it closed at six o'clock
on Wednesdays, which I vaguely recollected. But the lights were on. I
put my hands up to the glass to block the glare from the streetlamp
and get a better look. The store had forty, maybe fifty people inside.
All women. Coats were spread on a couple of old church benches and
there was a table of serve-yourself wine at the side with a cupcake tower
sponsored by the bakery next door. Nobody seemed to be taking tickets or names. I expected to see signs about an author appearance or a
table piled with books for a signing. Everyone looked younger than I
was, many in the same boots she'd been wearing—yours was a high-
rent neighborhood where all the boutiques carried the same things.
The two women standing next to the window had fresh new babies
wrapped to their chests in swathes of striped fabric. They swayed from

side to side as they chatted, in exactly the same rhythm, and I remembered that feeling, that tick of metronome that never quite leaves your hips when the weight of your baby is against you.

She was near the back, smoothing her thick, dark hair as someone put a hand on her shoulder to say hello. They hugged, her blushed cheek pressed against her tall, blond friend. She had a bright face, huge dark eyes wreathed with heavy mascara, and her mouth was locked in a smile. She seemed to remember what she'd brought for the blond woman—she reached in her purse quickly and pulled out something gray and knitted, and the friend pressed it against her chest in thanks. Another woman joined and handed them each a glass of wine.

The room began to fill and soon I couldn't see her from outside anymore. My heart sank. I needed more. I should have been terrified to walk through that door—surely she must have seen a picture of me at some point and knew what I looked like—but I went inside and added my coat to the heap. I recognized the staff person closing the till and leaned in to speak quietly to her.

"Do you know where the host of this party is?"

"It's not really a party. It's a moms' group. Just a drop-in thing. Sometimes they have speakers come or brands give them free stuff. We just lend our space and hope to get a few sales out of it."

"So everyone here is a mom?"

"I guess they don't have to be, but not sure why else they'd come." She shrugged and excused herself to the back with a tray of cash. I looked around and suddenly heard the symphony of mom problems around me—sleep training, starting solids, sleepers with zippers instead of snaps, preschool waiting lists. I poured wine into a small plastic cup and meandered to the opposite side of the room, to a spot where I could still see her. I looked at my phone, hoping nobody would speak to me, and glanced up to watch her every few seconds. She seemed to be telling a story, using her free hand to make tiny, panicked flutters, like butterfly wings. The two other women nodded and laughed. One of the others leaned in and rolled her eyes as she spoke and they laughed again. She touched people a lot, I noticed. Their arms, their hands, their waists. She was affectionate, I could tell. I thought of your bare feet under the sheets, always trying to find mine at night, always trying to rub against my calves, to feel my warmth, and of the way I pulled away across the bed. Farther and farther and farther away.

"Your first time?"

Someone with a very high ponytail and bright red lipstick popped up in front of me holding a postcard that said *Mom's Night Out* with a collection of small business logos.

"Yes, actually. Thanks."

"Great! I can introduce you to some people. How'd you hear about us?"

She put her arm at the small of my back and led me toward the middle of the room, not interested in the answer.

"Sydney, she's new," she said loudly, and pointed to me urgently above the crowd as though I needed a tag stapled to my ear so they could keep track of me. Sydney's eyes lifted and she squeezed through the crowd to come over and introduce herself.

"And you're . . . ?"

"Cecilia." It was the only name that came to me. I looked over their heads toward the back, where she had been, but I couldn't see her—she wasn't with the other two women anymore. I scanned the room and started to feel sick.

"Well, welcome, Cecilia! Congrats for getting yourself out of the house tonight! How old is your little one?"

"Thanks—you know what, I just wanted to stop by and get some information. I'll try to stay next time." I lifted my phone, as though someone had been texting me, as though I were a person who was needed. "I've got to run."

"Of course. Come back again." She took a sip of her wine and turned around to squeal hello to someone else.

My coat was still at the top of the pile but I dug through them anyway, buying time, looking over my shoulder to find her in the thick crowd. I had to go—I had been there long enough. I pulled my hood up and went outside where the snow flurries whipped around the street. I sat on a bench across from the bookstore and put my head between my knees.

She was a mother. You had found a better mother for our daughter. The kind of woman you always wanted.

65

The second time I was nervous.

I'd bought the long, brown wig at a theater supply store. You would have described it as mousy, but mousy was the look I was going for. My heart raced as I tucked my blond hair into the silk cap. I wasn't sure I looked different enough, but I couldn't think of what else to do. I practiced a happier smile in the mirror, and then hung my head. *You fool. You absolute fool.* For wearing the wig, for thinking I'd get away with it, for believing you had answered me truthfully when I asked if she had a child—any one of those. All of those.

When I got there, Sydney, the unofficial leader of the group, was at the door handing out samples of natural diaper cream to whoever walked in. I touched the ends of my new hair.

"Hi! Is this your first meeting? Welcome!" She spoke slightly over my head, as though she were looking for someone better to come up behind me. I nodded and thanked her and put the diaper cream in my bag. There was a speaker setting up a presentation they were calling "A Natural Household, a Natural You." The room was full of chairs. I got my wine and surveyed the crowd. I pretended to browse the bookshelves while I kept an eye on the door, watching as groups of

women congregated, complimenting outfits and asking about one another's kids. The brown strands blurred my periphery and made me
want to swipe at the hair like pesky flies—I wasn't used to being a brunette yet. The high-pony woman who had spoken to me last time sought
me out from across the room. God, had she recognized me? My cheeks
burned and I turned to find someone else to talk to, anyone, but everyone around me was in conversation. I slipped into a group of three
women who were discussing a "no time-out policy" and smiled, about
to introduce myself, when she tapped me on the shoulder.

"I'm Sloane. Here's a card. Cupcakes are from Luna's. Wine is from
Edin Estates. Next week we're having a sleep expert, she's *amazing*.
Are you on our Facebook page?" Relief. I took the postcard from her
hand, again. I chatted with the small group and watched the door, but
she never came in. Sloane called everyone to take a seat and the presenter began. I sat in the back row near the door, intent on leaving once
I could duck out unnoticed. The wig was itchy and I had no interest
in being there, if not for her.

Just as I was about to stand, I felt the cool air blow in from the door
behind me. There she was, waving an apology to the speaker, tiptoeing
to the bench as she unzipped her coat. I turned slowly back to face the
front of the room and crossed my legs, holding my breath. There was
an empty seat beside me. She slipped into it, a wave of her sweet perfume floating over me.

"Sorry," she whispered as she knocked my leg with her purse. I
smiled and kept my eyes on the presenter, although my heart was pounding so loudly that I couldn't hear a word the woman said. I dropped
my eyes to the side, looking at her ripped jeans, the boots they all wore,
the expensive bag she'd put on the floor.

"I follow her online, she's amazing." Her whisper startled me. I
nodded enthusiastically as she pulled out a small pink notebook with

the word JOY in gold foil on the cover. She jotted down notes about how to make spray bottles of nontoxic house cleaner while I pretended to care with an occasional nod. Her hands were long and beautiful. I folded mine, speckled with sunspots and hundreds of creases. I was forty—she looked at least a decade younger. She didn't wear any rings. I sometimes still wore my wedding ring, but had taken it off that night.

The presentation seemed endless. When it finally wrapped, I turned to her.

"That was so good. She's great."

"Right? I have a friend who does literally everything she says, and I swear she is *never* sick." She put the notebook in her purse and pointed to the table. "Do you want a glass of wine?"

I followed her while she touched various people hello along the way. A shoulder, an arm. Kisses and hugs. She poured two glasses and lifted her chin toward a clearing in the buzzing crowd. I followed her over. She released a huge breath.

"That's better. It gets so crowded in here. I shouldn't wear wool." She pulled at the neck of her burgundy sweater and took the tiniest sip of wine. "Oh, sorry, I'm Gemma. I don't think I said that yet."

"I'm Anne."

"How old are your kids?"

I had a plan for this part. I was a single mom with two young girls, a two- and a five-year-old. Red and blonde. Soccer and ballet. I had rehearsed their names out loud.

"I have one. He's four. His name is Sam."

The words echoed. I felt him bright inside me and my head became light, like I'd sniffed a drug I'd been off for years. I looked down, afraid for her to see my eyes. I pictured him at home having dinner with you and Violet, wondering where I was, if I'd be home in time to tuck him in. He would have been full of stories and silliness now. *I love you to the big, big moon and back, ten thousand trillion times, Mommy.*

"I have a boy, too. He'll be five months tomorrow." The echo of Sam's name in my ears died and my eyes snapped up. She took another nonsip, just wanting the taste on her lips. Her breasts, I noticed then, were torpedoes. Filled with milk.

"Sorry, did you say five months?"

She jumped as wine splashed on her suede boots—I'd let my arm fall. I stared at the empty plastic cup in my hand.

"Oh, dammit." She looked around for something to clean herself with. "I have wipes," she muttered and looked through her bag while I stood frozen, silent. I watched her pull the wet wipes from the package as I ran through the calendar. It was November. I went back through the months. You had moved out in January. Almost a year ago.

"So he was born in June?"

"Yes, June fifteenth. . . . Let me just find some napkins, these aren't working."

"Shit, sorry." I ran to the cupcake table and came back with a fistful of napkins and bent to pat her boots dry. She'd taken them off and was sitting in a chair, her feet turned in. I rubbed at the darkened suede and apologized profusely.

"I have this thing—this tremor in my hand sometimes." It was remarkable how easily the lies came to me.

"Oh—that's okay." Her tone changed at the thought of my new disability—she put her hand on my upper arm, as I'd seen her do to the other friends she had made in the room. "Don't worry one bit. They'll dry."

We both stood up. She was nearly a foot taller than me in her damp socks. I had to look up to speak to her.

"I—you—five months old, that's so little!" I was amazed with myself for speaking. For holding it together. "You look great."

"Thanks. I'm tired. He's a terrible sleeper. I can't wait to hear the sleep coach speaking next week. Or maybe you have some tips for me. Did you sleep train? The 'cry it out' method? I just don't think I can do that. I can't stand him to be upset."

This boy she spoke about was yours. She had given birth to your son. You had been given another chance. And then it hit me—the thirty-eight weeks it takes to grow a baby from conception. That she conceived in September, the month before you were fired from your job. That you would have known she was pregnant well before the time I asked you to leave. You knew the whole time. You knew.

"Um, you know, he just sort of slept. I didn't have to do much."

"Oh, really? Like from how old?"

The room felt thick. I thought of her pushing the baby out. Of you watching your new boy come to life.

"Maybe four months or so? I can't really remember."

"I'm thinking of topping him up at night with some formula. They say that helps to fill their bellies. But I'm not really sure what kind—"

"And the father?"

"Sorry?" She leaned closer—she thought she hadn't heard me correctly, the question was so odd.

"I mean, do you have a partner?"

"I do. He's great. He's a great father. He just sent this, actually." She smiled and pulled out her phone. Her lips moved slightly as she searched for a photo to show me, as though she were talking to herself. She held the picture up and lifted her eyebrows, waiting for my reaction, like it might be a photo of a huge, unwieldy erection. The baby was swaddled, asleep in a crib. The sheets had stars and moons. I couldn't see the baby's face from the angle of the photo. I took the phone from her and stared at the wrapped-up human who shared our dead son's DNA. "He can get him to sleep so easily. They really love each other."

"Very sweet." I handed it back and touched my hair, remembering the wig. I needed to get out of there—it was too hot, too loud all of a sudden.

"And you? Do you have a partner?"

"I don't— I . . . he was never in the picture. So. Single mom." I nodded, confirming the lie to myself, hoping she didn't ask more.

"You know, Anne, you look familiar to me."

"Oh?"

"Yeah, I feel like we've met before."

"Maybe." I turned toward the coat pile. I had to leave.

"Where'd you go to school?"

"Oh, a small place out west—"

"Do you do yoga?"

"Yeah, maybe that's why. I've tried a bunch of different studios, so maybe we crossed paths?"

"No . . . I don't think that's it."

I started making my way out. She followed.

"I'm out and about in the neighborhood a lot, maybe we've just—"

"Oh. Shit. I know." She snapped her fingers. I held my breath and looked at the door.

"It's just a resemblance—my spin instructor. You look a *lot* like her."

I *phoned you in the cab* on the way home. Four times. I knew you wouldn't pick up. I ached to speak with you, to ask you if he looked like Sam. If he had the same pout, the same smell. I'd forgotten to ask her the baby's name. I realized that we hadn't spoken to each other since the baby was born. Maybe you thought I'd taint your life somehow if you heard my voice, take something away from the experience you deserved. She seemed like a wonderful mother—I could tell just by being near her. She felt like a very, very good mother.

66

I wonder if you watched as her vagina, swollen and burning, opened up to release a new being, half of you, into the hands of a doctor who congratulated you on your son. A boy, for the second time. I wonder if your eyes filled with tears as they placed the slippery baby on her sweaty chest and saw him gape toward her nipple. I wonder if you held that woman's shaking hand while they yanked thread through the skin of her perineum, pulled and tugged until the damage was dealt with. I wonder if you took her by the elbow and led her to the toilet in her room, where she cried in pain and hovered with shaking thighs, blood pouring from her, her insides heavy, her vulva pulsing, her body so weak after an experience so strong. Did you squirt warm water up into her bloody parts like the nurses taught you before? Did you get into that wide hospital bed with her, and the baby, and wonder how you'd ever loved a different woman? Did you put your phone on silent so she wouldn't hear my texts as she was trying to get colostrum into the baby's mouth? Did you argue to circumcise his penis, like you did with Sam? Did you take her home to bed the next day, in soft jersey cotton pajamas she'd bought just for the occasion? And was that bed you took her to the place where you made this baby, the place where you came inside her with such euphoria that you didn't give a shit what happened afterward?

I couldn't sleep for days after meeting her.

I couldn't sleep until I went into the basement.

I brushed off the layer of dust on the storage container. Inside were Sam's things. Onesies, blankets, footed pajamas, a few other little things he loved. Benny the Bunny. I carried the box upstairs to the foot of my bed and began my ritual. Night-light on. Organic lavender lotion on my hands, the kind I used to rub on his skin after his bath. The white noise machine was at the bottom of the box. Ocean waves. I placed it on the bedside table.

I closed my eyes and tried to remember every last thing of his inside. The soft mint-green one-piece from your mother. The pajamas that matched Violet's. The muslin blanket with the hearts on it. The tiny red socks. The flannel blanket from the hospital. I could list them all, I could do it again right now, a game of memory. None of it had been washed. So much of him was in those fabrics.

This was an indulgence I'd allowed myself only a few times since Sam died. I saved it for when I needed it most.

I lifted each item slowly to my face and inhaled as deeply as I could until my nose stung, letting my mind soak up whatever it could find . . . banging pots on the kitchen floor while I made oatmeal, sucking soapy water from the wet facecloth in the bath, cuddling for stories, naked, happy, the risk of a diaper-free bum on our duvet. I craved these little silent movies of him. It didn't matter to me that these memories were not exact, that most of them hadn't happened precisely as they did in the scenes that played through my head—I just needed to see him, and then I could feel him with these things in my hands. If I focused just enough Sam could be right there next to me, and I could feel alive again.

When I finished caressing each of his things, I chose the pajamas he wore the most, thin in the knees from crawling after Violet, stained at the neck from blueberry jam. The light-knit blanket from his crib. And Benny. I used to be able to find him in that fur, distinctly, breathing him in to fill my brain like an anesthetic. But now Sam's scent was nearly gone and Benny felt a bit damp and musty. I ran my thumb over the stained part of his tail that looked like nothing but old rust now.

I'd kept an unused diaper, too. I laid everything out on the bed, each article as it would have been: the diaper inside the pajamas, the blanket laid underneath, Benny tucked in near his neck. And then I picked him up and I cradled him in my arms, and I smelled him, and I kissed him. I turned off the night-light. I tucked in the corners of the blanket so he was wrapped and warm. I swayed to the ocean waves and hummed the lullaby I always sang. I rocked him back and forth. And when he was still and heavy, when his breathing was long and deep, I carefully slipped into bed so as not to wake him. I moved the pillows, made a safe spot. And I slept there, with him in my arms.

In the morning, I put everything carefully back. I carried the box down to the basement. Back in the kitchen, I put the kettle on the stove, pulled up the blinds, and began another day alone.

67

My father told me he was going to drop me off at my mother's house on Sunday for lunch. I was stunned. We hadn't spoken much about her in the two years since she left, and I hadn't seen her since the time at the diner with Mrs. Ellington. He told me she had called the week before and extended the invitation. I didn't seem to have a choice, the way he told me about it, but I remember wanting to go despite her betrayal—I was curious. Maybe he was, too.

When she opened the door she looked past me to the driveway, searching for my father through the reflection on his windshield. She watched the car until it turned off the street and then looked down at me. I wore my hair a different way, in two long braids, and my face was speckled with new freckles from the summer sun.

"Nice to see you," she said, as though we'd run into each other at the grocery store.

I followed her in. Her house, modest on the outside, was filled with fancy items I hadn't seen before, not even at the Ellingtons'. Proper runners on the tables and glass statues on pedestals and pictures lit from above with their own special lamps. None of it felt real to me. It felt like a set, like actors would sweep in any minute and take over the stage. Richard called for us and she shuffled me to the kitchen, where he handed me a dark pink drink in a cocktail glass.

"I made you a Shirley Temple." I took it from his huge hand and they watched me have a sip.

"This is Richard. Richard, this is Blythe." She sat at the table and looked around her kitchen, prompting me to do the same. Everything looked pristine, unused. Maybe it was.

"I've ordered some sandwiches."

Richard stared at me and then back at my mother. She raised her eyebrows at him as if to say, *Happy now?*

He asked me a few questions about the first week of school and told me he liked my name, and then excused himself to make a call. My mother unwrapped our lunch from cellophane and asked me what I had been up to. *For the past two years, or just this weekend?* I wanted to ask. But it was clear that we were supposed to pretend—just like the house she had set up. Just like this life she had wanted to show me for some reason. She leaned over the counter to reach a knife and her blouse touched a blob of mayonnaise.

"Shit," she hissed and rubbed at the stain with a dish towel. "I've worn this once."

I ate my turkey sandwich and listened to them talk about somewhere on the coast of France. They'd gone for the summer. I wondered where all the money came from, why they lived in that boring house in that mediocre neighborhood a half hour outside the city. I'd always imagined she left us for an urban, bohemian life full of people who were as beautiful as she was. That was clearly not Richard. But he certainly didn't match the glass statues and the elegant china either. He looked as out of place as I knew she was.

Her hair and her skin and her lips and her clothes were different— even her voice. New textures and smells and pitches. Every part of her that I'd once known had become glossy and coated and smelled like a department store. I later saw piles of tissue and fancy shopping bags folded in her closet from stores I hadn't heard of before. She'd given me a haphazard tour of the house, after which we lingered in the bedroom. There weren't any pills on her bedside table. I noticed she had a small suitcase in the corner, open, her things strewn on top. She saw me staring at it.

"I haven't had a chance to unpack. We stay in the city a lot. Richard has business there. We lived there for a while, actually." She took off her stained silk blouse and looked through her closet for something else to wear. She sighed. "I hate it here, but—"

But what? I wondered. Her bra was black and lacy. I had a humiliating urge to put my face between her breasts, just to smell her skin, as if that crevice could possibly have reminded me of childhood.

Later that afternoon, after I came down quietly from the bathroom, I watched from the hallway as Richard grabbed her waist from behind and pulled her into him. She reached up and put her fingers in his waxy, graying hair.

"I missed you. Don't disappear like that again," he said. She pulled her hand away from his.

"I wish you hadn't called him."

"Well, it worked to get you home, didn't it?"

Richard had invited me over, not my mother. I was a ploy to get her back from the city. But there must have been a small part of her that wanted to see me, that still cared what my father and I thought of her.

I counted to ten and walked into the kitchen. My father would be back soon. I thanked them for lunch and watched for his car from the window. I waited for her to say something—*Come back soon. I'm glad you came. I've missed you.*

She waved good-bye to me from outside the doorway, making sure to give my father a chance to have a good look at her.

He never asked me about the visit—not the house, not Richard, not what she served for lunch. But at dinner, as we did the last of the dishes together in silence, I said to him: "It wasn't you who made her unhappy." I needed him to know. He didn't reply—he folded the damp dish towel on the counter and he left the kitchen.

That was the last time I saw my mother.

68

When Violet was with me, it was like living in the house with a ghost. She rarely spoke to me, but she made her presence felt. She left lights on, taps dripping. She seemed to change the air in the room. I knew the feeling of resentment well by then, enough to recognize it in the thickness of the space around her.

Who did she blame for the separation? The obvious answer would be me, if she blamed anyone at all. I think she liked the splitting of our family into two. She seemed to flourish in her new role as a child of divorce, quietly delighting in the amnesty she'd been given from me. We hadn't heard from her teachers in a while. I wondered if we were in the calm before the storm.

On the way to school one morning I reached back and handed her a muffin. She was fishing for something under her scarf but stopped to take it from my hand. When I turned back around she pulled out a delicate gold chain with a small round pendant, similar to the one you'd given me years before that I never wore anymore. I watched her touch it tenderly in the rearview mirror.

"Where did you get that?"

"Gemma."

She hadn't said her name aloud to me since that first lunch at your office. I desperately wanted to keep up my secret relationship with Gemma, so I never asked Violet about her. I could not incite any possible reason to be mentioned in your household.

I*t didn't take me long* to establish a connection with Gemma. She was chipper and high energy and enjoyed being asked about herself. She had a habit of going into long talks and then, midthought, squeezing her eyes closed to say, "I've really gone on, haven't I. What about *you*?" and then touching both of my wrists in the most delicate way, as though she were patting the paws of a bunny. The gesture was charming, and I understood the reprieve you found in her while we were standing inside the quietly crumbling walls of our marriage.

We began sitting together during the weekly presentations and then mingling with the women afterward. I stayed as close to Gemma as I could so that I never missed a chance to hear something new. She was a puzzle I was putting together slowly, week by week. My heart raced the entire time I was with her, eager, desperate to learn more about her. I often found myself staring at her, visualizing what you looked like next to her. How you touched her. How you fucked her. How you watched her nurse your baby and soothe him to sleep and tickle him in the morning and how utterly happy she made you.

"I love it actually—I love being a stepmom."

I snapped out of my fantasy and saw her clearly again. She had never mentioned Violet before. I had been waiting.

"She's eleven, which can be a tough age for some girls. But she seems to like me. I'm lucky. I mean you hear the horror stories of stepchildren . . ."

Someone else jumped in and changed the topic. Later, when we were alone, I asked her about what she'd said.

"I didn't know you had a stepdaughter."

"Oh, I haven't mentioned her? Her name's Violet. She's a sweetheart. My husband is very close with her, so she's with us a lot."

"And you get along, it sounds like?'"

"No issues at all. We just work so well, our little family. My husband dotes on us. He loves having the four of us together."

"And what about her mother?"

"She's not really in the picture much. It's a long story. She has some issues and so we sort of keep our distance."

I nodded and was quiet, hoping she'd say more.

"There's some history there and I stay out of it. Seems like she's not the most loving human being, from what I gather. Although who are we to judge, right?" She sighed and eyed the room.

I wanted more. I wanted to know every last lie you had told her about me. "Violet's lucky to have you, then."

"That's sweet of you, thanks. I love her like she's my own."

I searched her face for the truth. I was looking for the same uneasiness that had consumed me about Violet. But Gemma swayed to the music overhead and put her empty cup on the cash desk. "Shall we go?"

I cleared my throat and followed her to the door. "And so Violet, does she like the baby?"

"She adores Jet. She's the best big sister."

I hugged her good-bye, feeling her swollen milky tits against mine.

69

I'd gotten a new phone with a different number so that Gemma and I could text each other during the week. At first it was a quick series of boring pleasantries—*Will you be there? Great, me too!* And afterward, *So nice to see you! Have a wonderful week.* Later, she would text me for advice, standing in the aisles of the pharmacy while she looked for the right cold medicine, or wondering whether Jet should wear reusable or disposable swim diapers for his Mommy and Me lessons. She was a confident woman, loquacious and lively, but there was a part of her that constantly wanted reassurance when it came to Jet. She wanted to be a perfect mother, to do and buy and give the very best, and she often looked to me for advice. I found this vulnerability endearing. The way she consumed herself with her son's well-being, constantly evaluating herself and what she provided for him.

She loved being a mother, yes, but she also loved *to* mother. To dote, to care, to fuss, to love, to hold, to feed. She thrived on it. When I asked if she had thought about weaning the baby soon—he was nearly a year old by that point—she shook her head vigorously. I should have known—she once told me that every time she nursed him, she felt an emotional surge she had never experienced before he was born, something from deep within her that she couldn't explain. I told her it sounded like she was describing an orgasm.

"You know what, Anne—it's even better."

We laughed, but she was serious.

"I'd love to meet Sam," she said to me one Wednesday night as we put on our coats. "Wouldn't it be fun to get them together?"

"That would be so nice."

She never followed up on the idea, although I had a suite of well-thought-out excuses if she had. Schedules. Illness (she was terrified of germs). Last-minute plans to be out of town. Carrying on together felt so much easier than I thought it would.

One evening she called me at nearly twelve o'clock on a night when Violet was at your house. She was worried. Jet had a terrible chest cold and was having trouble breathing. She didn't know what to do: Should she take him into emergency? Should she run another steamy shower?

"What does your husband think?" I knew you weren't married—we weren't even divorced yet—but she called you her husband anyway.

"He's not here—he's out of town for work and he's not answering."

"Oh." I was surprised you'd left Violet with Gemma for the night and not said something to me about it. I thought of our loose agreement, of how fair I'd been about the splitting our time. We were supposed to let each other know if we'd be leaving Violet with someone else. You had started to take advantage of her preference for you, asking for an extra night here or there, not telling me when she'd be leaving the city with you for a weekend away. You knew you had the upper hand now. "So, you're alone?"

"His daughter is here. If I take him to the ER, I'd have to wake her up and bring her, too. But she has her first basketball practice before school tomorrow morning and she'll be exhausted. Maybe—she's eleven—maybe she can stay alone? The hospital is literally only four blocks away. She never wakes up, ever. But, God, I'd feel awful if she does and can't find me." She blew out a long stream of air, thinking. "No, no I'll have to wake her up if I go."

I don't know what came over me.

"Leave her. Leave her there alone, she'll be fine. Nothing will happen. Put the monitor in her room and watch her from there. She's old enough. I would take him in right away if I were you."

"Really? Shit. You think?"

"Yes, for sure. Just go. You won't be long, she won't wake up. You can't risk it—he's just a baby. You can't take the chance. You'll never forgive yourself."

I never would have left her alone. But I wanted you to be angry with her. Furious. I wanted her to do something you would think was terrible.

"Oh, I don't know, Anne."

"Just take him," I said with urgency. "I can hear him, and he sounds pretty awful. I'm worried."

I felt sick with myself when I hung up the phone.

She texted me in the morning to say they'd sent her home, after a four-hour wait, advising her to run a hot shower and hold him in the steam. He'd been fine.

The next week when I saw her at the mom group, she told me you had freaked out when she admitted to leaving Violet alone. I pictured you spitting mean words at her through clenched teeth, the way you did when you were truly enraged. *I thought I could trust you with her. I thought you were a better mother than that.*

"He's right, Anne, I probably shouldn't have done that. I wasn't thinking straight."

"I'm so sorry—maybe I gave you the wrong advice. But you were doing what you thought was best."

"Yeah. Maybe." She was more quiet than usual that night, and I knew she was upset with me. I texted her as I waited for a taxi to go home.

Everything okay? You seemed down tonight.

Just one of those weeks—nothing personal, I promise! ☺

She was too nice for confrontation. I felt ill at the thought that I'd betrayed her. She had slowly become the only person I needed.

70

I've left out an important part of our friendship. Perhaps the most important. When I was with Gemma, I was Sam's mother. He came alive in me again in a way I never thought could happen. Being with Gemma was like playing pretend and my imaginary friend was the love of my life. My sweet son. My gap-toothed, chatty little boy who tore through the halls of my house in bare feet and his favorite stained baseball shirt. He loved measuring tapes and garbage day and collecting sugar packets from restaurants. He asked me every day about Mother Nature and how she made the weather the way she did. We swam on weekends and went for muffins in the morning on our way to preschool. His shoes always felt too tight. His mouth was always pursed. He loved to hear about the day he was born.

On Wednesdays, I let myself wonder all day what I'd say when I got to the moms' group—that he'd been up in the night and I was exhausted, that he'd cried with the babysitter when I left. Maybe something the teacher had said about him when I'd picked him up from preschool that afternoon. Crafting the narrative around Sam was addictive—I cycled through story lines obsessively, thinking about what he'd be like and how I would care for him if he was alive. If

Violet hadn't killed him. Although I tried not to let her enter my mind on those days. They were sacred, just for him. And when Gemma sometimes brought her up in conversation, I bristled and listened, conflicted—I was eager for the open window to your life together, but hated that she existed in the periphery of Sam's second chance.

I loved it when Gemma asked me questions about him. She once told me my eyes lit up when she said his name and I had no doubt she could see my insides glow. Nobody ever mentioned him, and here she was, giving him space and time and worth. She wanted to know about him. To Gemma, Sam mattered. And so she mattered to me, deeply.

I hadn't thought about photos.

She asked me one day if I had a picture of Sam that she could see. She leaned over to look at the phone I held casually in my hand, expecting I could easily flick through hundreds of his pictures, like she had of Jet.

"You know what, I just cleared out my phone, actually. I was out of space again." I tried to look annoyed by this technological fact. I tossed the phone in my bag and calmly changed the topic.

That night I poured a glass of red wine and went searching online for pictures of four-year-old boys who looked like Sam. I flipped through social media accounts of strangers with open profiles. I spent hours scanning the lives of happy, bubble-blowing, wagon-riding, ice-cream-covered kids. I'd nearly finished the bottle when I found the perfect child. Dark curls, gap-toothed grin, and the same huge blue eyes. *Siobhan McAdams, mum to James by day, baker of cakes by night.*

I traced her face on my screen. She looked very tired. She looked very happy.

I saved a dozen of James's photos and placed one as the background on my phone—he was on a swing, hands above his head like he was on the crest of a roller coaster. Sam had loved the swings.

. . .

I picked up baby items from secondhand stores and sometimes brought them to Gemma, pretending they were things Sam had grown out of—I could never have parted with his real clothes or toys, and besides, you or Violet might have recognized them. She always hugged whatever I brought her, as though she were hugging Sam. I loved to watch her do that. I loved to watch her think of him.

One week she brought me a beautiful set of Froebel building blocks that I knew were expensive.

"Actually, it was my husband who suggested I bring them for you—someone gave them to us as a gift, but we already have a big set."

I realized she mustn't have told you about my role in the emergency room incident. I held the box to my chest in gratitude the way she did with the things I had given her. People do that, don't they, when they spend time together—take on each other's subtle gestures, begin to act like each other. I wondered if she had ever mimicked me without knowing it, maybe the way I had begun touching the ends of my Wednesday night hair. Or the way I clucked my tongue sometimes when I was thinking; I wondered if I ever crossed your mind if she did this, the thought fleeting, ephemeral, gone as quickly as it came.

On the way out, I asked her to thank you for the gift. And then I said something I shouldn't have—that I'd love to meet you and Jet and Violet sometime. This wasn't possible, of course, but I wanted to talk about you somehow. Gemma nodded and said she'd like that, too, that maybe I could come over for pizza, with Sam, like she'd suggested before.

"And how are things going with Violet?"

"Violet? She's good. Everyone's good." She was distracted, texting someone on her phone.

But I wondered if she was lying to me. I wondered if she ever looked at my daughter and had a feeling that something was wrong. I wondered if she ever suspected her son was in danger.

She kissed my cheek good-bye and I touched her arm, like she always touched mine.

We were getting far too close. I promised myself I would skip next week. I took the blocks home and put them in Sam's room.

71

I wasn't going to go. I texted her to say I wasn't feeling great—that Sam had had a restless night and I hadn't slept much the night before either. She texted back a sad face, and then again to say she'd miss seeing me. I didn't want to disappoint her.

We sat near the back and exchanged updates from the week in low voices, hers, a series of inconsequential problems that worried her, mine, sweet things Sam had said or done.

We'd been seeing each other at the Wednesday night gathering for nearly a year and knew most of the regulars, although Gemma and I had established ourselves as a pair at some point. The other women held two spots for us if the seating was tight, and asked one of us where the other was if we were late. I wondered why Gemma had taken an interest in me, of all the women there. The answer, I'm sure, was that I'd sought her out with such intention that I'd given her no choice. Still, I wanted to believe there was something about me that she was drawn to—she thought of me as a wonderful mother, capable and loving and committed, and befriending me gave her great comfort as she navigated that first year with your new son. It made me feel like I was a clandestine part of the new family you had built, one step removed from the clutches of your judgments at last.

We said good-bye to the others and I wrapped my scarf around my neck.

"My husband's here." Gemma pointed to the door. There you were. Standing outside, staring at me. I clutched the wool in my hands and caught my breath. Slowly I turned so that my back faced you. You'd been watching us.

"Come. I'll introduce you." She put her hands on my shoulders and guided me to the door. I didn't know what to do.

"Gemma, I—I have to use the bathroom—"

"Oh, just come out quickly. We're going to catch a late movie, but I want you to meet him while he's here."

I lowered my eyes and tried to think. What could I do? I pulled my scarf up high around my chin and yanked my hat low over my forehead. I fished the long, brown strands of hair out from under my coat and spread them over my shoulders. As if you wouldn't have recognized me. The woman you loved for twenty years. The mother of your children. I stood there in front of you, as naked as I had ever been. She kissed you. She didn't have to reach up like I did. Your eyes felt like bullets. I swallowed and tears pooled on the lids of my eyes, although it could have been from the bitter cold for all Gemma knew.

"Fox, this is Anne. Anne, this is Fox."

My head floated away like a candlelit paper lantern into the night sky—I was no longer standing there, no longer locked in your stare, waiting to be massacred by whatever you would say next. It's the only way I could survive the shame, the fear, the regret of you knowing what I'd done. I left myself. I watched from above.

"Nice to meet you." I offered my gloved hand to you. You looked at Gemma. And then looked back at me. You didn't take your hands from your pockets. I'd bought that coat for your birthday.

She turned to you with genuine concern, as though the only reason you could have been so rude is if you'd had an aneurysm. You slowly pulled your hand from your coat pocket and took mine in yours. We hadn't spoken in a year and a half. We hadn't touched in even longer. The skin on your face was red from the cold and you looked older. Maybe less sleep with the baby, maybe the stress of the job you had now. Or maybe I had just lost track of time—despite everything, in the memories that came to me the easiest, you were still the man I was in love with years ago.

"You, too." You glanced over my head as you spoke and I knew then you were going to spare us all the humiliation. I doubted you were doing it for me.

Gemma looked uncomfortable. Her usual soft, fluid mannerisms disappeared, and she tensed. I could see it even under her thick down coat. I think she understood that something wasn't right, but it was too cold to stand still for long, and there were other women catching her eye to say good-bye. The three of us turned away from the perilousness of one another. I slipped through the crowd that lingered on the sidewalk and then began to run. I didn't know what else to do. I needed to be as far away from you as I could be.

72

I don't know if Gemma told you what happened next.

I imagine you waited until after the theater to tell her. Or maybe it was days. Maybe you had wanted to spare her the disappointment as long as you could, until you felt too dishonest keeping quiet any longer. Or maybe you didn't want to admit that you'd been married for so long to a woman who would do something as unthinkable as I had. As unhinged. Shame by association. I didn't hear from Gemma that week and I didn't dare reach out. Her unusual silence was proof that you'd told her who I was. I stopped going to the Wednesday night group.

Maybe she told you very little about the year of friendship we shared. But it meant a great deal to me. I hadn't had a friend like her before, someone for whom my fondness felt so warm and easy. She was like a temperate summer day. She felt to me like you once had. Before. It wasn't until she was gone from my life that I realized how lonely I was.

My curiosity ate away at me until I worked up the nerve to ask Violet one day.

"How's Gemma?"

"Why are you asking?"

"Just curious."

"She's fine."

"And the baby?"

The baby. We had never discussed him. Her fork stayed in her mouth and she stared at the vegetables on the plate, wondering, I'm sure, how I knew—maybe she was processing the shift in power, that she no longer harbored this secret.

"He's fine." Something about the way she cleared her throat afterward made me feel uneasy. She excused herself from the table and neither of us mentioned Jet again that evening. Before bed she asked if she could stay with you for the weekend—your parents would be visiting. I still hadn't spoken to your mother since I discovered the affair. She called every so often but had stopped leaving me messages by then.

"All right, but your father should be the one to ask me that."

She shrugged. We both knew there was no place for protocol in this mess we'd created. My phone chimed from the other room. It was Gemma. She had sent me a text:

Can we talk?

I bent over in relief.

We met the next day for tea near the bookstore. I didn't sleep the night before, playing out versions of what I'd say, how I'd possibly explain myself. I was most nervous, insanely, for her to see me in my own hair, without the mousy brown wig I'd come to love wearing. I focused my sea of nerves on confronting this one thing—my hair. Not my twisted manipulation, not the deranged way I'd brought my son back to life, not the shocking ease with which I lied, as though I were having mindless chitchat with strangers during a morning of errands.

I saw from the door that she had ordered a cup of tea for each of us. We didn't hug as usual when I said hello. I slipped into the chair and reached for the ends of my hair and then remembered—I was

Blythe, not Anne. I straightened the collar on my shirt instead. I'd worn something I knew she liked—she'd mentioned so once, fingering the sleeve to feel the weight of the linen.

"I don't know what to say." I hadn't planned to speak first, but there it was.

Gemma nodded, but then shook her head uncomfortably and I understood. I chewed on my lip as she poured a bit of milk into her cup. She waited a moment and then slid the milk and sugar across to me. We listened to my spoon clink against the china as I stirred. It was clear she didn't want to speak and so maybe she just wanted to know what I'd say to her if I were given the chance.

"I don't expect you to ever forgive me. There's no excuse for what I've done."

She looked over me and watched the world pass by the café. Her eyes followed each person, like a teacher silently counting her students as they came in from recess. I wondered if she regretted asking me to meet. I wondered if I should just shut up.

"I'm ashamed of myself, Gemma. I'm deeply ashamed. I look back now and I can't believe what I did, I can't believe I'm capable of something so . . . psychotic. I . . ."

I waited for her to tear me apart. Her eyes moved away from the window and studied my hair. I'd worn it the same way for years. I wondered if she noticed the wiry gray strands among the ash blond. I wondered if she thought I looked older this way.

"If there's anything I can answer, anything—"

"I'm sorry about your son. I'm sorry you lost him."

Her words shocked me.

"I can't imagine losing Jet." She touched her lip.

I exhaled and touched mine, too, wondering where her compassion came from. She should have loathed me. Dead child and all.

"Fox never told me what happened." She looked down at her tea and swirled the cup. "All I know is that he had a son, that you had a son, together, and he was killed in an accident. I've always assumed it was a car crash. Was it?"

I'd told so many lies. I couldn't tell another one. I opened my mouth and the truth came out. I told her exactly what I remembered. Step by step. My memory of her pink mittens on the handle. The sound of the car slamming into the stroller. That he was still strapped in when he died. That we couldn't even see his body after. That the stepdaughter she loved and trusted, the sister of her own child, had pushed that stroller into oncoming traffic and killed my son.

She didn't react as she listened. She was still and looked me in the eye the entire time I spoke. I thought I saw her swallow, the way people do when they're tempering something, a realization they wished they weren't having. I saw a hairline crack crawl through the ice. I leaned toward her.

"Gemma. Do you ever think there's something different about Violet? Have you had even a hint of worry that your son wasn't safe being alone with her?"

She pushed her chair away and the screeching sound on the tiles made me cringe. She placed a twenty-dollar bill on the table and then carried her coat outside into November's early falling snow. She didn't even stop to put it on.

73

Inside the house we all used to live in, there is one pair of shoes at the door. The kettle perpetually steams. I use the same water glass six times before I wash it. I break dishwasher tabs in half. The hangers in each closet are spaced two inches apart and there's nobody here to move them. There are splotches of tea on the hallway floor that I haven't yet wiped, although I think about doing it every day. I put inordinate importance on organized drawers, and the plants are overwatered. There are forty-two rolls of toilet paper in the basement. I nearly always forget to remove this item from the list of groceries I reorder every other week online.

I hope for a mouse, and I know this is strange, but I often yearn for the comfort of a regular visitor, the crinkle of a bag in the cupboard or the scatter of claws on the hardwood; brief, nonverbal, predictable company.

On some weekends, I turn on the Formula 1 races. The pitchy hiss of the engines and the British commentary take me back to Sunday mornings before swim lessons, when I'd bring you eggs and coffee, toast without the crust for Violet.

. . .

I've grown used to the loneliness, but there was someone who only came over when Violet was at your house. He was a less than successful literary agent whom Grace introduced me to. He liked to fuck me slowly with the bedroom windows wide open, listening to the footsteps on the concrete of the sidewalk. I think feeling close to the strangers outside made him come faster.

I'm starting with that, but it won't make the right impression. He was measured and intelligent, and he was a reason to cook at night, to open a bottle of wine. He used up the toilet paper. He added warmth to the bed when I needed it on occasion. I liked the fact that he never asked about Violet—they didn't exist to each other. I hadn't met a man who was easier to be around, in that sense, than he was. He didn't like to think about the fact that I had children—that my body had birthed and had fed. You thought of motherhood as the ultimate expression of a woman, but he didn't; for him, the vagina was nothing other than a vessel for his pleasure. To think of it otherwise made him physically queasy, the way others felt when they gave blood. He told me this once when I told him I had an appointment for a Pap smear.

He read my writing and we talked about what I could do and what could sell. He wanted me to write young adult, something commercial and angsty that would work with the right cover. Something, in other words, that would work for him to represent and monetize. Sometimes I wondered about his motives, in that respect. But I was on the cusp of the age when women worry about disappearing to everyone but themselves, blending in with their sensible hair, their practical coats. I see them walk down the street every day as though they're ghosts. I suppose I wasn't ready to be invisible yet. Not then.

1972–1974

Henry's sense of parental responsibility seemed to have died with Etta. His heart was too broken to care for anyone else. He blamed himself for Etta's suicide, although he was the only one who did—Cecilia knew he loved Etta, and that he had tried. Nobody said a word to Cecilia about what happened. Nobody knew what to say.

She barely went to school after that, but she was smart enough to keep her truancies below the point where they'd expel her. She had a hard time facing anyone there, and the feeling seemed mutual. She suspected all anyone saw when they looked at her was her dead mother hanging from a tree.

She spent most of her time reading poetry, which she discovered wandering the town's library during the classes she skipped. The collection wasn't very big. She could make it through the entire two shelves in about two and a half weeks, and then she would start over again. She had dreams of finding Etta dead with her head in the oven, like Sylvia Plath, whose books she sometimes slept with under her pillow.

She began writing her own poetry, filling notebook after notebook, although she didn't think any of it was any good. She did this until she turned seventeen, the year before graduation. She had decided by then that she needed to make her own money if she wanted to leave town and become someone new.

She took a caregiver job with Mrs. Smith, an elderly woman who lived a few doors down. Mrs. Smith had left a HELP WANTED sign on her front door in printing that looked like a child's. She was deaf and nearly blind, but she could still go about most of her business on her own. She needed someone to help with things that her hands couldn't feel their way through anymore, so Cecilia would mend her clothes with a needle and thread or pinch the right amount of spice into her stew. She wasn't used to helping anyone but herself, so she found this role unexpectedly satisfying, if a little tedious at times. But she liked that she could go around a familiar house without another person's demons threatening her day. There was a kind of peace and order there she had never felt before.

When Mrs. Smith died in her sleep, Cecilia was the one who found her, lying halfway off the bed. One shrunken breast had fallen out of her white nightgown. While she thought of what to do next, she took the tin from the woman's top dresser drawer. Cecilia had watched Mrs. Smith tuck her money away when she came from the bank each week. She found $680, enough for a ticket to the city, and room and board for a couple of months. Cecilia wondered if maybe Mrs. Smith had meant for her to have it—she had never tried to hide it from her, and she had no next of kin. Or at least this thought made her feel less guilty when she took every last dollar.

Henry drove Cecilia to the train station the morning after. He didn't say a word, not even good-bye. But she knew this was only because he couldn't. She kissed him for the first time in her life, once on each of his hairy cheeks. He didn't shave much after Etta died. She whispered to him the only possible thing there was to say: thank you.

Outside of his car, Cecilia straightened her nicest outfit, a plum corduroy skirt and blouse that she'd bought secondhand. The rest of her things were packed in Etta's teal-colored monogrammed luggage, a gift from Henry that she'd never used. There was nowhere Etta had wanted to go.

Cecilia had turned eighteen and knew she had a classic sort of beauty, a kind her mother never had. She suspected it would work to her advantage more in the big city than it ever had back at home. No sooner had Cecilia stepped out of the taxi than she saw Seb West, the doorman at a fancy hotel she couldn't afford to stay at. The hotel was the only place she'd ever heard of in the city—she hadn't known what other address to give the taxi driver. Seb held out his white-gloved hand to take hers, and they barely let go after that.

Seb showed Cecilia the city and introduced her to his friends. One of them helped her get a poorly paid job at his uncle's high-end livery service. She helped with bookings and kept the office tidy and went for lunch with the other women who worked there. One of them told her about a small studio for rent above an art gallery that had gone out of business, but she still couldn't afford the cost of city living on her own. Seb moved in with her to split the rent, and he paid for almost everything else in Cecilia's life. They were officially a couple.

She reveled in the freedom of the city. Having somewhere important to be in the morning. Getting coffee from the vendor on the street, reading poetry in the park during her breaks. Meeting people who had no idea where she came from. Or from whom.

Cecilia was right about her beauty and the kind of attention it attracted. Men's eyes followed her down the street and around the office, and she was always being touched—a hand here, a hand there. She felt both powerful and vulnerable at the same time. Seb and Cecilia would go out for drinks often, or to poetry readings at underground bars. She felt like prey the minute he turned his back. Even Seb's friends who knew they were an item would place their hands a little too low when they squeezed past.

One night, his friend Lenny, who Seb thought hung the moon, shoved her against the wall of the bar and stuck his tongue down her throat while Seb was in the bathroom. Cecilia pushed him away and wished she hadn't liked it.

But being wanted in that way was thrilling for her. It made her feel wild for the first time in her life. So she let this kind of thing happen often with Lenny.

Soon they began meeting during her coffee breaks at work. Cecilia loved what he had to say. He told her he could help her get into modeling, and that her looks shouldn't be wasted working at a dead-end office job and sleeping with a doorman. He liked to say there was something about her, something he couldn't quite put his finger on. She told him she loved poetry and hoped she might one day find a job at a publishing house, maybe even get something of her own published. She had never told Seb any of this. Lenny said he had a friend with big connections whom he could introduce her to. He talked to her about leaving Seb and moving in with him.

One week later, Cecilia learned she was pregnant.

As quickly as she found the city, she lost it.

Seb had no savings and he insisted they move into his parents' house in the suburbs until he had more money put away. He was thrilled to start a family. He'd had a happy childhood with memories of big Thanksgiving dinners and camping vacations.

Cecilia was devastated.

When she finally found the courage to tell Seb she wanted an abortion, he told her never to mention it again. He said she could move back home for good and ask her stepfather for the money, if the idea of having a baby with him was that terrible.

Cecilia couldn't stop thinking about her mother hanging from the tree. She felt trapped and she felt foolish. And so she gave in.

74

There was nothing to distinguish the slow stretch of time between when I lost Gemma and what happened next that tugged her back into my life. The year was unremarkable. Violet was going on thirteen, but I wasn't with her much—you had somehow maneuvered things so that she came only once a week. At one point I emailed a lawyer, someone an acquaintance had used in her divorce. We set up a call and I watched my phone ring on the table when the date and time came. I had no fight in me, and besides, it seemed Violet was happier living without me.

So I was surprised when the teacher called me to ask if I would chaperone a field trip to a farm. It was the night before the trip—another mother who did this sort of thing regularly was sick and had to cancel. The thought of Violet treating me with her usual chill in front of her classmates filled me with dread. But I agreed to do it. I knocked on Violet's door to tell her I'd be going. She had no reaction at all. She didn't look up from the beaded bracelet she was stringing with patient fingers. Her hands looked so different from mine.

I sat somewhere in the middle of the bus, beside a father who mostly read emails on his phone while we bumped our way out of the city, listening to the cloud cover of teenage excitement. Violet was several rows behind me on the other side of the bus in the window seat. The girl she sat next to was tall with a burgeoning chest. Her back was turned to Violet as she leaned across the aisle to whisper with a pair of brunettes in matching French braids. Violet's eyes tracked the rolling countryside.

She looked like she wasn't paying attention to the whispers, but I knew she could hear every word: I saw the ball in her throat slowly slide up and then down. I remembered how that felt, to be excluded. I hadn't thought Violet cared about fitting in with the cool crowd at school. She seemed to me far more comfortable on the periphery, and mostly on her own; she wasn't like the other girls her age. She never had been.

When we got to the farm I dropped back behind the group and watched her. She walked in lockstep with the girls from the bus, but they didn't speak much to her. When they stopped at the entrance to the apple orchard, Violet looked around to place me. I gave a small wave from the back of the group. She flipped her ponytail behind her shoulders and inserted herself stiffly into the small group of girls who were talking loudly over the farmer's instructions about how to pick the apples properly so the bud wasn't damaged for next year's crop. The teacher handed out plastic bags.

We had one hour in the orchard before they were going to teach us how to make pies. I wandered away from the other parents, who mostly kept their distance as well, and found the McIntosh trees. Several rows over I saw the red of Violet's jacket weaving between the narrow trunks. She was alone, holding her bag in one hand and reaching with her other arm up into the branches. There was a gracefulness in her movements that surprised me. She felt the skin of the apples, looking for imperfections. When she plucked one, she would smell it and turn it around in her fingers. She looked so mature, the plumpness in her cheeks gone, the line of her jaw more prominent. Despite the budding femininity that was beginning to define her, she moved just like you. I saw it in the way she shifted her weight and how she folded her arms behind her back. But she held her head just like me—tilted, with a tendency to glance upward when she was thinking of her response to something, finding the right word in a vocabulary that seemed to grow even faster than her long legs.

The breeze picked up every so often and distracted her, wisps of her dark hair whipping across her face. She placed the bag at her feet and pulled out a hair elastic, collected her ponytail again, and then ran her hand over the top of her head. She kept her eyes on the ground. I wondered what she was looking at, maybe a bird or a rotting apple. But as I walked closer, I realized she was staring at nothing; she was lost in thought and she looked sad.

Once she sensed my presence, she picked up her bag and walked toward a clump of students who had given up on collecting, eating their apples instead. I watched her sit down and cross her legs and bite into her own.

The teacher whistled with his fingers and started to wrangle the students. I watched Violet follow her class to the barn. As I made my way inside I lost track of her in the crowd of kids and scanned the benches as the students took their seats. I saw the girls from the bus sitting together at one of the tables.

"Has anyone seen Violet?"

One of them looked up at me and shook her head. The others were spelling their names on the table with the curls of apple peel. "You guys are friends with her, right?"

Another girl glanced around the table, looking for permission to speak. "Sure. I guess. I mean, kind of."

Two of them giggled. The one who spoke nudged them to be quiet.

My heart was pounding by then. I looked around the barn but still couldn't see her.

"Mr. Philips, do you know where Violet went?"

"She went to the bus to lie down. She has a headache—she said you were taking her."

I jogged out to the parking lot, but the bus driver wasn't there and the door was locked. The lot attendant said he hadn't seen a student wandering around. I ran to the stables at the back and asked if anyone had seen a brunette girl. I checked the hay piles on the other side of the stables and then saw a roped-off corn maze in the distance.

"Has anyone gone in there? I'm looking for my daughter." I was yelling then. I sounded frantic. I was trying to catch my breath.

A young guy repainting the ENTER HERE! sign shook his head.

That was when I knew she had left. She was punishing me for coming. We had learned to walk wide circles around each other in order to coexist—that was our unspoken agreement. But being on the field trip violated that rule. I ran back to the barn. I found the teacher and told him she was missing, that I thought she'd left somehow. He said he'd check the premises and asked another parent to alert the manager of the farm.

He didn't tell me not to worry—he didn't say, *She must be here somewhere.*

I saw a table of boys looking around, aware that something was wrong. One of them walked over to me and asked what was happening.

"We can't find Violet. Do you know where she might have gone?"

He was quiet. He shook his head and walked back to his friends, and they all looked over at me. I thought they knew something. I went to the table and leaned over the end and took a deep breath so my voice wouldn't crack. "Does anyone know where Violet went?"

They all shook their heads, like the first boy, and one of them politely said, "Sorry, Mrs. Connor, we don't know."

I could see then they had fear in their eyes, too.

The dad I'd sat beside offered to circle the grounds with me again. By then my head was spinning. My legs were numb. I'd felt this way before, when Violet was two and had scampered too far away at an amusement park, only to be found minutes later at the cotton candy cart. That had been minutes. Minutes during which I knew she was probably safe, probably a hairline out of sight.

And then there was Sam. I tried not to think about him. I tried.

"I can't breathe," I said, and the dad sat me down on the pea gravel.

"Put your head between your legs." He rubbed my back. "Does she have a cell phone?"

I shook my head.

"Have you checked your phone?"

I didn't respond. He reached into my purse and found it.

"You've missed six calls."

I grabbed it from him and put in my password. It was Gemma's calls I had missed.

"Violet," I said in a cracking voice when she answered. "She's gone."

"I got a call five minutes ago. From a truck driver." She paused, as though she might not tell me more. "She's at a rest stop on the side of the highway. I'm going to get her." She hung up without saying goodbye. The dad helped me to my feet and we went to find the teacher to call off the search. I sat in the tiny gift shop with a bottle of water and tried calling you again and again, but you didn't answer.

An hour later, we were back on the bus and took the same spots we'd had on the way there. The volume was noticeably lower now, the effect of the fresh air muffling the volcano of energy from before.

Nobody said anything about Violet—it was as though she hadn't ever been there. When we arrived back at the school parking lot, I crouched at my seat and watched the students make their way off the bus. I checked the back to make sure nothing had been left behind and found the bracelet on the seat where the braided girls had been. The purple and yellow and gold beads Violet had been diligently stringing the night before. She must have made it for one of them. It was untied, abandoned. I turned the beads back and forth between my fingers.

"Hey," I called out to the three girls. They sat on the school steps waiting for their parents to pick them up. "Did you drop this?"

Two of them stared at the ground.

"I said, did one of you drop this?"

I held it out in the palm of my hand and they all shook their heads. I closed my hand around the bracelet and stared at the girls until a car pulled up. They looked straight ahead and didn't say a word.

At home I put the bracelet deep in my bottom drawer where I knew Violet wouldn't find it. Everything that had happened that day changed how I saw her. She was powerless among her friends, and she didn't want me to see that. She was no longer the girl who could so easily intimidate others, who could effortlessly hurt people with what she said or did. They could see through her now, and for a moment, I almost felt bad for her.

I called Gemma that night, although I wasn't sure she would answer. I straightened in the kitchen chair when she did.

"I just wanted to check on her. How's she doing?"

"She's been quiet. But fine." I heard her cover the receiver and whisper something. She was silent. I imagined her turning to you and rolling her eyes. *She doesn't get it—she was running away from HER.*

SHE is the problem. I imagined you gesturing for her to hang up. I imagined the bottle of wine you would have opened now that the kids were in bed. I looked around my dim, quiet kitchen. I wanted to remind Gemma that I'd once been the mother she herself had turned to, before she had it all figured out. That she'd searched my face for the secrets of how to mother her own child. I had lied to her. But I was still the same woman she had called her best friend. I couldn't help myself.

"How are you? How's Jet?"

"Good-bye, Blythe."

75

For a long time after the field trip, I didn't see Violet. I filled my time writing, agreeing to see the agent when he asked to come over, although at some point I started to feel even lonelier when he was there.

He would run the shower while I checked the weather. Rainy and cold. Bring an umbrella today, I would say. He would ask about my plans. Writing, calling someone to clean the gutters. Did he have time for breakfast? He did not—a meeting at eight o'clock, remember? Would he want to come over that night? He couldn't—dinner with a new author. He would come tomorrow instead. Would I make that lamb stew? He would step past the partition into the shower where he could have been anyone behind the wet, distorted glass—it was then I would watch him. He would leave the bathroom door open so the steam wouldn't fill the mirror. I didn't like the streaks the towel left when he wiped it before he shaved. I didn't like the speckles of his shavings in my sink. Before he was done, I would leave to boil water for the tea. Downstairs he would kiss me good-bye and I would barely lean into him. I'm not sure he ever noticed.

On a random day in June, Violet called to ask if she could stay with me for the weekend. She hadn't wanted to stay the weekend since the beginning of the school year. I canceled my plans with the agent and told her to tell you she'd be with me. The overnight bag she put in the trunk when I picked her up from school was full of clothes I'd never seen before. I was missing so much of her life. The gold sparkly leggings made me sad—they were something I should have bought her if I'd seen them in a store, but I didn't think to buy her things anymore.

We went to the movies and had ice cream afterward. We didn't speak much but there was something about her that was less agitated. Less bristly. I was cautious. I gave her space. At one point we were in the car and a skit came on the radio, something about a cat in heat. I wasn't sure she knew what that meant, but we looked at each other and laughed and I felt my stomach sink. Not for the moment we shared, but for how foreign it had felt—how much we had missed.

She was the same age I was when I last saw my mother.

I usually said good night standing in her doorway. That evening, I sat on the end of her bed and I put my hand over her feet under the blanket. I squeezed them. I had done this when she was younger, before she stopped letting me touch her. She looked up from her book and met my eyes. She didn't pull her feet away.

"Nana misses you. She said so the other day."

"Oh," I said gently, surprised Violet would tell me this. Your mother and I still hadn't spoken.

"I miss her, too."

"Why don't you call her?"

"I don't know." I sighed. "I think it will make me feel too sad to talk with her. I bet she loves Jet, doesn't she?"

Violet shrugged dismissively. I wondered for a moment if she was envious of the attention he got in your house, but then it occurred to me that maybe she thought I was better off not hearing about your son. Her eyes flickered as they wandered the room, and I wondered if Sam had crossed both of our minds then. I wanted desperately to mention him, to put him there in the bedroom with us. I looked back down at the shape of her feet under my hand. I felt strangely calm.

"Is there anything you want to talk about? Anything at school, or . . . anything else?" I didn't want to leave her room. I didn't want to take my hand off her.

She shook her head. "No, I'm good. Night, Mom." She opened the book to the page she'd held with her finger and settled her back into her pillow. "Thanks for the movie."

I fell asleep that night on the couch, still in my clothes, thinking about how nice it was to be around her. I wondered if things were changing.

I woke up to light footsteps on the wooden floor above. It had been six years since Sam died, but my instinct to wake in the middle of the night at the slightest noise was still just as strong as when he was born.

Violet was walking on her toes, moving from her room to mine.

The door opened. Was she looking for me? I wondered if she would call for me. Her steps became even quieter. She was near my dresser now. I heard the hanging brass handle touch the wood. And then again when it closed. She'd been brief. Efficient. I wondered which drawer, what she was looking for. The bracelet I'd found tossed aside on the bus months ago was in there. Of course. I should have thrown it away— I never would have imagined she'd find it. I couldn't remember the last time she'd gone into my room. I heard her steps carry her back to bed. I waited, giving her time to fall back asleep, and then I went upstairs quietly. I put on my nightshirt and checked the drawer—the bracelet was still there. She hadn't taken it if she had seen it.

*S*he *was pleasant* over breakfast. Not friendly, not chatty, just pleasant. I dropped her off at your house and watched from my car as she ran up the driveway and flew through the door. I could see Gemma through the living-room window, rushing to greet her, to welcome her home.

That was when the idea first came to me. To drive back later, after the sun had set. To watch you all at night.

77

After you and I met, I stopped going to my father for the things I needed the most. Comfort, advice. He became less useful to me. This must have become apparent to him in the way I glossed over the details of my life when he called, changing the conversation back to him. I didn't let him in anymore. I'm ashamed of this—I knew I was the only thing he had.

On the day he dropped me off at my college dorm, he kissed me good-bye on the head and walked away quietly. When I looked out the window hours later, he was still there, leaning against a tree, looking up at my building. I closed the curtain before he saw me looking out. I think often about that—the way he stood there.

The month of graduation, it occurred to me one morning that he hadn't called at all since I'd been home for the holidays. I planned to phone him that weekend and then never did, although I told you I had, and that he was eager to see me. Instead I showed up at his house unannounced the evening after my exams. I told him I had to drop some things off from my dorm room. We exchanged a few cordial words and then he went to bed early. I decided to stay one more night. The following evening, I cooked us a chicken the way I knew he liked it. I waited for him to come home from work, but the hours rolled on. When he came in just after ten o'clock, he smelled like booze and sat at the kitchen table, looking at the cold plate of food while I leaned on the counter. I think we both thought of my mother then. I poured us each a drink of whiskey and sat down. I hadn't planned on asking him, but I did:

"Why did she leave me?"

H*e was gone* before I woke up in the morning. My head pounded from the bottle we'd finished together. I drove back to campus and packed the last of my things. You and I were moving in together the next day. It became hard for me to think about my father after that night. I was desperate to leave my past behind. He was too much a part of my mother and me, although he had never been the problem.

When the police called to tell me that he'd been found dead in his home, that they suspected he'd died in his sleep from a heart attack, I handed you the receiver and lay on our warm parquet flooring in a beam of morning sun. We'd been living in our apartment for four months by then.

"I'm glad you went to visit him," you said, crouching down to touch my hair.

I turned away from you on the floor. I could only think of the last thing my father said that night, staring at the bottom of his glass. We'd been talking and drinking for hours.

I would look at you and say to Cecilia, "Aren't we lucky." But she couldn't see—

He'd caught himself midsentence and left the table without saying anything else. He'd been telling me about the days after I was born. I'd hung on his every word.

Now I realized my mother and I had broken his heart.

. . .

I *went home to organize* the funeral and approached the house cautiously. Mrs. Ellington had a spare key and had cleaned up before I got there. I knew right away because the house smelled of lemons and she always cleaned with lemon oil. His bedding was different. I recognized the clean sheets from the spare bed in the Ellingtons' house.

Mrs. Ellington came by in the afternoon to keep me company. Daniel and Thomas helped me clear out the house the day before the funeral and I gave it all away—I wanted it empty. I wanted everything gone.

I *listed the house* I grew up in the following season for a price below market value. I felt nothing to see it go. Mrs. Ellington came over the day I signed the papers.

"He was very proud of you. You made him very happy."

I touched her hand. She was kind to lie to me.

78

Three days after the pleasant visit with Violet, Gemma called. I could tell by the pitch of her voice that she was upset.

She'd found Jet in the laundry room that morning playing with a sharp blade. He'd been just about to cut through the jeans he was wearing when she walked in.

"Is it yours?"

"What do you mean?" I had been walking home from the pool. I'd gone to see Sam's tiles. I hadn't yet processed what she'd said—I was still surprised to have seen her name on my phone.

"Did the blade come from your house?"

I thought of the one I'd taken from Fox's tin four years ago, tucked at the back of my dresser drawer, wrapped in a scarf. I hadn't touched it since. Violet. I wondered if that's why she had gone into my room. If she'd somehow known it was there.

"I can't think of where else it would have come from. Fox doesn't keep them here. Violet said you still have his old modeling tools in the basement, lying around in the open. Near where her laundry was."

"That's absurd," I said, starting to feel warm. I imagined her giving the blade to Jet while Gemma was downstairs and then walking away to wait for his scream. My face grew hotter.

"You should know better, Blythe. One of them could have been hurt."

She huffed and hung up. She'd become mean. She used to just pity me. Now, she didn't like me.

I swore under my breath and hustled home. I pulled off my boots and ran upstairs to my room and opened the drawer. The scarf was there but the blade was gone.

I stopped sleeping for weeks after that. When I did, I dreamed of Sam. His fingers were sliced one by one as he wriggled in my arms, screaming. I don't know who was doing the cutting. Violet, I suppose. And then I could feel the ends of his fingers rolling around my tongue as I sucked and chewed them. Like a mouthful of jelly beans. I spit in the sink when I woke up, expecting I would see blood. That's how real it felt to me.

Violet came over the following month. We were quieter this time, less pleasant to each other. The coldness was back. She knew Gemma had called me. I knew she'd taken the blade, but I didn't know if I should confront her about it. I didn't know what to do. I was exhausted from not sleeping and it was easier not to think about it.

I decided to let it go, until one day she asked me a question. I was bleaching the bathroom mat in the laundry tub downstairs. She pointed to the poison symbol on the bottle of bleach and opened her mouth for a moment before she let the words out: "That means someone could die if they drank even a bit of it, right?" She paused again. "Why do you have something so dangerous down here?"

"Why are you asking?"

She shrugged. She wasn't looking for an answer—she left the laundry room and I heard her phone you to pick her up early. The anxiety crawled up my spine, that familiar, crippling panic that nearly closed my throat. I had been there before. I had barely survived it.

I put the bottle back in the cupboard where I kept the other cleaning supplies. I scanned the shelf. I made a mental note of what was there.

I called Gemma again and again that afternoon as my chest pounded. She answered in the evening.

I told her what Violet had said about the poison. I told her about the blade missing from my drawer.

I told her I was only looking out for her and her family. That I was worried about Jet. That we had to think about Violet differently. That I was afraid something was going to happen again—that I had an instinct. I put my head on the table while I waited for her to speak. I was so tired of thinking about Violet. I didn't want her to be my problem anymore. My fear.

Gemma was quiet. And then she spoke calmly:

"She didn't push Sam, Blythe. I know you believe she did. But you've made it up. You saw something happen that never did. She didn't do it."

She hung up the phone. I heard the keys in the door—he was coming to stay the night. I called him into the kitchen and I took my clothes off. We fucked on the table while he lifted up my limp, hanging breasts that had been sucked to their death, like he was imagining where they once had been.

80

I'd thought about going back to the corner for years. The idea would come to me as effortlessly as the thought to go see a movie on an empty Sunday afternoon. *Well, there's always that. I could do that today.* And then I'd talk myself into cleaning the bathroom or organizing the kitchen cupboards instead.

The day I'm speaking of, though, was different. I'd grown sleepless again and milled about the house without purpose, unable to do much more than stare at things: the saltshaker that needed refilling, the time on the stove that was still an hour ahead, the pile of junk mail that sat inches away from the recycling bin. I heard Gemma's voice over and over for months, a muffled echo, like someone had wrapped my head in aluminum foil. She had spoken to me as though she knew something I didn't. As though she had been there the day he died. *How do you know what happened?* I wanted to scream into the phone. *How could you possibly know?*

But I have to admit, I began to doubt myself more as time passed. The conviction I'd carried for years was losing its weight somehow. I was having a harder time seeing that day clearly in my mind. Sometimes I woke up in the morning and it was the first thing I did—search my memory for the replay. Had it faded? Was it further away than it was the day before?

I could have walked—we didn't live that far away. But driving made it feel as far away as I needed it to be. I circled the neighborhood a few times and then parked my car one block from where it happened. I closed my eyes and leaned back into the headrest. I stayed there for a while.

And then I walked. I looked up from under my hood and saw the sign for Joe's coffee shop. The letters were a glossy new black where they'd once been faded and chipped. I put my hand on my chest to see if I could feel my heartbeat through my coat. Each pump of blood felt like a weep.

I turned around and faced the intersection.

Everything about it looked different than it had in my memory. And yet how different could one intersection look from another? The gray cracked and faded asphalt with soft tar lines like veins, yellow iridescent paint marking the crosswalk people might not use. The stoplights rocked in the wind and the walk signal chimed as the traffic rumbled up from behind me.

I scanned the pavement, looking for a mark. Blood. Debris. And then remembered that time was real, that 2,442 long, empty days had passed. I waited for a break in traffic. I walked onto the road and crouched in the spot where he had died—just left of center in the right-hand lane, a few yards ahead of the crosswalk. I ran my hand over the asphalt and then pressed it against my cold cheek.

I looked over at the curb and imagined the stroller rolling off. The grooved dip at the edge that I had remembered so clearly was not there. The edge of the cement was smooth and tipped to the street; I could see the elevation from where I crouched, and it wasn't as slight as I'd remembered. I walked over to the sidewalk and took a cylinder of lip balm from my pocket. I put it on its side and I watched it roll from the tip of my boot, slowly at first but then with more speed, until it came to a rest in the middle of the road. The light turned green and the tube bounced away under the bellies of passing cars. A middle-aged man in a suit slowed down to eye me as he walked by. I looked away and stood up.

My mind replayed the scene again. Coming out of the coffee shop. Standing on the sidewalk. Holding the tea in my left hand. The handle of the stroller in my right hand. Touching his head for the last time. The feeling of the hot steam rising up to my face. Violet beside me. The yank on my arm. The scorch on my skin. Violet's pink mittens on the black handle. The back of Sam's head moving farther away. How fast did he go? Did it have momentum? Could it have rolled so far without a push? Had she touched that handle?

I watched the scene play out in every possible way, over and over, right there in front of me. It could have. It could have happened.

Someone bumped my elbow passing by, and then someone else, and I suddenly found myself standing there in a stream of people, their hands clutching take-out containers and coffees. I felt invisible among these human beings who had real lives and jobs and went places that mattered and were expected to arrive by other people who needed them. *Fuck you all*, I thought and wanted to scream at them. *My son is dead! He died right here! You walk by here every day like it's nothing!* I was angry and exhausted. I turned around and stared at the coffee shop.

It was the last place I had looked into Sam's eyes while he was alive. Everything about it was different now. Through the window I saw the wood floors had been replaced with white herringbone ceramic tiles and the walls were framed with panels of chalkboard paint where plaid wallpaper had once been. I tried to remember what the tables had been like before the tall stainless-steel ones. It was quiet for lunchtime—it used to be such a busy place.

I walked inside and noticed that the door chime Violet and Sam had loved was gone. Joe was still there, his back turned to me as he fiddled with an espresso machine.

I took a deep breath. "Joe," I said, and he looked up slowly. His shoulders fell. He came around the counter and held his hands out for mine. He squeezed them.

"I always hoped you'd come back in."

"Things look different," I said, looking around.

Joe rolled his eyes. "My son. He's taking over the place—my back is bad and there's too much standing around here." He smiled at me. "How are you?"

I looked out the window to the intersection.

"What do you remember about it?" I swallowed. I hadn't planned to go in there, I hadn't planned on talking to him.

"Oh, sweetheart," he said and put his hands on mine again. He looked out the window with me. "I just remember how distraught you were. You were in shock. Your daughter clung to your waist and wanted to be held, but you couldn't bend down. You couldn't move."

Violet had never done that before—she had never clung to me, never turned to me for comfort in the way other children did with their mothers. Gripping, wanting.

We sat together at a table overlooking the window and watched the traffic lights change and the cars go by. The sky was white.

"Did you see it happen?"

He winced, but didn't look away from the street. He was thinking about what to say to me. I turned away and then saw him shake his head in my periphery.

"Did you see how the stroller got there?" I tried again and closed my eyes.

"Just one of those terrible, freak accidents."

I opened my eyes and looked down at his hands folded on the table. He squeezed them together, like he was getting through a shot of pain.

"I've thought about you a lot over the years, how you could possibly move on after that." His eyes became glassy. "I've always thanked God you had that little girl to live for."

When I got home, the door slammed shut behind me in the gusty November wind and nearly caught my fingers. I sank to the floor and threw my keys against the wall. I thought of Sam, of how his face was just starting to change from the generic pudge of a baby to who he would one day be, of the smell of my sweet milk that was always in the crevice of his neck, of the last tug of my nipple in his mouth when he was finished. Of the way he searched for my face in the dark while he nursed.

I closed my eyes and tried to feel the weight of his body on my lap. I could get there; I could be there. The morning television show playing in the background, the steam of the kettle from the kitchen. The faint sound of Violet's bare feet upstairs. The running water in the bathroom sink while you shaved for work. The feel of my unwashed hair. The ascending cry from the other room. That life, banal and stifling. But comforting. It was everything. I'd let it all go.

Maybe I'd let him go, too.

81

There had been half a bottle of wine consumed that night, yes. But I'd been thinking about calling you for days. I curled up on the couch while he slept upstairs. On your side of the bed. I wished he hadn't stayed the night. It was nearly midnight.

I had talked myself through different versions of what I could say to you, but nothing felt right. I didn't want to apologize for the mother I'd been to her—I wasn't sorry. I didn't want to say I was wrong—I didn't know if I was. I just wanted you to know that something inside of me had changed. And I wanted to see our daughter more.

Gemma answered your phone the third time I called. "Is everything okay?"

Maybe it is, I wanted to reply. Maybe it finally is.

But instead I asked to speak to you. You were beside her in bed, I could hear the sheets move as you rolled over to take the phone.

"I need to see her more. I want to do better."

I asked you about the painting, the one you took from our bedroom when you moved out. I hadn't planned to ask you about this, I hadn't even thought about it that night. But suddenly I wanted it desperately. I stood up and paced the room while you let me sit on the line in silence. I imagined it hanging on a stark white wall in the hallway of your beautiful new home, Gemma touching the gold frame gently while she walked by, thinking of her own small child and the way he touched her face.

"I don't know where it is."

82

I picked Violet up from school the next week. She was sitting alone on the cold steps, a boulder in the waterfall of children bounding down around her.

"We can do anything you want this afternoon," I'd said as she buckled up. "You pick. But we're going with a new schedule. Every Wednesday and Thursday night with me."

I watched her text furiously from the corner of my eye.

"I want to go home," she said eventually, looking out the window.

"We will, but let's do something fun first. What are you in the mood for?"

"No, I mean home. To Gemma. And Dad."

"Well, you're my daughter. And I'm your mother. So we're going to try to act like it."

I pulled into the parking lot of a gas station and stopped the car. I didn't know where to take her. She was turned toward the passenger door, texting, and I realized I hadn't known she'd been given her own phone.

"Who are you texting?"

"Mom and Dad."

I didn't give her a reaction—I knew she was looking for one.

Instead I filled the car with gas and drove us out to the highway.

Two hours later we stopped for takeout at the first drive-through off the exit ramp. I didn't know she was vegetarian now—she would only eat the fries. She never asked where we were going, not for the whole two hours. Instead she leaned her arm against the window and slowly pulled strands of her hair through her fingers, flattening them out and running her hand along the silky ribbon like the bow of a violin. This was something I, too, had done as a girl.

My heart felt soft when I pulled into the lot and took a ticket from the machine. I hadn't been there in a very long time. I got out of the car and waited in the cold for her to join me, but she didn't move. I opened her door and put my hand on her shoulder.

"There's someone I want you to meet."

She didn't say anything as we checked in at the front desk. I handed over my ID and clipped the visitor passes to each of our coats. She followed me quietly to the elevator and down the hall of the fourth floor. The smell was stale and aseptic but for the waft of urine every now and then. It crushed me to breathe in that air. I knocked softly on the door of her room.

"Come in."

She sat in an orange slip-covered chair with her legs crossed, an empty crossword on her lap. The lights in the room were off and the pen in her hand had the cap on. A loosely knitted blanket hung around her shoulders. She opened her mouth to speak but then just sighed. She'd forgotten what she wanted to say. And then:

"You're here! I've been waiting for you!"

Violet watched as I hugged her gently. I turned on the lamp behind her and she glanced up at the bulb, surprised by the light. I gestured for Violet to sit at the end of the bed.

"I'm so happy to see you." She reached her hand to me and I ran my thumb over her skin, as thin as rice paper. Her veins moved under my lips as I gave her hand a kiss. She smelled like petroleum jelly.

"You look so beautiful today." She spoke so earnestly that I suddenly really did feel beautiful. I thanked her. Her lips were dry and I reached for the cup of water on her bedside table and offered it to her. "No, thank you, dear. You have some. You're always so thirsty. Even as a little girl, you were."

Violet looked at me and I could see by her twisting mouth that she was upset. She was feeling uncomfortable, in this strange building with this strange stench and this woman she had never met before. She shifted on the bed and looked to the door.

"I want to introduce you to someone. This is Violet, my daughter." Violet looked quickly at the stranger in the chair and mumbled a hello.

"Oh. She's lovely, isn't she?"

"She certainly is."

"Do you know how I got here?" she asked me. Her face was worried.

I took her hand again. "You were driven here in a car. You lived not too far away from here, in a house on Downington Crescent. Do you remember?"

"I don't remember."

A nurse came in with a covered tray and put it on the small rolling table. "Dinnertime!"

"Leda, I want you to meet my daughter." She tugged at my hands and beamed at the nurse. "Isn't she beautiful?"

Violet looked at me for the first time. She stood up and walked toward the door, her hands on her elbows. Her chin lowered, and I wondered if she might cry. The nurse smiled at me and then turned down the bed, fluffing the thin pillow. She dropped two capsules in a foam cup on the bedside table and then lifted the cover on the dinner tray. The room filled with the awful smell of hot, canned vegetables. Violet turned away from us.

"Oh. I've got to eat and get ready for bed now." She slowly stood up from her chair and tried to fold the blanket that had been on her shoulders. She went into the bathroom and shut the door. I arranged her dinner setting for her and put her crossword book on the dresser. Violet eyed me quietly until the toilet flushed and then we watched her settle herself back in the chair.

"We'll get going, then." I leaned down to kiss her cheek. "I'll come visit you for the holidays. Have you seen Daniel or Thomas? Have they come by lately?"

"Who are they?"

"Your sons." I'd lost touch with them long ago.

"I don't have any sons. I only have you."

I kissed her again as she stared at the knife and fork, wondering what to do with them. I put the fork in her hand and helped her stab a green bean. She nodded and then brought the bean to her lips.

We got in the car and I let it run for a minute. I waited for Violet to take out her phone and start texting. She didn't. Instead she looked straight ahead while we found our way back to the highway under the dark sky. I wondered if she'd fallen asleep. Halfway home she finally spoke to me.

"Who was that woman? She wasn't your mother. She was Black." Her tone was biting. Like I had been trying to fool her. Like I had wanted to make her feel stupid somehow.

"She was the closest thing I had."

"Why don't you find your real mother?"

I paused, thinking about how to answer her truthfully.

"Because I'm scared to know who she became."

I looked away from the road to her shadowed profile. Sadness squeezed my throat. For nearly fourteen years I'd wanted to find something between us that wasn't there. She had come from me. I had made her. This beautiful thing beside me, I had made her, and there was a time I had wanted her, a time I thought she would be my world. She looked like a woman now. There was feminine wisdom growing in her eyes and she was about to thrive without me. She was about to choose a life that did not include me. I would be left behind.

1975

Cecilia knew early on she wasn't meant to be a mother. She could feel it in her bones as womanhood set in. When she would see a child with his hand in his mother's, dragging his feet along the ground, she'd look the other way. This was a physical reaction for her, like wincing when the water was too hot from the faucet. As far as she was concerned, she didn't have that thing other women did—she didn't feel nurturing or see the joy of a chubby little thigh. And she certainly didn't want to see herself reflected in another living thing.

Her period had come every month since she was twelve, like a faithful friend reminding her: You bleed. You shed. You don't need a baby inside you. Don't listen when the world tells you that you do.

She had dreams and freedom. But then she gave it all up.

When the baby moved inside her, sometimes Cecilia wondered if her feelings were changing. Once she stood naked in the mirror and watched the lump of the baby's foot move across the top of her stomach, tracing the arc of a crescent moon. She laughed out loud and the baby moved some more. She laughed some more. They were having a moment of fun, the two of them.

They sedated her for the labor. The baby didn't want to come out, so they cut Cecilia three ways and used forceps that made the baby's head look like a triangle. When Cecilia came to, the baby was already wrapped in flannel somewhere in the patch of newborns.

"You had a girl," the nurse said to her, like it was exactly the thing Cecilia wanted to hear.

Seb wheeled her to the window and knocked on the glass to get the nurse's attention.

"She's that one." Cecilia pointed right to the baby, three rows in, four to the left.

"How do you know?"

"I just know."

The nurse picked up the baby and held her high for them to see. She was wide-eyed and still. Cecilia thought she looked just like her old doll, Beth-Anne.

The nurse asked through the glass if she wanted to feed her. Cecilia looked up at Seb and asked if they could go outside instead. He took her out through the front doors of the hospital in her slippers and nightgown, the IV pole rattling on the cement. He gave Cecilia her cigarettes and she stared at the parking lot while she smoked.

"We could get in the car now and go. Just us." Cecilia put out the cigarette on her knee.

Seb grinned. "Those painkillers must really be working." He turned her around to go back inside. "Come on. We have to pick a name."

They took the baby home and put her in a bassinet on the kitchen table of his parents' house. Cecilia's milk never came in. The baby grew fat quickly on formula, and Cecilia thought she looked like Etta. She hardly cried at all, even at night like other babies did. Seb said to Cecilia nearly every day, "Aren't we lucky."

83

Her brush was tangled in my long, wet hair. My mother sat on the toilet and pulled strand after strand from the bristles. I told her again she could cut it out—I was eleven years old and I wasn't concerned yet about how I looked. But she insisted I wouldn't like my hair cut short. I wondered why she cared so much about this, but not much else. I was quiet while she yanked at my head. The radio played in the background and the static cut in every few seconds. I stared at the faded rainbows on my nightgown.

"Your grandmother had short hair."

"Do you look like her?"

"Not really. We were similar in some ways, but not in our looks."

"Will I be like you when I grow up?"

She stopped pulling at my hair for a moment. I reached up to feel the tangled brush, but she pushed my hand away.

"I don't know. I hope not."

"I want to be a mom, too, one day." My mother stopped again and was quiet. She put her hand on my shoulder and held it there. I arched my back—the gentleness of her touch felt strange.

"You know, you don't have to be. You don't have to be a mother."

"Do you wish you weren't a mother?"

"Sometimes I wish I were a different kind of person."

"Who do you wish you were?"

"Oh, I don't know." She started pulling at the knot again. Static filled the radio, but she let it hiss. "When I was young I dreamed of being a poet."

"Why aren't you?"

"I wasn't any good." And then she added, "I haven't written a word since I had you."

That didn't make any sense to me—that my existence in the world could have taken poetry away from her. "You could try again."

She chuckled. "No. It's all gone from me now."

She paused, my hair still in her hand. I leaned back into her knees. "You know, there's a lot about ourselves that we can't change—it's just the way we're born. But some parts of us are shaped by what we see. And how we're treated by other people. How we're made to feel." She finally pulled the brush free and whisked it against a fistful of my hair until it was smooth. I cringed while she finished. She handed me the brush over my shoulder and I uncrossed my bony legs to stand.

"Blythe?"

"Yes?" I turned around in the doorway.

"I don't want you learning to be like me. But I don't know how to teach you to be anyone different."

She left us the next day.

84

The morning after we visited Mrs. Ellington, I heard Violet call Gemma from the bathroom while she ran the shower to muffle her words. I didn't linger outside to eavesdrop—I went to the kitchen and made her breakfast. I sat across from her with a cup of coffee and watched her eat.

"What?" She lifted her spoon up, annoyed, dripping milk on the table. She hadn't spoken to me since we were in the car. I noticed a thin bra strap on her shoulder peek out from the neck of her sweater.

"I'm glad you have Gemma in your life. I brought you to meet Mrs. Ellington so you could see that I understand. I want you to feel loved by someone you trust. Someone you can turn to. And that person doesn't have to be me, if you don't want it to be."

She dropped the spoon in her cereal bowl and then shoved her chair out from the table, spilling my coffee. I caught her just as the front door was closing.

"Wait. You forgot your coat. I'll drive you," I said, trying to turn her around. I hadn't expected her to react like this—I thought I'd extended an olive branch, a mutual understanding: I was not who she wanted and I had conceded.

"Of course you're happy to hand me over to Gemma. You wish you never had me, don't you?"

"You know that's not true."

"You're a liar. You hate me." She tried to pull her arm from me, but my grip was strong. I thought of Sam. Of his crushed body in the stroller. I could feel the pain of that day, and every day of missing him since. I could feel the years of crippling blame and terror and doubt. And then I could feel my mother. I yanked her closer, twisting her arm harder than I should have. Adrenaline shot up my legs and I jerked her hard again, pulling her closer to my face. I'd never experienced the physical rush of hurting her like this before. I promise you.

I realized then how satisfied she looked. The corner of her lips turned up slowly as she winced. *Go ahead. Keep hurting me. Leave a mark.* I let go of her. And then she ran.

She wasn't there on the steps when I went to get her after school. I idled the car and went into the office to see where she was. They told me she'd gone home sick. That you had picked her up.

I texted you. *I thought we had an agreement on the schedule.*

You replied. *I don't think it's going to work.*

That night there was a soft knock on the front door, so soft that I almost didn't get out of bed to answer it. I slipped on my robe and walked carefully down the stairs in the dark. I opened the door. Nobody was there. But there was a large bubble-wrapped package with a note taped to it. I opened it on the cold floor. The painting. Sam's painting. The note was from Gemma.

You deserve to have this. It's been hanging in Violet's room since Fox gave it to her, but she took it down this

afternoon. The frame is cracked. And she punctured the
canvas. I'm sorry for that.

I didn't know how much it meant to you.

Please, give her space.

I hope you understand.

Merry Christmas.

Gemma

You hadn't yet made it back to your car. I would recognize the shape of you anywhere, the round of your shoulders, the slight lift in your elbows while you walked. I didn't think before I called your name. You didn't think before you turned around. And so there we were, staring at each other. Strangers, family. I waited for you to turn away toward your car. But instead you came back. To the porch you rebuilt, to the home you had loved. The home we still shared on paper. You looked up to where the trim around the door had spliced, a shard of wood jutting out like a blade.

"You should get that fixed."

"Thank you. For bringing this back." I gestured behind me to the painting, half unwrapped in the entryway.

"Thank Gemma."

I nodded.

"You can't call my wife anymore. You have to move on with your life. You know this, right? For the good of everyone."

I knew. But I didn't want to hear it from you.

You turned away from me, and I thought you might leave then. I stared at the side of your face, trying to decide what I felt for you now. It had been so long since we'd been near each other. You didn't feel real to me, you felt like a character in a life that had never been mine. I wanted to reach for your chin, to touch you, to see how you felt between my fingers now that you loved someone else, now that you were a father to a child who was not ours.

"What?" you asked, feeling my eyes on you.

I shook my head. We shook our heads at each other. And then you closed your eyes and you started to chuckle.

"You know what, I thought of something on the way over here." You took a seat on the top stair and spoke toward the road. I sat next to you and wrapped my housecoat tight. "There was this thing I never told you about." You chuckled again and let your shoulders fall. I had no idea what you would say.

"Do you remember that time, just after Sam was born, when all of your nice clothes from the closet disappeared? And we couldn't find them anywhere?"

"It was that cleaning service you hired, that stupid discount place." I scoffed. I remembered. I thought I was going crazy; all of my nice blouses and sweaters had disappeared at some point. I had lived in my oversized sweats for months after his birth, so I couldn't say for sure when it had happened, but their disappearance was the strangest thing. We had done a trial with a new cleaning company in the neighborhood and it was the only possible explanation I could think of. I was too tired and preoccupied to care much at the time. You told me not to worry, that we'd replace everything.

You hung your head and began to laugh. "Well, one day"—you squeezed the bridge of your nose between your fingers and your shoulders shook—"one day I went in your closet to get a sweater you asked for, and—" You couldn't finish. You were in tears. I hadn't seen anyone laugh so hard in years.

"What? This is annoying, just tell me!"

"I opened your closet door and everything was . . . it was all cut up." You could barely spit the words out. The tears spilled down your face. You shook your head and wheezed. "The arms, they had all been snipped and the shirts were cropped. I touched one thing after another and thought, *What the hell?*" You wiped your face with the back of your hand. "And then I looked down, and there Violet was, hiding under the bottoms of your dresses, holding out one of those modeling knives from my desk. She'd done it. She'd just gone to town like Edward fucking Scissorhands. So I threw the clothes out and never told you."

My jaw fell. My clothes. She'd massacred my wardrobe. While I sat downstairs on the couch feeding the baby, she'd been up there slicing every nice thing I owned. And you covered up for her.

"That is fucked up." It was all I could think to say. You looked at me and laughed again, delirious. You were infuriating. I shook my head and called you an idiot under my breath. You shouldn't have found it funny.

But then I cracked a smile. I couldn't help myself. I started to laugh, too. It was absurd. You still had that pull on me, that way of making me want to be like you. We howled like a pair of old dogs in the night. At the thought of such a strange thing to do, at the ridiculousness of hiding it from me. At the idea that after everything, we could be there, that night, on the cold porch, together.

"You should have told me." I wiped my nose on my housecoat and let the laughter settle.

"I know." You were calm by then and something changed in your face. You looked me in the eye for the first time in years. We sat there together in the heaviness of everything we would not say. I had to look away. I closed my heavy lids and thought of our son. Our beautiful son. I thought of Elijah, the boy from the playground. I thought of the children she bullied. Of the nights she stared at Sam in the dark while he slept. Of her detachment. Of the blades. Of the mother lion she threw out the window on the way home from the zoo. Of my mother's secrets and her shame. Of my expectations. Of my deadening fears. Of things that were normal, of the things I read into. What I had seen. What I had not seen. What you knew.

You cleared your throat and stood up.

"She wasn't always easy. But she deserved more from you." You looked down the street toward your car and zipped up your jacket. With your hands in your pockets, you took one step down the stairs, away from me. "And you deserved more from me."

W*hen I went* into the house there was a message on my voice mail. It was an older woman, she didn't say who she was. There was a rattle to her voice and a hollow sound in the background. She'd called to let me know my mother had died that day. She didn't say where, or how. She paused and muffled the receiver, interrupted, maybe, by someone. And then she left her phone number. The last two numbers were cut off by the tone—she had taken too long to speak.

85

As she stands in the window of your home on Christmas Eve, reaching for the curtain, I get out of my car, these pages in my hands. I stand in the middle of the road in the falling snow lit from the yellow streetlight and I watch her.

I want her to know I am sorry.

Violet drops her arms to her sides. And then she lifts her chin and our eyes find each other. I think I see softness fall in her cheeks. I think she might put her hand to the window, like she needs me. Her mother. I wonder, for a fleeting moment, if we'll be okay.

She mouths something, but I can't make it out. I walk closer to the window and shrug my shoulders, shake my head—*Say it again?* I ask her. *Say it again?* She mouths the words slowly this time. And then she lunges forward. Her hands push against the window, like she wants to break through the glass, and she holds them there. I can see her chest rising and falling.

I pushed him.

I pushed him.

These are the words I think I can hear.

"Say it again!" This time I shout. I'm desperate. But she does not say it again. She notices these pages I carry in my arms. I look down at them, too. We look back at each other, and I can't find that softness in her face anymore.

Your shadow appears at the back of the room and she walks away from the window, away from me. She is yours. The lights in your house go out.

A year and a half later

Many seasons have passed since she's noticed how nice the warm wafts of early June air feel in her lungs. She stops outside her house and breathes again, deep into her soft belly, the way she practices at the end of every session with her therapist. She puffs out the air, counting one, two, three, and then fishes for her keys.

Saturday afternoons are much like any other day of the week. She plucks the green heads off a quart of strawberries that she cuts into halves and eats for lunch, slowly, at her kitchen table. Soon she will bring a small glass of water upstairs into the room that had once been her son's. She will cross her legs and then lower herself to the meditation cushion placed squarely in front of the window. She will stretch her back and then she will sit there in the afternoon light for the next forty-five minutes, and she will think of nothing. Not him. Not her. Not the mistakes she has made as a mother. Not the guilt she carries for the damage she has done. Not her unbearable loneliness.

No, she will not think about any of that. She has worked too hard to let it go.

I am capable of moving beyond my mistakes.
I am able to heal from the hurt and pain I have caused.

She will say these affirmations aloud and she will put her hands to her chest, and then she will flick her hands, she will release it all.

When it is time for dinner, she closes her laptop and she chops herself a salad. She allows herself to put on some music, just three songs—some of her joys are still measured. But tonight she'll move her shoulders ever so slightly, she will tap her foot. She is trying, and trying has become easier.

After dinner, as she does every night, she turns on the light at the front of the house. She does this in case her daughter decides it is finally time to see her.

Upstairs, she hums a verse she had listened to in the kitchen. She undresses. The bath fills with hot water and the mirror steams. She is leaning over the counter, wiping the glass, wanting to examine her bare face, to pat the loose skin under her eyes, when the phone rings.

She is startled and clutches a towel to her breasts like there is an intruder in the next room. The phone glows from the end of her bed. *My daughter*, she thinks. *It could be my daughter*, and she floats in that hope for a moment.

She slides her finger on the screen and lifts it to her ear.

The woman is hysterical. The woman is desperately searching for words it seems she will never find. She walks to the other end of her bedroom and then to the corner, as though she's looking for better reception, as though this will help the woman to speak. She hushes into the phone and as she does this, she realizes who it is she is soothing. She closes her eyes. It is Gemma.

"Blythe," she finally whispers. "Something happened to Jet."

Acknowledgments

To Madeleine Milburn, thank you for being an exceptional agent and human being, and for your passion, vision, warmth, and thoughtfulness. You are a life changer.

To the very special team at the Madeleine Milburn Literary, TV & Film Agency, especially Anna Hogarty, Georgia McVeigh, Giles Milburn, Sophie Pélissier, Georgina Simmonds, Liane-Louise Smith, Hayley Steed, and Rachel Yeoh, thank you for all that you do.

To Pamela Dorman, thank you for believing in this novel and in me. Learning from you has been an honor and a pleasure, and I feel incredibly fortunate to be one of your authors. Thank you to Brian Tart and the team at Viking Penguin, whose hands I'm so lucky to have this novel in: Bel Banta, Jane Cavolina, Tricia Conley, Andy Dudley, Tess Espinoza, Matt Giarratano, Rebecca Marsh, Randee Marullo, Nick Michal, Marie Michels, Lauren Monaco, Jeramie Orton, Lindsay Prevette, Jason Ramirez, Andrea Schulz, Roseanne Serra, Kate Stark, Mary Stone, and Claire Vaccaro.

To Maxine Hitchcock, fellow Oscar-mum, thank you for your certitude, for your thoughtful hand in making this novel better, and for being such a delight in this process. Thank you to Louise Moore and the wonderful group at Michael Joseph for your support from the beginning: Clare Bowren, Claire Bush, Zana Chaka, Anna Curvis,

Christina Ellicott, Rebecca Hilsdon, Rebecca Jones, Nick Lowndes, Laura Nicol, Clare Parker, Vicky Photiou, Elizabeth Smith, and Lauren Wakefield.

To Nicole Winstanley, thank you for the pivotal guidance you've given me, as a publisher and as a mother, and for your generous confidence in me along the way. Your belief in this book means the world to me. To Kristin Cochrane and the fantastic team at Penguin Canada and Penguin Random House Canada, thank you for championing this book so strongly and for making this former publicist's dreams come true, especially: Beth Cockeram, Anthony de Ridder, Dan French, Charidy Johnston, Bonnie Maitland, Meredith Pal, and David Ross.

To Beth Lockley, whose brilliance is matchless and whose friendship I have cherished dearly for over a decade, thank you for encouraging this book since it was a seed of an idea, and for the kind of genuine support I wish every woman could have in her life.

To the international publishers who came on board with such keenness, thank you.

To Linda Preussen, thank you for helping me learn how to write a better story, and to Amy Jones, thank you for the meaningful vote of confidence.

To Dr. Kristine Laderoute, thank you for so willingly lending your psychological expertise.

To Ashley Bennion, the treasured other half of our writing group of two, thank you for reading countless drafts, for the hundreds of email exchanges, and for your years of support on and off the page.

I'm lucky to have wonderful friendships with some truly remarkable women. Thank you to each of you for your support, and for always asking, "How's the writing going?" even though the answer is usually avoidant! In particular, thank you to Jenny (Gleed) Leroux, Jenny Emery, and Ashley Thomson. And to Jessica Berry, for your insightful help with this story, and for your incredible enthusiasm that has made this whole journey even better—thank you.

To the Fizzell family, thank you for your love and support.

To Jackelyne Napilan, thank you for your loyal and loving care.

To Sara Audrain and Samantha Audrain, thank you for being so thrilled, and for making slow summer days with a book our status quo. To Cathy Audrain, who ensured we were a family of voracious readers, thank you for your incomparable love and devotion. To Mark Audrain, thank you for the writer's gene, for your unwavering belief in me, and for being so very proud, always. It is a gift to have been raised by parents like mine, and I am grateful for them every day.

I started this novel when my son was six months old. Motherhood and a writing life mark the same new beginning for me, and both have been a joy and a privilege. Oscar and Waverly—you inspire me endlessly, and this is for you. And finally, thank you to my partner, Michael Fizzell, for making everything possible, and everything better.

A PENGUIN READERS GUIDE TO

THE PUSH

Ashley Audrain

An Introduction to
The Push

Blythe Connor's difficult childhood left her uneasy about
parenthood, and once her daughter, Violet, is born, she's eager not
to repeat the mistakes of the past. Except she can't let go of a
disturbing, nagging thought: Violet does not seem like other
children. She's distant, stubborn, antisocial, angry. Bad things
happen around her, and it can't all be in Blythe's imagination.

Blythe's husband, Fox, refuses to see what is increasingly clear to
Blythe, and the conflict cracks their marriage open, revealing what
the stresses of parenthood can do to a partnership. Isolated and
ignored, Blythe begins to doubt her own perceptions. But when her
worst nightmare becomes reality, and everything she fears about
Violet crystallizes into one tragic moment, she must reckon with
the repercussions—and with the unsettling notion that she may
have been right all along.

In laser-sharp, powerful prose, *The Push* is an utterly unput-
downable novel that explores what parents owe their children,
whether we are formed by nature or by nurture, and whether we can
ever really outrun the scars of the past. An intense psychological
drama that grapples with universal fears about who we are and
what we, as parents, can ever do to influence our children, *The Push*
will keep readers guessing until the very last page.

A Conversation with
Ashley Audrain

The Push *is a searing look at motherhood—both the raw, personal experience and the societal expectations and cultural pressures that surround it. Why did you want to tackle this topic?*

I have long been fascinated with motherhood—how society perceives mothers, how they perceive themselves, how motherhood changes women, why women want to be mothers in the first place—and so I always felt this would be the focus of my novel. Many things about motherhood are softened when we talk or write about them. When I became a mother myself, this especially stood out to me in writing and in film—the washed-over birth scenes and the idyllic children, the tired but fulfilled mother. I wanted to write from a darker place of motherhood, because it can be very ugly and terrifying at times, even if you are privileged to be raising children in the best of circumstances.

Where did the idea of The Push *come from?*

I started writing the novel when my son was six months old, a time when I thought a lot about the expectations of motherhood: how we are meant to feel, who our child will be, what life will look like. But what if those expectations are entirely different from reality? There is a lot of fear in motherhood, despite it being something we're taught is the most natural role there is. I find satisfaction in exploring our common fears, perhaps as a way of understanding them better in myself. I think a lot of us have flashes of nightmarish thoughts cross our minds as we're raising children, no matter the circumstance, and I found it fascinating to let my

4

mind wander further down that path, considering the "what if" scenarios in the lives of these characters.

The narrative of Blythe's experience is interwoven with memories of her own childhood, and her mother's childhood. Why did you decide to explore her family history in this manner, and how did you land on the style?

It's hard to understand Blythe without understanding her past, and I wanted to explore the idea of how we learn to mother and what we carry from the women we come from, consciously or not. I experimented with the best way to weave this into the narrative— the story of Blythe's grandmother Etta and her mother, Cecilia, stands on its own in a way, but I wanted to draw parallels in the experience of all three women as daughters and mothers. I also wanted there to be some ambiguity about how much of her past Blythe knows for sure, how much she was told, and how much she has puzzled together herself; I think this is true of how we all understand our family histories.

As with any story about children behaving badly, The Push *touches on the idea of nature versus nurture—of how our personalities are formed and what we owe to each other. What do you think of this age-old question, and how* The Push *addresses it?*

The degree to which nature and nurture shape a person fascinates me. What makes a person with a loving, positive upbringing behave unconscionably? How does a person with a traumatic childhood completely break the cycle of certain behaviors with their own families? The evolving science of inherited trauma is particularly interesting, the way a severe emotional experience can physically alter the cells and behavior of that person's own children. In *The Push*, we, as readers, alongside Blythe, examine how she was inevitably shaped as a mother, and how Violet is being shaped by Blythe. The answers to these questions aren't clear-cut, of course, which I think contributes to the ambiguity in the novel along the way.

Blythe's actual experience of parenthood turns out to be very different from her expectations. Becoming a mother is not what she thought it would be, and her child is not who she imagined her to be. Though Blythe's experience is very specific, do you think this is common among parents?

Someone once told me that her friend confessed she didn't like her own child very much—not just because of a particularly tough phase, but because she genuinely didn't like who she was. I had never heard such a candid feeling expressed by a mother before. There is increasingly more discourse among women about the failed expectations of motherhood, but there are still taboo truths that few women will share, like regretting the decision to have a child, or not feeling the love they thought they would. Motherhood is so often discussed in clichés: "The most important job in the world," or "The days are long, but the years are short." What if it feels like the worst job in the world? What if the years feel like decades? Those opinions aren't a part of the mainstream language around motherhood, but I think a lot of mothers can relate to them.

The Push is also the story of a marriage, and the pressure that parenthood can place on partners. Can you speak a little bit about Blythe and Fox's relationship in the book, and how it breaks down over time?

When Blythe and Fox begin their relationship as young adults, they each find something specific in each other that fills a need— but with that comes lifelong expectations of each other that neither can uphold. The resentment that grows in their relationship becomes too much for either of them to bear. I think an interesting debate about Fox is whether he's a good parent: did he sacrifice his relationship in defense of his daughter? Which role—parent or partner—should be the priority in a family unit? Balancing those two roles is something a lot of parents in a marriage can relate to, especially after experiencing the ways parenthood inevitably changes a relationship.

Did you do any specific research for The Push, *and were there any important takeaways?*
    I did most of my research in the later revision stages, when I was conscious of ensuring certain things made sense from a psychological perspective. A psychologist who reviewed the novel directed me to a particularly interesting paper from 1975 in the *Journal of the American Academy of Child Psychiatry* titled "Ghosts in the Nursery"—what a compelling metaphor for the relationship between a parent's own early childhood experience and the treatment of their children. And while reading about theories on matrilineal relationships, I found a quote that eventually became the epigraph about how a woman who is pregnant with a daughter carries the egg cells of her grandchildren inside of her. I love the way this quote represents the foundation of the novel.

There are many moments in the book when Blythe feels like she's lost her mind, like she's the only one who can see the truth. Yet to the reader, she never feels like one of those unreliable narrators we're now so used to seeing in psychological thrillers. How did you manage this delicate balance?
    Perhaps it's because the novel is written as a memoir of sorts in Blythe's voice, and she addresses the intended reader—her husband—as "you" throughout. This is her side of their story. This narrative perspective feels quite personal and intimate, and we get the sense that she really believes this version of the events. There is nothing disingenuous about her intention, although there is certainly doubt along the way as to what is fact and what is fiction. I want the reader to have a substantial amount of empathy for

Blythe—I didn't want her to be another trope of a bad mother who can't be redeemed. I hope readers can see parts of themselves in her along the way.

The Push *might be particularly relevant for mothers, but it's also about all the fears and anxieties that weigh on women in general—and what happens when they aren't heard or believed. Can you speak to this a little bit, and how it connects to our current moment?*

We're still living in a time when women's voices are often devalued, ignored, or questioned without merit. We've seen this in the way society treats women who speak out publicly, as an example. There's no question this broader societal attitude has an impact on an individual level in the domestic lives of women. Being ignored, not believed, or even gaslighted can be a form of trauma. The idea of the "crazy woman" or the "hysterical mother" has existed for a long time, and it creates fear and silences women, particularly where there is a power imbalance. In *The Push*, Blythe experiences a form of this from everyone around her: what she believes is inconvenient and has difficult consequences, so they shut her down. There are impacts on her own mental health because of this, and she is pushed to a place that is hard to come back from.

The Push *is the ultimate page-turner, easy to devour in one sitting. What are your tips and tricks for cultivating suspense? Are there writers or stories in the thriller genre that you particularly admire?*

Thank you. The pace and intensity of the novel is likely influenced by the way in which I wrote and revised: in short blocks of time, often racing against the clock for when I had to get back to my young children. I like to read stories that have short but powerful chapters, ones that make me pause for a moment before I turn to the next page, and I hope that's reflected in the structure of *The Push*. I've always gravitated toward darker, more psychological stories that explore the contemporary lives of women, especially mothers. I love a book I can't put down because I want to uncover the "why" of what's happened as much as the "what," but I also want the writing to be so compelling that I savor each sentence at the same time. There are so many brilliant writers perfecting this kind of suspenseful read: Leila Slimani's *The Perfect Nanny*, Celeste Ng's *Little Fires Everywhere*, and Elizabeth Kay's *Seven Lies* are a few favorites . . . but I could go on!

What do you hope readers take away from The Push?

I hope *The Push* is a novel that keeps people up far too late reading at night—that's the kind of book I love to discover. I also hope for *The Push* to create conversation among readers. About the expectations of motherhood, about what we owe our children, and about what happens when we don't believe women's truths.

QUESTIONS AND TOPICS
FOR DISCUSSION

1. In the book, Blythe struggles with feelings of inadequacy as she fails to live up to the perfect ideal of motherhood. How do societal pressures contribute to those feelings? How do you think society views motherhood—what it should look like, how it should feel, even who should be a mother—and what kind of burden does that place on women?

2. Does being a "good mother" always require selflessness and unconditional love? How much of ourselves do we owe our children?

3. What are your thoughts about Blythe as a mother? Did she fail Violet? Sam? What could or should she have done differently?

4. The theory of inherited trauma—that we carry the scars of past generations—is explored through Blythe's mother and grandmother, who struggled in similar ways to Blythe. How much do you think we carry forward from the experiences of the generation before us? Is it possible to break the cycle completely?

5. Nature versus nurture is a big theme in *The Push*. Are we born, or are we made? And, especially, when children turn out to be violent or dangerous, how much blame lies with the way they are raised?

6. Blythe writes that both she and her mother "had only one version of the truth" when it comes to what they can remember

about their own upbringings—there isn't anyone left who can tell them a different side of the story. Do you think we subconsciously reframe what we remember about our past? Did you believe everything Blythe remembered about her childhood?

7. Blythe says of her early relationship with Fox: "I had nothing when I met you, and you effortlessly became my everything." What did you think about the quality of their relationship from the outset? Is there something dangerous about a love so all-consuming and addictive?

8. Do you think Fox ever lied about not believing Blythe in order to protect Violet? If so, do you think trying to protect his daughter was a good enough reason to doubt his wife?

9. When Blythe and Fox speak for the last time, Fox tells Blythe, "[Violet] wasn't always easy. But she deserved more from you. And you deserved more from me." What do you think Fox lacked as a husband?

10. Were you surprised by the nature of Blythe and Gemma's relationship? Even though it was based on a lie, do you think there was real friendship and understanding there?

11. Do you think Gemma was always being truthful with Blythe about her feelings for Violet?